"Who are you?"

Robyn's eyes fastened on his lips. An errant frisson of a thrill skated over her skin. How could
this be a dream?

"An avenging angel," Kiel said.

"Of course. Did you leave your wings at the
door?"

"No." His brow rose. "I don't do wings, except
under extreme circumstances."

She smiled. "I don't fall into bed with strange
angels, either. I'm a widow," she confided, then
frowned. "But I guess you know all that if you're
an angel, huh?"

"I know, Robyn."

The firelight behind him set a halo about his hair.
Or maybe, expecting angel accoutrements, she
was only making that up. Kiel was way too sexy to
be an angel. The way he made her feel was how
only one man on earth had made her feel—
her husband!

Dear Reader,

The word *angel* conjures up chubby cherubs or wizened old specters, not men who are virile and muscular and sinfully sexy. But you're about to enter the Denver Branch of Avenging Angels to meet some of the sexiest angels this side of heaven!

Whenever there's injustice, the Avenging Angels are on the case.

Carly Bishop brings you another irresistible angel in *The Soulmate*. As an Avenging Angel, sexy Kiel faces an assignment unlike any other—he has to avenge his own death!

I know you'll love Kiel—and all the Avenging Angels! We hope you haven't missed any of this super-special quartet!

Regards,

Debra Matteucci
Senior Editor & Editorial Coordinator
Harlequin Books
300 East 42nd Street
New York, New York 10017

The Soulmate
Carly Bishop

Harlequin Books

TORONTO • NEW YORK • LONDON
AMSTERDAM • PARIS • SYDNEY • HAMBURG
STOCKHOLM • ATHENS • TOKYO • MILAN
MADRID • WARSAW • BUDAPEST • AUCKLAND

To my dear Aunt Sody
for your
Grit and grace under a lifetime of fire

ISBN 0-373-22370-6

THE SOULMATE

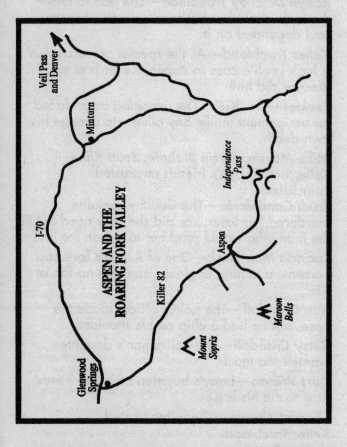

ASPEN AND THE
ROARING FORK VALLEY

Veil Pass
and Denver

Minturn

Independence
Pass

I-70

Aspen

Killer 82

Maroon
Bells

Mount
Sopris

Glenwood
Springs

CAST OF CHARACTERS

Robyn Delaney Trueblood—She had to know the truth about her husband's death...her very soul depended on it.

Keller Trueblood—As the special prosecutor in a high-profile case in Aspen, Keller had to die—or did he?

Ezekiel—Or "Kiel." The avenging angel faced an assignment unlike any other—to avenge his own death.

Mike Massie, Jessie Blahnik, Scott Kline—Keller and Robyn's friends mistrusted coincidence.

Trudi Candelaria—The wealthy socialite murdered her lover...or did she only need to kill the man who would send her to prison for life?

Lucinda Montbank—One of Aspen's foremost citizens, a mining engineer, she was no fan of Kiel.

Ken Crandall—The police officer made the case, but he had a chip on his shoulder.

Betsy Crandall—The policeman's daughter wanted too much.

Curt Wilson—Betsy's boyfriend figured it was time to cut his losses.

Vincent Ybarra—The judge trusted Keller Trueblood.

Chapter One

"You guys ever asked yourselves why a mine shaft collapses on a particular day after standing there for a hundred-and-six years?"

Robyn Delaney Trueblood blanched. Before the comment she and her friends had been swapping gossip about the decadent life-styles of the Aspen, Colorado, rich and famous. Now her laughter died in her throat, and for a moment, a pin dropping would have rocked her condo.

Her husband, Keller, had died one year ago tomorrow in the collapse of a shaft of the Hallelujah silver mine, and her friends had gathered together tonight at her place to help her finally lay Keller's memory to rest. To celebrate his life, not to wallow more over his loss.

Robyn's best friend and local TV News producer, Jessie Blahnik, glared at Mike Massie, a Denver criminal defense attorney. "Stow it, why don't you," Jessie snapped.

"Because I want to know," Mike persisted, undaunted by Jessie's raised eyebrows. "I mean, look. Keller was winding up his prosecution of Trudi Candelaria. The dame murdered her lover, the internationally famous ski jumper, Spyder Nielsen. One day, Keller goes poking around in a mine shaft with Robyn that has withstood the test of time, marauders, hikers and mining fiends for well over a century—"

"Mike, everyone who grows up in Colorado knows old mines collapse. Besides, the last thing Robyn needs is your—"

"No...Jessie. It's okay," Robyn interrupted. "I've asked myself the same question a million times. Why that mine shaft? Why that day? Why did Keller have to die and not me?" Her head dipped low. She hadn't exactly come out of the Hallelujah unscathed, either, but losing Keller had nearly killed her where the old, rotted timbers had failed.

She straightened her shoulders and finished her wine. She no longer needed to cry about it. "It was more dangerous than we knew, or we went too far—beyond where there were any modern reinforcements. But the only real answer I know, Mike, is that there is no answer. Things just happen, things we have no control over."

"Exactly," the third and last of her remaining guests, Scott Kline, put in. A writing buddy and colleague of Robyn's, Scott wrote for the Denver *Post.* "It's like asking why the *Challenger* had to blow up. Or, why did the *Titanic* have to sink? Or, why didn't Abe Lincoln sneeze?"

"Other than that, Mrs. Lincoln...how did you enjoy the play?" Mike muttered darkly, nursing his tequila and lime. "This one ain't over, folks."

"Massie, what are you talking about?" Jessie demanded.

"The murder of Keller Trueblood, Esquire, special prosecutor in the case of *Colorado v. Candelaria.*"

A chill swept over Robyn's flesh. "Murder?" The pit of her stomach dropped like a stone. She stared at Keller's oldest and best friend. Cocksure, arrogant, full of himself—maybe. He'd probably had one too many margaritas, but Robyn had never known Michael Massie to indulge paranoid, unlikely, off-the-wall crime theories.

Massie slugged down the dregs of his tequila and lime. "What would you say if I told you that Stuart Willetts put his condo in Aspen on the market yesterday?"

"How about, 'So what?'" Jessie jibed.

"And," Mike went on, "the day before that, he moved in with Trudi Candelaria—right into Spyder Nielsen's bed."

"I'd say you're so far out in left field you might as well be in the Rock Pile," Jessie retorted, referring to the cheap seats in the Denver Rockies baseball park. "How do you know any of this?"

"Because I grew up in Pitkin County, Jess," Mike snapped. "Because I know people. The regular live-in maid, Frau Kautz, who spent twenty years with Spyder, is on a week's holiday. Candelaria has hired temporary help, and people *I* know know other people who've witnessed Willetts's possessions being moved in. I'm telling you, as far as Candelaria and Willetts were concerned, Keller had to die."

Jessie shook her head, put down her drink, picked up her purse and stood up. "Come on, Michael. It's late. I'll drive you home and you can sleep it off."

But however easily Jessie tossed off Mike's query, Robyn couldn't. Murder was her stock in trade. She wrote true-crime novels—which was how she'd met Keller in the first place, interviewing him almost four years ago in the course of researching her book, *Where Angels Fear to Tread.* Keller had been the prosecuting attorney in that murder trial. They married fourteen months after Keller brought in a stunning conviction, and a few weeks after Robyn's book hit the stands.

So Robyn *knew* murder. She'd spent hundreds of hours over the course of her career in maximum security pens, interviewing murderers. Even more hours went into poring over transcripts and research with the families, friends and associates of killers and their victims. She had a Ph.D. in sociology and three true-crime bestsellers to her credit.

No one could ever know what was in another person's heart, but Robyn understood that most people didn't get to be killers overnight, or without passions and reasons and rages that drove them to commit such terrible, final acts as murder.

Stuart Willetts had been Keller's second chair—his assistant—in the prosecution of Trudi Candelaria. If Stuart and the accused, Trudi Candelaria, were now involved, as Michael Massie was suggesting, the question begged to be asked—had Trudi and Stuart conspired to get rid of Keller so the murder indictment against her could be scuttled?

"Jessie, wait. Sit down for another minute, okay?" She waited until her friend gave in and sat back down before posing her question to make absolutely sure she understood his point. "Mike, are you saying Keller's chief deputy prosecutor is having an affair with the defendant, with Trudi Candelaria?"

"That's exactly what I'm saying. Yes. I'd bet Willetts had the hots for the Candelaria dame from day one—and she damned well knew it."

"Wouldn't Keller have seen that kind of thing going on?" Robyn asked. "I can't believe he wouldn't have taken Willetts off the case in a New York minute if he thought there was any impropriety like that."

"Maybe." Mike shrugged. "I'm not knocking Keller, Robyn. Not at all. But Willetts swims with the rest of us sharks. He knows how to present himself and how to play his cards close to the chest. Tip his hand? I don't think so. That's why Keller picked him in the first place."

Jessie shook her head. "Mike, you're making shark bait out of minnows. How could Stuart Willetts possibly have known that Keller and Robyn were going to that mine on that particular Sunday? What could he possibly know about making a mine shaft collapse?"

Robyn grimaced. "He knew we were going, Jessie. He was at dinner with us at Planet Hollywood in Aspen that Friday night. I wanted to go see the Hallelujah. I was working on a story about the silver miners, remember?"

"Of course. It was Mike who put you in touch with Lucinda Montbank."

"Yes." Montbank was a well-known name in Aspen. The Montbank fortune was made in silver mining a century ago, before gold became the standard. Now, of the Montbanks, only Lucinda remained, and the rights to the Hallelujah remained in her possession. She also possessed substantial real estate holdings in a town where multimillion-dollar homes were the norm.

"I asked Keller to go with me to the mine. I remember this all very distinctly because Willetts was giving me a hard time about not going hang gliding with Keller and him instead."

"Okay," Jessie granted. "Supposing that's true, what about the technical knowledge? How could anyone be sure Keller would die in that mine? How would you even go about making a mine shaft collapse?"

"Come on, Jessie." Mike got up to pour himself a cup of coffee. "This is Aspen we're talking. That kind of information qualifies as local lore. There's the library, the Historical Society. Hell, some crusty old miner living in a shack up by Marble could do it for a few bucks on a bet."

Scott Kline plunked his cocktail glass down on the table. "I hate to admit it, but this scenario is beginning to make sense. Willetts had to know that if Keller died, the defense would lobby for the charges against Trudi to be dismissed—or for a mistrial at the very least."

"Which is exactly what happened, isn't it?" Robyn asked.

Mike nodded. "Willetts beat the land-speed record for conceding to a mistrial. At the time, I thought he was just being cagey. That he would reinstate the murder charges and start over."

"He never did, did he?" Robyn asked. It seemed hard to believe, now, that she hadn't followed the news after the mine collapsed, but she had been in a Denver hospital undergoing the first of three operations to restore her leg to some semblance of working order.

Even if she hadn't been knocked out for weeks on end with pain medications for the operations, she and Keller had agreed it would be vital to both their careers to keep their professional paths from crossing after they married. She'd made a point of steering clear no matter how juicy the Spyder Nielsen case became, and to pick up the threads after it was all over, after Keller died, wasn't in her heart.

"That's right," Mike concurred. "Willetts never reinstated the charges. He bailed out on the pretext that the evidence against Trudi had proven too shaky to make the charges stick."

"Maybe it wasn't a pretext at all," Robyn protested. "Maybe Stuart Willetts just knew when to cut his losses. I overheard Keller on the phone one night in a pretty heated conversation with the main detective. Maybe the case wasn't stacking up."

"Yeah, well, you can put that spin on it," Mike said, sitting back. He hung both arms over the back of his chair. "But now Willetts has moved in with the merry widow. Lover, I guess," he corrected himself, "since Trudi and Spyder weren't married.

"I think," he concluded darkly, "you have to ask yourself this question. If you were an obscenely wealthy jet-setter like Trudi Candelaria, why would you give a guy like Willetts the time of day—unless he was the one who kept you out of the slammer?"

"Love?" Robyn suggested.

Massie gave her a look. "Get a grip, Robyn. You and Keller may have been soulmates unto eternity, but the *only* person Trudi Candelaria gives a rat's ass about is Trudi."

THE FOLLOWING AFTERNOON, Monday, on the anniversary of Keller's death, Robyn departed the Rocky Mountain Rehabilitation Center for the last time.

Her outpatient treatment program had run its course, though her leg wasn't back to one hundred percent. The prognosis said it never would be. Most nights a numbness around her foot and ankle kept her awake, and in the mornings she would awaken feeling as if she hadn't slept very well.

Last night she hadn't slept at all.

After a year spent in a hellish round of operations and physical therapy, she could get around without her cane for most of the day. She could drive, take small hikes and even manage an hour on a stair stepper. As for her emotional fitness, she was making do with a little seashell night-light plugged into the wall, where for months she hadn't been able to endure the lights being turned off at all.

There was no darker place than a mine shaft that has collapsed, and before her rescue was effected, more than the pain of her leg, the blackness had invaded her heart, mind and soul, leaving her unable to cope with the dark at all.

That was passing, too. The tiny light of the seashell kept her rational in the dark now.

What she couldn't seem to do, what had motivated the small party last night, was to get over losing Keller.

She didn't buy into New Age anything. Not crystals, not dream catchers, not the advocates of creating your own reality, not Richard Bach and *Jonathan Livingston Seagull,* or even Aspen's most famous resident, John Denver. All of which put her at odds with half of the bestsellers of the decade—and a lot of what Aspen in the 1990s was all about.

Robyn Delaney believed in what she could see, hear and touch, and not much of anything else—with one exception. That she *belonged,* body, mind, heart and soul, to Keller Trueblood. She felt churlish and ungrateful with her friends, hateful and disconnected from her family, because all she wanted was the one thing she couldn't have. She couldn't have Keller back in her life.

She felt cut off, adrift in a sea of strangers, who even if they were dear and caring friends, would never understand her as Keller had.

Now, after Massie had trotted out the possibility last night that the collapse of the old Hallelujah silver mine had been a deliberate attempt on Keller's life, her despair had shifted shape on her. She made her living drawing such inferences, pulling together threads of motive and secret agendas and the deadly passions of real people.

Her head throbbed. She still had waking flashes of rotted timbers collapsing with a horrible cracking noise.

Her leg had been crushed.

Keller had died.

The thought that his death was murder and not an accident seemed paranoid but way too coincidental—as Robyn's beloved Austrian grandmama Marie would have said long ago, *crazy-making.*

Robyn had to find out if there was any substance to her suspicions. To do that, she had to return to Aspen.

The heat of the late afternoon sun at Denver's mile-high altitude sapped even the marigolds and mums, which were wilting on their stems. The cottonwoods seemed to gasp and shed leaves in small clumps. Fire bushes glowed red.

Robyn left the shade of the striped awning and waved with her brass-handled cane to the evening therapy staff and nurses just arriving. The parking lot had cleared out with the departure of the day crew. She made a beeline for her midnight blue coupe and unlocked the door.

Heat rolled out in waves, but she sank gratefully down into the leather-covered bucket seat. Her therapy session had left her muscles behaving like overdone spaghetti. The steering wheel blazed from the sun beating down inside the windshield.

"Holy hot," she muttered. Switching on the engine and then the air-conditioning, she left her door wide open to blow out the hot and bring in the cold. She turned to put her shoulder bag in the passenger seat when a wiry, wild-eyed teenager darted up to her car.

His head was shaved and a ring pierced his eyebrow. He planted his huge, gangly hands on the doorsill above her and demanded she hand over her purse. "An' while you're at it, the rock on your finger."

Keller's wedding ring? Her temper snapped. "Not a chance." Not Keller's ring, not anything else that remained of her shattered life. Not if the hounds of hell were after her. After the year she had just put in, three long operations and countless hours of grueling physical therapy, Robyn Delaney was not only tough as nails, she spit in the eye of death.

She had the vague impression of a statistic flying through her head proving how unlikely she was to get away with her life while resisting a mugger. Too bad. If she died defying this cretin and went to heaven, then, maybe, she could have Keller back again. Part of her wanted that so fiercely that she just didn't care what happened.

She tossed her long black French braid over her shoulder and glared up at the would-be mugger. "Get your mitts off my car, you miserable little toad," she demanded.

"Yeah?"

Oh, here was a brilliant one, she thought. "Yeah." She tried to pull her car door closed, but the wiry body stood rooted to the pavement.

Though momentarily startled at her resistance, the mean-ass kid regrouped—and he wasn't joking. He reached down with his overgrown hand, grabbed the shoulder of her silk tank top and twisted until it cut into her armpit. "Maybe you don't get I'm gonna hurt you, bitch, if you don' hand over the goods," he snarled.

The material bit into her flesh. She stifled her cry and groped automatically for her cane. He dragged her from the car and threw her to the baking-hot pavement.

Something cracked inside of her. She knew crime and criminals and all about the dark places in twisted human souls. She knew all about their victims, too, *their* pain, *their* impotence—and for once in her life, she desperately needed to strike a blow against the lowlifes who preyed on other people.... Against a creep who thought he could take Keller's ring from her.

Adrenaline poured through her. Her heart raced, and a voice in her head squeaked hysterically at her foolish bravado, but Robyn tuned it out and lashed out at her attacker with her cane and all the pent-up rage inside her.

Her blow landed on his shoulder, but it just enraged the mugger. She screamed and clenched her fist so he couldn't strip Keller's ring from her finger. No power on earth could have opened her hand. Her attacker backhanded Robyn and the fragile flesh inside her mouth split and bled.

He might have knocked her senseless and taken Keller's ring from her, anyway, but a security guard bellowed at the mugger and came running full out. Robyn seized upon the distraction he provided and drew her leg up hard and high in the mugger's crotch. He lashed out in his pain but missed her face and lit out running from the security guard.

The guard, a man named Shelton whom she'd spoken with often enough in the past year, offered Robyn his handkerchief while a couple of other security types tackled the kid. She stood up with Shelton's help, retrieved her cane and, for an instant, indulged the primal satisfaction of having bested a predator. A second or two later, her nerves let her down and Robyn began quaking like an aspen leaf in a very stiff wind.

Sure, now, chimed that same annoying little voice of caution in her mind. She shook her head and scraped loose tendrils of hair back from her face. "Thanks, Shelton."

The security guard, a burly, ruddy-skinned ex-cop, steadied her. "Robyn, what's wrong with you? Are you nuts? You know better than to take on a mugger!"

She clasped the guard's wrist and gulped as her courage dissolved away to nothing. Tears bit at her eyelids. Her elbow was badly scraped and burned by the pavement. Her face hurt like blazes. "I . . . yes. Maybe I am, but I'm all right. He just ticked me off, you know? I'm in no mood to play a wilting violet."

"How about a *dead* violet?" Shelton jibed, but then relented. "You're pale as a ghost, Robyn.... Are you sure you're okay? Maybe you should come back inside."

Robyn shook her head. "I'm fine, really. Thanks." She let go of the security guard's steadying arm and turned properly in her seat. She didn't want to worry him, or trigger a call from her well-meaning psychotherapist, so she made all the proper noises to reassure Shelton that she would be okay.

She didn't say, at least out loud, that she was still so angry inside at Keller for dying on her she thought her being a ghost would at least be a better alternative to surviving him. Maybe the movies had it right and *Keller* was now a ghost. Well, she could be one, too, and together they could haunt the Halls of Justice.

She bid the guard goodbye, whipped on her sunglasses against the fierce glare of sunlight and sped off. Aspen was at least a four-hour drive, maybe more.

She wheeled onto Colfax and headed to a neighborhood meat market. She hobbled a bit getting inside. The butcher, Cory Janns, a first cousin of Keller's, nearly came through the refrigerated display case at the sight of her blackened eye and battered face.

"Holy cow, Robyn!" he exclaimed, wiping his hands on his white apron. "What happened to you?"

"A mugger happened to me, Cory." She worked up a nonchalant smile that hurt her face. "You should see the other guy. Do you think you could give me an ice pack or—"

"A piece of beefsteak," he said. "Hold on. I'll fix you right up." He slid open a door of the refrigerator case and pulled out a hunk of tenderloin, eyeing her eye. "Jeez. The family's going to come unglued."

She could imagine the Trueblood family brouhaha—not to mention the reaction from Keller's mother, a powerhouse in local charities who no politician ignored. No doubt the steely lady would soon be demanding the entire Denver police department bring Robyn's attacker to justice. "Cory, please don't say anything to May about this. I'm going up to Aspen for a few days—I'm on my way now, in fact."

She gave him an imploring look. Cory was a soft touch, and the first to say he was not the brightest star in the Trueblood family firmament. He wasn't likely to guess why she would be returning to Aspen. "Maybe you'll cover for me if the family notices I'm gone? Just say I decided to get away for a few days?"

He frowned. "They'll notice, all right, but I'll do what I can." He carved the meat and packaged it, then came around the refrigerator case to show her how she could hold it by the wrapping paper as a poultice to her black eye.

She exchanged hugs with Keller's cousin and departed, crawling back into her coupe. Her slacks were badly smudged, her blouse a wreck and her whole body ached, but she wasn't going to cave in and cry—or change her plans.

She turned onto York Street northbound and headed for the highway. She intended to be in the resort ski town by eight o'clock, and further up the mountain, to the eleven-thousand-square-foot home of the late and largely unmourned Spyder Nielsen, by nine.

This, she knew, was almost certainly Frau Kautz's last vacation day, giving Robyn the last perfect opportunity to confront Candelaria and Willetts without having to do some exotic end-run around the formidable house-keeper.

Today was the day. Now was the time.

Holding the small slice of tenderloin to her cheek, she merged into the heavy afternoon traffic on I-70 west-bound. The snarled traffic gave her pause and her cheek ached horribly, and at long last, despite her fierce deter-mination, the folly of her actions back in that parking lot hit her squarely. Tears threatened, and a lump clogged her throat.

"What's this about, Robyn?" she chided herself, sorting through her feelings.

It wasn't about the emptiness of the antique double sleigh bed she and Keller had shared, though there were nights when she ached for his touch. Nights when, for the sound of his voice or scent of his skin or the taste of his lips, she would have traded anything she possessed.

It wasn't that she didn't have enough friends, enough writing buddies, enough family, to make her feel looked-out-for and encouraged that in time, she would be fine.

It wasn't even that she still felt responsible. That if it hadn't been for her wanting to go poking around the old Hallelujah mine shaft in the mountains surrounding As-pen, Keller would be alive and well today.

What it came down to was perspective. A year had passed. Keller's own mother had gotten over his loss. Robyn simply had to pull up her socks and get on with living her life. Keller would want that. *Do yourself a favor,* he would say, *a little auto pro bono.*

Get a life, Robyn....

The only life she wanted was the one she had shared with Keller, but Robyn *had* tried. God knew she tried. Why else would she have arranged the small get-together last night? She'd been thinking a ritual gathering like that might be cathartic. That she could finally lay him to rest in her heart with a celebration of the life and times of Keller Trueblood.

It might all have worked that way, too, if one thing hadn't led to another, leading Mike Massie to suggest Keller had been murdered.

Driving in what she had lately decided to call an aggressive manner—better than admitting she was reckless—she darted in and out of clogged rush hour traffic through the heart of Denver. She didn't know why she bothered justifying her driving to herself. Who cared?

Who? Really? But the same obnoxious little Jiminy Cricket voice—it wasn't a voice, but how else was she supposed to describe thoughts popping around in her head that were decidedly not her own?—kept insisting her driving made her an uninsurable, undesirable risk at the wheel.

She moved in and out of traffic lanes, content to be beating the flow, even signaling each time to prove herself a safe driver—right up until all lanes of traffic came to a screeching halt just before the exits to the town of Golden.

She switched on the radio to listen for what the delay was all about, but after a few minutes, she turned the radio off and shoved a Rachmaninoff CD into the disk player instead.

Her bags were packed and stashed in the back seat. Her mind was made up. It really didn't matter what the radio sky-spies had to say about the traffic, or that she was going to have to stop somewhere and change her clothes.

She was going to Aspen, and she was going now.

AT THE LOGAN STREET address where the Denver Branch of Avenging Angels kept an earthly presence in a small brownstone surrounded by high rises, the office receptionist, Grace, sat at her desk. Part of her job was to steer mortals to other resources should they wander in. Part of it involved running interference for Angelo, head angel of the DBAA.

Clarence, the Guardian Angel of the human Robyn Delaney, required all Grace's celestial tact to handle. Angelo wasn't given to granting run-amok Guardian Angels an audience. Yet Clarence wasn't going away. Feathers, she thought, were going to fly.

Gray-haired, blue-eyed, dressed in a tailored white dress only because she missed the old days with the flowing white robes, Grace loved her job. The Avengers were the most exciting of all angels to be around, the ones who worked for truth and justice and got to set things aright in the mortal world. To all appearances they *were* mortal, as opposed to Clarence here, whose visage was only apparent to other angels.

There was no hierarchy in heaven that put Avenging Angels above Guardians, or even Cherubs for that matter, but human form was one delicious perk. To have a human body minus the aches and pains and infirmities! Because she worked in this office, Grace got human form as well—even if it was rather... matronly.

Clarence the Guardian was fit to be tied, though tied with what, Grace couldn't imagine due to his lack of real substance. Her sense of humor grew sorely tried, and she scowled at his lack of decorum. Clarence's earthly charge, Robyn Delaney, it seemed, was moving into dangerous territory, and Clarence had apparently arrived at the end of his heavenly tether with her reckless antics.

"Do *try* to get a hold of yourself, Clarence," Grace advised, breathing a grateful sigh of relief when Angelo summoned Clarence to his office. In a flash, the piping-mad little Guardian was gone from her reception area.

Now, Grace thought, if only Ezekiel would respond to his page.... In a moment of thinking about the Avenging Angel who went by Kiel, he popped in, materializing out of thin air.

"Gracie!" He gave her a dazzling grin. Ordinary daylight sparkled off his thick, wavy golden red hair, and his eyes reminded Grace of the skies over the Aeolian archipelago in the Mediterranean. "You rang?"

"On his nibs' orders," Grace answered, but she stifled her smile. Popping in as he had done reeked of disregard for rules meant to protect stray mortals from witnessing such unearthly events. It set Grace's teeth to clacking, too. "If you're going to materialize, you simply must do it elsewhere and use the door! You're an Avenger, Kiel," she reminded him sternly.

And unnecessarily. He knew his job, had taken to it like a duck to water. In an earth year, he'd avenged well over one hundred injustices, but his penchant for popping in and out unnerved her completely.

Still, she harbored a soft spot in her angel's heart for Kiel. Time had little meaning to angels over the millenia, but he had only recently made his transition to the celestial. His leftover earthly sensibilities charmed her angelic socks right off.

He went around calling the other angels "halos." Thought it was a catchier acronym than the DBAA. Heaven's Avengers Local One-o-one, for pity's sake!

He grinned as shamelessly as any mortal, and slouched like one. He *was* one in all save a technical sense, but he flirted like the very devil.

Grace was immune, naturally, having been around long enough to have bounced Methuselah on her knee, but if she'd ever had a son, which she hadn't, she'd have picked Ezekiel. On the other hand, she wouldn't have wanted a daughter anywhere near this earth angel.

Angelo's voice boomed out. "*Now,* Ezekiel?"

"Here I am—to stand and deliver," Kiel deadpanned for Grace, slouching against her desk. He materialized a bouquet of miniature pink and purple snapdragons for her vase, and despite her eons, Grace blushed with pleasure.

It wasn't on the recommended list of celestial powers to convert energy to matter, but Kiel had energy to burn and a very undeveloped sense of angelic restraint. "Have a good one, Gracie."

He bounded up the steps to the second-story balcony and sauntered into Angelo's office. A little guardian angel who reminded Kiel of Elmer Fudd in a temper tantrum, could hardly contain himself to one place, never mind a chair. Angelo took in Kiel's presence and introduced him to the Guardian.

"Ezekiel, DBAA, this is Clarence, DBGA—uh...Guardians, that is. Certainly one of the most...proactive Guardians in the history of the cosmos."

Clarence fumed, apparently divining *proactive* wasn't exactly meant to be a compliment. "One little traffic jam," he complained. He toted an abacus of some age, and when he manipulated the beads, his pudgy fingers flew. "One hundred-and-three fender benders. *Minor* ones at that. So what's the big deal?"

By way of answering what was the big deal, Angelo glowered, creating a small burst of light energy. Kiel stifled a grin. Clarence was a dead ringer for the literary depictions of a thirteenth-century monk—potbellied and sporting a fringe of scant hair which circled his rounded head.

The little Guardian tucked the abacus under his arm and drew himself up to his full three-point-five cubits to launch himself into Angelo's formidable face.

"I'll tell you what, Mr. Bigshot Avenging Angelo," Clarence went on. "Guardians often have the resources to watch over half a dozen mortals. What do *I* get? One. Easy, you say? Piece of angel food? Bah! My assignment, bless her demented, grieving little heart, is a bona fide fruitcake who requires my complete and unceasing attention." He sniffed. "Stopping traffic befitted the occasion."

Amused, interested, Kiel dropped his human form into the chair beside Clarence's. "Stopping traffic?"

Scowling, Angelo explained. "Clarence, here, in order to delay one mortal being, had traffic backed up on I-70 for thirty miles—"

"Thirty-two-point-six, to be precise," Clarence interrupted, adding, "there didn't seem to be any other way of stopping her. I'm telling you I was not acting outside my reasonable and customary powers."

Listening to the little Guardian piping up about his powers, Kiel could still think of a lot less drastic solutions—flat tires, overheated radiators, running out of gas—that would have affected a single mortal rather than hundreds of them. But the little Guardian was clearly at his wits' end. "What's happening with your mortal?"

Clarence sighed. "She's a dear girl—I'll say that right up front—but her husband died a year ago, and she's simply inconsolable. Can't say as I blame her, actually." He whipped out his abacus again and set the beads to crashing back and forth. "The odds against finding that kind of happiness—"

"Are astronomical, I'm sure," Angelo interrupted to forestall the complex calculations.

"Exactly," Clarence said, aggrieved to be cut off so summarily from his favorite occupation. "In fact, just this afternoon I popped a warning bubble over Robyn's head citing the precise odds of getting away with defying muggers, which she *completely* ignored."

Kiel didn't bother smothering his grin. This mortal-Guardian assignment sounded like the mismatch of the ages. One for the millenia.

"She jaywalks," Clarence hurried on. "She drives like a bat out of you-know-where. She ignores common sense warnings, fights back when she shouldn't—she got a terrible shiner this very afternoon.... *Terrible,* I'm telling you."

Kiel's amusement faded. "You couldn't have prevented that?"

Clarence rolled his eyes. "If Guardians could prevent human beings from their folly, we wouldn't need Avengers, now, would we? Mortals have their free will, you know."

Kiel gave a shrug; Clarence was right.

"Now," he squeaked, racing on, "she's got it in her head that her husband was murdered. If I didn't stop her, in a few hours she'd be in Aspen asking questions."

"And the problem with that would be what?" Kiel asked.

"Serious, that's what!" Clarence sputtered. "Pretty soon, whoever killed her husband would have to kill her to shut her up. You don't know Robyn. She won't quit. She'll end up getting herself killed, and then I'll be answering to St. Peter."

"Robyn, you said?" Kiel asked.

"Yes. Robyn Delaney Trueblood," Clarence supplied. "And I..."

Kiel straightened.

Clarence went on and on about quitting, giving up, throwing in the towel, crying uncle, whatever it took to get out from under his Guardian responsibilities to Robyn Delaney Trueblood. But Kiel had tuned the Guardian Angel out.

Robyn...

The name echoed through his being, stirring vaguely recollected mortal sensations. He lifted his head and turned his awareness inside himself as if trying to recall a favorite melody—but the images he sought were veiled and unfocused, somehow inaccessible.

He tried to shake off the frustration of knowing...and not knowing. The Avenging Angels often worked under such limitations. His fellow Avengers Sam and Dash—even that cute little button of an angel, Ariel—had just been on assignments to restore order and justice. The DBAA dockets were full, and it was often the case that the Avenging Angels assigned didn't know who the guilty party was. The Avengers couldn't just swoop in, name the culprits and strike them down. Instead, they had to work through mortals.

But this not knowing felt strangely personal to Kiel, as if in his mortal existence he had known Robyn Delaney Trueblood....

Chapter Two

"You have," Angelo muttered darkly, answering Kiel's unspoken thought.

"Have what?" Kiel asked.

"*Known* Robyn Delaney."

"In the biblical sense?" Clarence squeaked, gaping at Kiel. "You mean Ezekiel is Keller Trueblood?"

"*Was* Keller Trueblood," Angelo corrected him, projecting an image, like a hologram, of Keller and his wife, Robyn, into thin air for both Clarence and Kiel to see.

"Oh, my gracious sake's alive!" Clarence uttered, but Kiel could only stare dumbfounded at the extraordinary lifelike projection. He didn't recognize himself—the mortal he was supposed to have been. Kiel's earthly manifestations bore no physical resemblance to Keller Trueblood's image, but the woman, *Robyn,* fired Kiel's heart. A strange and foreign sensation poured through him.

Kiel's human manifestations didn't ever get too cold or overly hot. He didn't shiver, sweat, sneeze or even leave footprints. He was an unrepentant flirt, that was true, but if he'd ever had sexual congress with a mortal, with *Robyn,* he didn't remember it. In fact he had no recollections of a life here on earth before his assignment to the DBAA.

But the still, silent apparition of Robyn Delaney, caught up in this special dimension, mesmerized him, touched him deeply. Her hair was black as cooled, gleaming lava, her complexion fair and fine as the inside of a conch, and her rich brown eyes seemed to penetrate to the molten core of him.

His very soul lightened and soared at the sight of her insubstantial image. What was he supposed to do with such wonder and joy over an earthbound woman?

He tried to bring his attention back to a more objective focus, to the problem at hand. It had never before occurred to him to question where his soul had most recently been. Recalling his fellow Avenging Angel Dash's last assignment, Kiel had to wonder why he had no memory of a mortal life—or if it was true that Keller Trueblood had been murdered.

"Didn't Dash and the mortal Liz Carradine just avenge Agatha Orben's murder?" he asked.

Angelo nodded, making the projection of Keller Trueblood and Robyn Delaney vanish. "Yes, but—"

"And didn't Aggie arrive in heaven knowing she'd been murdered? Didn't she go straight to St. Michael demanding justice?"

Angelo frowned. "Again, yes—"

"Then why is it that I arrived not even knowing my mortal name?"

"These decisions," Angelo intoned, annoyed by these vestiges of Kiel's prosecutorial cross-examination skills, "are made upstairs, so to speak."

"Or else I fell through the cracks," Kiel muttered.

"Well, this is all very interesting," Clarence whined, stamping his foot at his inability to get a word in edgewise, "but could we please get back to what you're going to do about Robyn?"

"We'll take it from here," Angelo stated, waving the Guardian away. "Be gone!"

To Kiel's amazement, the quirky, bean-counting little Guardian Clarence stubbornly held his ground so as not to leave Robyn Delaney Trueblood stranded without heavenly supervision.

"I want your word on that," Clarence demanded.

"My *word!*" Angelo burst forth with a commanding demonstration of his fearsome angelic power. Sparks flew. A brilliant light more powerful than a million candles flashed. "My *word?*"

Clarence gulped. "I'll take that as a promise," he croaked, popping out before he could be commanded again to leave.

Angelo shook his head. Guardians, Kiel knew, performed a vital function in the scheme of things, but they could be a real pain.

"About your mortal existence, Kiel." Angelo didn't wax philosophic very often. Justice required decisiveness and action; in this instance, he parted with his usual peremptory ways. "It's often the case that the Heavenly Hosts wish to spare newcomers the anguish of knowing they had an early and unanticipated end to their human lives. It's true that Agatha Orben was murdered, but she had lived a long and prosperous life. You, on the other hand, were in your prime."

Kiel nodded thoughtfully. Even now the image of Robyn Delaney threatened his angelic equilibrium, made him wonder what it was to be human and in love. In heaven, it went without question that to be human was to be frail and needful. Vulnerable to grand and dark passions alike.

"The fact is," Angelo went on, "I've never assigned a case quite like this one. Your death... make that *Keller's* death, was a grave injustice, but there was an even earlier injustice, too. Keller Trueblood was prosecuting the murder of Spyder Nielsen when he died." Angelo briefly outlined the facts of the case. "By dint of some cosmic slip-up after Keller's death, that murder has gone unsolved and unpunished, as well."

"Some cosmic slip-up?" Kiel demanded incredulously. "How do these things happen?"

Angelo shrugged. "It's rare, but mistakes happen. Why, I can't say."

"Can't say," Kiel asked, uncertain as to whether or not Angelo, in his supervisory capacity, could be trusted to reveal the whole truth, "or won't?"

"Can't," Angelo promised. "Kiel, you must understand what's at stake. In all likelihood, loath as I am to admit it, Clarence is right. Robyn Delaney will be in grave danger if she goes after the truth of Keller Trueblood's death alone—and then we'll *really* have a tangled mess of injustices."

"So, I take the assignment," Kiel said, acting as if he was certain, to make up for the fact that he wasn't so certain at all. "I don't remember the first thing about being Keller Trueblood, so there shouldn't be a problem."

Angelo looked up at Kiel from beneath his shaggy white eyebrows. "Surely you can divine the possible complications.... You are the angel of Robyn Delaney's husband. We're not talking any old marriage, Kiel. It may have appeared ordinary, but Robyn and Keller were soulmates. Their marriage was made in heaven. Two people in love for all time. Robyn *is* inconsolable, and is destined to remain that way for so long as she lives."

Untouched in his angelic trappings by such human emotions, Kiel had no way of gauging the power of Robyn Delaney's feelings or the nature of her loss. "Am I supposed to reveal to her that I am...that I was Keller?"

The shelf of Angelo's white brows lowered. "That decision must be yours. I should think it might deepen her despair to lose you again when this case is resolved."

Kiel could see how dangerous it might be to Robyn's peace of mind if she knew, if despite all his precautions, she somehow came to *know* that Kiel was the angelic incarnation of the soulmate she had known as Keller Trueblood. To lose a soulmate twice in one lifetime... Kiel shook his head. He could not in any conscience put her through that.

"Why bring me in on this case?" Kiel asked after a while. "There have to be forty other halos around here who could avenge Trueblood's death."

Angelo scowled. "We can't afford to lose whatever insight Keller Trueblood possessed concerning the murder of Spyder Nielsen." He eyed Kiel carefully. "Unless I'm very much mistaken, you are already experiencing certain echoes of Keller's earthly experience as Robyn's husband. Yes?"

Kiel gulped, so to speak. He began to see the stickier implications.

Angelo nodded. "There is a pinprick, now, in the vast reservoir of Keller's memory. Hopefully, that will serve you well in avenging your own death, as well as preventing Robyn's."

"Let me get this straight," Kiel said. "If I take this assignment, I'm going to have greater and greater access to Trueblood's memory?"

Angelo shrugged. "We simply don't know. A case of an angel avenging his own mortal death has never arisen before."

Kiel didn't know panic, except as an interesting phenomenon in humans, but he thought what he was experiencing right now might qualify. Already wary of his reactions to a mere image of Robyn Delaney, he didn't want anything to do with Keller Trueblood's remembrances. "Why don't you just restore his memory to some other sap?"

Angelo glowered at Kiel's choice of labels. "That is impossible."

"Why?" Kiel demanded. "Humans get themselves age-regressed and claim other people's memories and lives all the time."

"Crackpots," Angelo muttered darkly. "We're not restoring Keller Trueblood's memory to you. It can't be done. But your soul is your soul, and your consciousness of earthly experience may expand to benefit your cause."

He paused and glanced skyward, shaking his head. "Look. This is all celestial psycho-babble to me. I just pass out assignments, and these orders come from *on high*. You may refuse this assignment, Kiel, but it's been hinted that one of Robyn Delaney's descendants will be crucial to the fate of mankind in the next millenium. That won't be possible if Robyn provokes her own murder."

Kiel stood and paced to the window overlooking the gardens in back. The last of the roses clung sweetly to the vine. Autumn leaves had begun to fall. Angels didn't need oxygen, per se, so it wasn't possible that his lungs were failing him. Still, he felt this sensation to the core of his angel being.

A curious, dangerous sparkling hummed through every cell of his human form. Kiel shut his eyes and let his memory reconstruct for him Angelo's three-dimensional image of Robyn Delaney Trueblood. The extraordinary bond he felt with her overpowered his considerable angelic detachment . . . and then he understood the strange emotion human beings called despair.

He would fight to save her life; and though he was her soulmate, because his natural life had been cut short and he was an angel, Robyn Delaney's children would not be his.

He drew a deep breath and allowed the peace of his heavenly existence to ease the painful mortal emotion, restoring his equilibrium.

The dice of God, after all, were always loaded.

ONE MOMENT THE TRAFFIC was at a standstill, and the next, flowing freely. Robyn had never seen anything like it. In fact, fifteen miles further up I-70, she began to wonder if there had been any delay at all. Maybe she was just so anxious to get on with confronting Stuart Willetts and Trudi Candelaria that she had imagined the whole thing—but no.

She hadn't imagined anything.

The sun went down behind the mountains early, casting a glow around the aspen groves. In Silverthorne she pulled off the interstate to fill her gas tank. Dark clouds had begun to roll over the mountains, obliterating the sunlight. The gas station cashier said she'd heard they'd closed Independence Pass and it was snowing even now on Vail Pass—both entries to Aspen.

What else could go wrong? Robyn thought, changing in the rest room into a clean pair of oatmeal-colored linen slacks and a turquoise silk blouse. But a late September snowfall in the mountains wasn't all that uncommon.

Reassuring herself that a few inches of snow would not make the roads impassable, she tossed her ruined clothing into the back seat of the car, then darted across the way into a French bakery near the warehouse outlet stores. She bought a small crusty baguette and a large coffee, then resumed her drive.

By the turnoff south of Minturn, high in the heart of the Rockies, Robyn knew the sudden storm was more than she had counted on. She hadn't packed for this. She stayed on I-70 westbound, and in Glenwood Springs she almost turned off and took a room at the famous Hotel Colorado. The natural hot springs in the area would have gone a long way toward easing the ache in her leg from taking on the creepy little mugger and then driving so far.

What would it matter if she didn't get to Aspen tonight? Willetts and Candelaria would not be any more guilty or less innocent.

Robyn simply couldn't endure the delay. She hadn't made her reputation by coddling herself. She wouldn't start now. She knew from long experience that if she waited, her advantage might crumble. Frau Kautz would return. Robyn might lose the element of surprise, or catch one and not the other at home—*Spyder's* home. For her purposes, she needed to catch Candelaria and Willetts together and off guard and without the interference-running Frau Kautz.

South from Glenwood on what the locals called Killer 82, Robyn wended her way up the Roaring Fork River valley to Aspen. Winding, steep, breathtakingly gorgeous in her headlights even against the pitch black of night, the road twisted and climbed through the mountains until the pink glow of Aspen in the distance began to shine through the snow.

She couldn't see the lights of private airplanes twinkling above Sardy Field, but the landing approach sent them so close to the highway that she could hear the whine of jet engines in descent, landing in rapid succession before the storm made it impossible.

Short of Main Street, she turned back on the McClain Flats Road, back toward some of the most expensive properties anywhere on earth. She might have taken the county road itself outside of the town of Snowmass, but there was no marker for the road Spyder lived on.

Robyn backtracked slowly. She knew that many of these ritzy communities were gated, with at least a security guard and a boom to lower and raise, but not the one she sought. Spyder Nielsen was extravagant to the extreme in many ways, but not in this.

No one who didn't belong on his estate or serve there even knew where Spyder's property lay—not, at least, until he'd been murdered. She turned onto a road she would not have seen in the dark and snow without knowing exactly how far she'd come back.

No snowplows had been through, but so far, it hadn't mattered. She hadn't hydroplaned or been unable to brake. She would make it just fine.

In keeping with the rugged, natural environs, there were no street lamps. Her headlights reflected back at her off the blowing snow, and she passed through steep patches that in another few months would be impassable without four-wheel drive.

Spyder Nielsen's estate lay yet another four miles ahead. One mile up the narrow, winding road the snow began to drift. Robyn's tires began to slip on icy gravel beneath the snow. She pressed on the gas pedal and plowed through a small drift, but on the other side of the barrier, her speed sent her into a sickening spin and her coupe careered backward, slamming the rear of the car into the mountainside.

"Damn it!" she cried, jolted hard, banging her fist in frustration off the steering wheel. A part of her knew she should take a cosmic hint and give up confronting Willetts and Candelaria tonight, but she refused to be stopped.

Nothing would have stopped Keller. Nothing had *ever* stopped Keller—not until that mine shaft collapsed—and nothing could stop her short of her goal now, either. The engine had died, but she was able to switch on the ignition again. She tried rocking the car back and forth to gain momentum and escape the drifts, but every maneuver she tried to pull her coupe back onto the road only buried her tires deeper.

The car refused to budge. She knew she would never be able to see in the dark how she could work her way free and back onto the road.

She pared down the contents of her shoulder bag to a small voice recorder, her identification and a toothbrush, then pulled a disposable rain slicker over her head, the only garment she had that might come close to protecting her from the elements, got out of the car and began hiking up the deserted and treacherous mountain road.

The thick, wet snow soaked through her canvas espadrilles. The rain slicker, her only protection, barely held up. Her limbs began to feel leaden and her fingers frozen, then fiery and finally numb from the cold. The wind sliced through her linen slacks and plastered the slicker to her shoulders. One shiver after another shuddered through her body, and Robyn began to cry.

Her tears made the going even tougher. She couldn't see where she was going, much less gauge her steps. The rugged mountain road was meant for four-wheeling, not hiking. The terrain created drifts and the ice-encrusted gravel gave way beneath her feet.

Getting out of her car was the worst decision she had made in a string of impulsive, irrational choices. She wasn't getting better, she was getting worse. She wasn't getting over Keller, she had merely uncovered whole new vistas to obsess in. She loved him more than life. She didn't want to go on without him. She didn't want to be brave anymore, or strong.

It was just too hard pretending to be fine when her heart ached so much that she just wanted to lie down and die.

When her leg collapsed beneath her and she fell, she struggled back to her knees, anyway. Something inside her would not say die. Some primitive part of her brain refused to give up and let her heart have its way.

She swiped at her tears, but her hands were cold and wet from falling in the snow. She would follow the road back to her car and wait in the warmth from the heater for help to arrive. How long could it be before someone drove by?

Days.

She shoved the thought away and pulled the strap of her purse back onto her shoulder. She tried to stand, but this time her ankle, stiffened by the numbing cold snow, twisted and threw her into a patch of scrub oak. She fought off more tears, willing herself to crawl back to her car if that's all she could do.

At last she saw the lumpish shape of her car, covered by snow in the time since she had taken off on foot, but her leg collapsed beneath her one last time. The extreme

mountain cold and damp ate away at her will. A dangerous euphoria threatened her thinking. Her body was so
cold that her mind shut down the pain signals. She had
finally found the way to end her anguish with no one
around to shame her out of it or stop her.

All she had to do was fall back and let the cold sap her
body heat a little longer, and then she would be free and
clear. Hypothermia would save her from feeling anything ever again.

She fell asleep, startled awake and drifted off again,
and finally, finally succumbed to the overwhelming illu-
sion of warmth and peace.

Her tears froze on her lashes, and her eyes fell shut. It
wouldn't be long now.

She dreamed she heard the laboring sough of a stallion, and that she could feel the pounding of hoofbeats
through the snow-blanketed earth.

Caught in her frozen dream, a golden horse and rider
seemed to materialize in her hallucinations from out of
the snowy darkness. A peculiar lightness seemed to em-
anate around them. The rider wore a long sheepskin coat,
boots, jeans and a light-colored Stetson pulled low over
his eyes.

"Keller!"

Untold joy suffused her sleeping mind and frozen
heart. She was going now. She would not have to endure
an hour longer.

Keller had come for her.

"ROBYN." KIEL UTTERED her name and scooped her up
from the hard snow-covered earth and cradled her against
his body. He held her close, sheltering her, knowing it
would take a miracle, and a fast one, to bring her back

from the brink of a fearsome and terrible decision. She wanted to die, to let go, and she would unless he could find some way to lure her back.

He carried her back toward the golden stallion. Supporting her weight in one arm, he grabbed the leather horn, lifted a foot to the stirrup iron and swung high into the saddle. The stallion sidestepped, searching for footing. Kiel wedged Robyn's limp body between his and the swell of the saddle pommel, then urged his mount up the steep, treacherous slope.

He guided the stallion further from the upscale ski resort town of Aspen, Colorado, beyond civilization and onto national forest service land. In a valley not too distant from Spyder Nielsen's home, Kiel constructed a log cabin safe house in his mind and it materialized in the next instant.

Dismounting, he carried Robyn through waist-high drifts to the warm and welcoming cabin. The door closed behind him. A fire crackled in the stone hearth fireplace as the need occurred to him.

Had Robyn been conscious, he might have been a little more circumspect about utilizing his extensive powers, but she wasn't and he feared for her life. Her hypothermia was meaningless in his arms; her normal body temperature was already restored and had been from the moment he plucked her from the snow, but the will to live had all but fled her fragile spirit.

He strode across the room to the feather bed and sat, still holding Robyn in his arms. By the light of the fire, he began to peel away the wet, bone-chilling clothes from her body. He knew at this moment it was in Robyn Delaney's subconscious power to choose to live or die, and he feared her choice. He could help keep her alive. He could even speed the healing process, but without her will, her choice, he could do nothing.

He dropped her sodden, ice-crusted clothing on the floor and, holding her against his body, threw back the covers. Wrapping her tightly in the down quilt, he tucked her body between the flannel sheets, knelt at the side of the bed and took her raw and bleeding hands into his.

He focused all his angelic powers upon bringing the life-sustaining resources of her body to bear upon the scrapes and abrasions on her palms. As he watched, the healing began to take place. A little longer, and fresh new skin, whole and sweet, overtook the bleeding places, restoring her hands until the shape of them caught at his memory. Or rather, Keller's memory—but it was Kiel who turned her left hand over and recognized the wedding ring, the square-cut sapphire surrounded by half-carat diamonds, that Keller had vowed upon to be hers forever.

His throat thickened, another first for him, like the flash of despair he had experienced. He separated himself from the emotions as a ghost slips from a dying body.

"Robyn, listen to me," he urged. "You must come back. Don't go. Don't go." Her body was still and stiff as a sculpture in ice. Her body temperature was normal, but she lay still as death.

He maintained a cocoon of radiant heat around her, then let his awareness traverse her body, searching for other injuries he had not seen. When he sensed the damage to her face, an unangelic rage stirred in him.

He tilted her chin upward. Firelight illuminated the bruised and swollen cheek her Guardian Clarence had mentioned. As an angel, Kiel could not swear but he had never been as sorely tempted. Again he focused her body's own healing power upon the battered flesh below her eye, and that injury healed, as well. Still she showed no signs of fighting to live.

Kiel jerked back the covers and ran his hand from her calf up her thigh, along her slender waist and torso, and he knew from the lifelessness he sensed that Robyn Delaney had given up.

"Don't do it, Robyn!" he urged. "Try. Come back to me!" He shook her shoulder, and for a moment her beautiful brown eyes opened and fixed on him. "Robyn, do it for Keller. Hang in there."

Her eyes filled with tears. Her chin quivered, and she swallowed and caught her lip between her teeth, looked away, then again deep into Kiel's eyes. Her small whimper sounded to him like "Keller."

Unblinking, she reached to touch his cheek, but her body had been pushed past its limits. Her hand fell away. "Hold me. Please. Hold me."

Already kneeling, Kiel bowed his head, instinctively seeking guidance, the wisdom of a power greater than his own. Robyn Delaney hovered between life and death, and no radiant cocoon of warmth, no direction of her life forces, no therapy, no miracle save love was going to bring her back this time.

He knew how far she had come, how many times since her leg was crushed in that mine shaft that she had battled back from death's door. She could have given up and joined Keller Trueblood in eternity a year ago, but she had chosen life then, a dozen times since then—and even this night when she fought to get back to her car.

Body and soul, her resources were spent. She needed the intimacy of another human body, the reassurance of love and life and purpose and meaning in order to go on living. She needed the love of Keller Trueblood one last time, and Kiel was as close as she was going to get.

He took this reasoning for the divine guidance he sought, and stood to tear off his clothes and join her in that feather bed in a place that had no real existence in space and time.

He drew her on her side flush to his body, and deep, cell-level memory took over, fitting her head to his breast, her breasts to his torso, her pelvis to his stomach, her thighs to his male flesh. He crossed one leg over hers, taking her more fully into his body's embrace.

At last her body began to respond, burrowing closer, instinctively seeking contact deeper than flesh and bone, and after a few moments, a deep shuddering took her in its powerful grip. Even then, Kiel knew it was not from the hypothermia but the hollowness of her soul where the love of Keller Trueblood had lived. Her hands began to move over Kiel's human form in deeply instinctual ways, seeking union in the only vein left to her.

He made love to her. His touch, his kisses, had nothing to do with lust, which, like swearing and all the seven deadly sins, were forbidden him. His soul was Keller's, united for all time with Robyn Delaney's. Making love to her was an expression of deep and abiding love, one precious moment in which he could give her reason to go on.

His human flesh grew hot and turgid. He stroked her, trailed his lips from the jagged course of her terrible scars to her breasts, to her sweetly bow-shaped lips, and slowly, slowly, he seduced her back from the terrible brink.

She called out Keller's name when Kiel penetrated her body.

Afterward, when she had fallen deeply asleep, Kiel prayed that this union of his and Keller's soul with hers would have the flesh-and-blood result of a child.

But, being an angel, Kiel was required absolutely to be truthful, so he admitted to himself that he had not prayed on her behalf but for himself, instead.

Chapter Three

Robyn wavered in and out of consciousness, still caught up in the remnants of a dream. Could she awaken in her dream and still be asleep? It must be so, for her eyes opened and her gaze fixed on the man in her dreams sitting quietly on the stone hearth of a log cabin.

A tide of sensual memories flowed through her. Her heart began to thump.

She watched him through her lashes. Nothing about his physical appearance reminded her of any man she had ever known—least of all Keller, who had been long and too lean, darkly handsome and deeply tanned. He was, Keller had always joked, a candidate for that weather-beaten leathery look in old age.

This man's softly curling hair gleamed like polished bronze. His skin was fair, his eyes a stunning, deep shade of blue, his body more muscled than Keller's had been. He seemed ageless to her. He held something white in his hands—ivory, maybe—turning it over and over as if some treasure was concealed inside.

She had never expected to awaken from that moment when she saw Keller, when she believed that she had crossed over from life into the Hereafter with him. But sometime after seeing him, she had been compelled to turn back.

She'd expected that when she woke the dream would be over. She would discover that she had not really been saved from freezing to death by a mysterious rider and been warmed by his body. That she had not seen the light of Keller's eyes in those of a complete stranger, and that she had not made love with him.

But she had. Her body told her that.

In her dreams, it was Keller touching her, Keller whose lips trailed fire and life, Keller whose touch incited her body and invited, no, *commanded,* that she edge back from extinction, Keller whose thrust she recognized and craved like no other, ever. But this man was not who she had believed he was.

Her cheeks flamed, but she could not sustain the flash of deep, piercing anger because something more deeply substantial, more meaningful than his physical appearance, spoke to her heart.

So much so that she knew.

Making love with this man was more the brushing together of her soul with his than a physical mating, which scared her more than if she'd gone out looking to have Keller's memory blotted from her heart.

Lying naked and afraid of what she had done beneath a fluffy down comforter, she closed her eyes. The feather bed cradled her. Pillows, soft as clouds, cushioned her head. Her ankle felt whole and healthy. Her cheek didn't ache, either, so she knew she must be in that netherworld of not being quite awake. But her heart still thumped, and the stranger consumed her dreamy dismay at finding herself still occupying her body, even in a dream.

She opened her eyes again. He had begun to whittle the piece of ivory. "What is your name?"

He looked up. His intense blue eyes focused on her in a way she didn't understand, as if he didn't expect her to have to ask such a question. "Kiel," he said.

"Kiel what?"

"Just...Kiel."

"And who are you, *just Kiel?*"

His lips curved.

Her eyes fastened on his lips. An errant frisson of a thrill skated over her skin. How could this, *this,* be a dream?

"An Avenging Angel," he said.

"Of course." She drew a pillow up tight against her tender breasts. She clung to her dream as if her sanity depended upon it. "That's possible in a dream. Isn't it? Did you leave your wings at the door?"

"No." He raised his brow. "I don't do wings, except under extreme circumstances." He gave a half smile. "Even then, I don't check them at the door."

She smiled dreamily. "I don't fall into bed with strange angels, either—except in near-death experiences, I guess. I'm a widow," she confided, then frowned. "But I guess you know all that if you're an angel, huh?"

"I know, Robyn."

The firelight behind him set a halo around his golden red hair. Or maybe, expecting angel accoutrements, she was only making that up in her dreams, too. The troubling thought occurred to her that angels didn't go around making love to mortals, even in dreams. Kiel was way too sexy to be an angel. The way he made her feel, looking at her, was how Keller had always made her feel, only more so. More earthy. Sexual. Rooted in what was real. Love.

But she must be wrong about dreams. Anything could happen, couldn't it? He could know what was in her heart if this was her dream. Isn't that what all women wanted in a mate, a man who understood what was in her heart?

She sat up, pulling the comforter up to cover herself. "Maybe that's what this is all about. My poor little lost psyche fulfilling my deepest needs in my dreams."

His eyes betrayed a glint of terrible guilt.

"What?" she asked.

"I'm sorry, Robyn."

She swallowed. She didn't understand. "Sorry for what? Being in my dreams?"

"Not exactly." Dressed in jeans and a green-and-blue plaid woolen shirt, barefoot, male, freckled, strong and testy enough to make a believer of her, he stopped whittling and set aside the chunk of ivory and his knife. "This isn't a dream."

"Oh. Well." She straightened her backbone. "In that case you need to pop out, or whatever earth angels do, and I need to be on my way."

She tossed aside the comforter and stood, naked, her body still rosy in the afterglow of sleep and one dangerously sensual dream. She figured Kiel, the-figment-of-her-imagination-angel, would fade in a trice. That she would wake up in her own bedroom with Keller's outrageous pen-and-ink cartoon sketches on the bookshelves, the thick gray-and-peach Aubusson carpet, the too-neat, half-empty sleigh bed and the scent from a vase of white roses that she had bought herself because Keller wasn't around to bring her flowers anymore.

The only trouble was, when she stood, naked as the day she was born, Kiel didn't fade. Reality crowded in on her. A bare plank floorboard creaked beneath her feet.

The bed was rumpled. The scent of burning pine logs permeated the cabin.

And the Avenging Angel Kiel stared an instant too long at her body.

He stood and raked a hand through his fiery golden hair, then turned to plant his hands on the mantel and stare into the fire instead. "Get dressed, Robyn."

She panicked. Would an angel have a gritting voice of a frustrated human male? No. Keeping a sharp eye on his broad, plaid-clad back, she snatched up clothes from her open suitcase, then stared at the designer jeans she didn't remember packing and a beautiful Scottish wool pullover sweater of Keller's she wore only at home. The remains of her euphoria vanished into thin air. "What are these?"

"Your clothes?"

"I want to know what is going on right now!" She put on the underwear, jeans and Keller's sweater, then jerked on warm socks. "Who are you, really? How did these things get in my suitcase? For that matter, where is *here?*"

He sighed, then picked up the poker and sent sparks flying up the stone chimney. "I'm an angel, Robyn. An Avenging Angel." He seemed to know the precise moment she was dressed and he could safely turn around again. He put the poker back in its place and sat down, taking up his knife once more. "The clothes are yours—"

"No," she contradicted him fiercely, ignoring for the moment his delusions of being an Avenging Angel. "The sweater belonged to my husband—to Keller—and I only wear it when I'm ... alone." Her head dipped low. Embarrassment nagged at her for betraying herself. Again.

That she would wear Keller's sweater to drive away her loneliness told a pretty pathetic tale.

"I must be going crazy." She pressed her lips together, and lifted her chin. She couldn't question how Keller's sweater got in her suitcase if she wasn't willing to accept the possibility of an angel—an Avenging Angel—intervening in her life. "I must have put the sweater and jeans and socks there myself."

"I thought the sweater would be a comfort to you." Kiel whoever-he-was sat back on the hearth. His eyes never left her.

She swallowed. "How would you know that?" She met his gaze defiantly. He seemed to be waiting on her to accept the absurd, but he would have a long wait.

He tilted his head. "Robyn, I know this is a stretch to believe—"

"It's more than a stretch, buster. It's either loony tunes or a miracle." She had made her reputation drawing together the threads of unlikely events, crimes, motives. She knew how battered and bruised hearts became so twisted that a woman could drown her own children or a husband kill his wife, but those weren't things that led to a great deal of faith. "I don't believe in miracles."

"Not in any, Robyn?"

Her chin tilted stubbornly. "Not unless I count Keller's presence in my life. But then Keller was ripped right back out again, so that would be a miracle gone awry, wouldn't it?" she demanded. "Not a miracle at all, but some cruel cosmic joke I can't ever forgive!"

He lowered his wildly blue eyes. Didn't have an answer for that, did he? she thought. She felt perilously close to panicking. She latched onto her anger instead, watching him leaning back against the stone fireplace, his legs outstretched. His bare feet were utterly masculine, therefore completely human. And whether she'd packed those clothes herself or fallen into bed in some hypothermic stupor, she wasn't ready to be carted off by men in white jackets.

She plopped herself down in the wooden rocker a little way away with her cosmetic bag and began tugging at the laces of winter hiking boots she had not packed, either. "Suppose you start at the beginning. With the truth, this time."

His fingers toyed with the knife but his eyes focused on hers. "Angels can't lie, Robyn." His voice was still laced with that human male grittiness. "It doesn't matter whether you believe I'm an angel or not. I've been sent to prevent your death."

She went along for the hell of it, wisecracking to pretend she had a choice. "Wouldn't that more properly be the province of Guardian Angels?"

Kiel's lips curved. "Usually." His smile made her skin prickle. "The truth is, Robyn Delaney, *your* Guardian threw up his hands in despair."

She blinked. "I hope you're kidding."

"I'm not."

"You're saying there *are* such things as Guardian Angels?"

"Yes." He nodded. She knew he was looking again at her black eye and swollen cheek where the mugger had backhanded her. "Yours gave you up for a hopeless cause. He didn't know what to do for you anymore."

For an intelligent woman, she had made some fairly reckless decisions. She knew that. Her fingers went to her cheek. It didn't hurt at all, or feel the slightest bit swollen to her fingers. She snatched up a compact from her tapestry bag of makeup and flipped it open. Her black eye was completely clear, and her cheek unbruised.

"Oh, my God." Her hands began to shake. She snapped the compact closed and let it fall into her lap. Her hand waved aimlessly in the direction of her cheek. "Did you do this? Fix this?"

"Not exactly. I made your own healing go a little...faster, is all."

She took a deep breath and blew it out. She could no longer cling to the notion that this was all a dream. Kiel didn't seem to fit the manic mold, which might have explained his delusions of being an Avenging Angel.

She had a preoccupation with reasons, a passion to know why people behaved as they did, what drove them, a need to understand how things happened. Right now she couldn't explain anything, not her clothing, not her cheek being healed, not this place.

Or even why she had allowed Kiel to entice her back from the promising brink of the Hereafter where she could have had Keller back again. Why had she been so willing to see something of Keller in this stranger? Queen of the Lonely Hearts, Robyn Delaney Trueblood....

If her eyes weren't deceiving her and she hadn't gone over the edge, then what he claimed must somehow be true. She needed answers.

She needed them now. "Where are we?"

He paused in his whittling and looked around the cabin. "This place doesn't really exist."

"Humor me. If it did exist, where would it be?"

"A ways from your car, tucked away in a remote valley beyond Aspen."

Then, Robyn thought, she was still within striking distance of Spyder Nielsen's place. "And you just materialized out of thin air? On—"

"You were half frozen to death."

"A golden stallion?" She rolled her eyes. "Please."

He tilted his head. A smile played at his lips. "Not your fantasy, huh?" He looked at her from beneath his brows, daring her, somehow, to deny it.

Her cheeks flamed. It was her fantasy, one of them, to be swept away like a movie heroine on a galloping steed in the arms of a strong and silent sort. Keller would have known that, but Kiel had no business messing with her fantasies. She couldn't seem to break off eye contact with him. "I don't do..." She swallowed. His fingers caressed the piece of ivory. Heat flared at her throat. "I don't have... fantasies. I'm all grown up now."

"Do you believe only children have fantasies?"

"No." She opened her compact again to make sure of what she already knew. She lowered the mirror. "But if I wanted to fantasize myself an Avenging Angel, I would have chosen the angel that Keller became."

His jaw tightened, and his hand closed in a fist around his whittling. She hadn't meant to insult him, but she had definitely struck a nerve. An angel with an ego.

Great.

"Look," she said. "I'm sorry. I didn't mean to offend you—or suggest you're not a perfectly wonderful Avenging Angel..." She jumped up in frustration. "Good Lord, what am I *saying?*" She wrapped her arms around herself. "I need some coffee. I need out of here."

She clumped in her winter hiking boots across the wooden floor to a kitchen nook, refusing to question the fact that there even was coffee—and on an earthenware dish, a slice of a raspberry crumb cake she would cheerfully die for.

She snatched up a sleek gray percolator from the gas burner of a gourmet iron cookstove crafted to resemble a century-old antique. She poured herself a mugful, then took a bite of crumb cake, which was real, and a sip of percolated coffee, which was black and strong and brimming with caffeine, the way she'd been drinking it since Keller died. She had to remind herself that this place supposedly did not exist.

The refrigerator was shiny and black and ultramodern, the sink a dove-gray ceramic, the countertop beveled marble. She opened the blinds over the square oak table, which was set against the wall beneath a picture window.

Snow had drifted high, covering the ground and the branches of blue spruce and spindly lodgepole pines. She saw no road or any access to the cabin, but maybe the snow concealed a trail.

She wrapped her fingers around the steaming mug. She would bet if she stuck her nose out the door, the snowflakes would light on her face and melt like the real thing, too.

Why didn't she feel real fear, trapped God-only-knew where with a man who claimed to be one of His angels? *Because it's true?*

He still sat on the hearth, whittling, watching her. She leaned against the marble counter, polished off the piece of crumb cake and resorted to her questioning technique to anchor herself again.

"Why this place, Kiel?"

Putting aside the ivory and pocketknife, he got up and came over to pour himself a mug of coffee. He stood near her, taller by inches, solidly masculine and warm. He leaned against the counter opposite her and crossed one bare foot over the other. Her pleasure in his proximity alarmed her.

"You might have died, Robyn. You were dangerously close. I had to do something, and this—" he gestured around the cabin "—was one of my options."

"What does that mean? That, being an angel, you could have blinked me home if you wanted to?"

He gave a half smile. "In a manner of speaking."

"Or back into my car?"

"Yes."

"Or to a hospital?"

His eyes darkened. "Haven't you spent more than your share of time in hospitals, Robyn?"

"Yes, but—" She broke off, swamped by the memory of his sensual ministrations, of his lips tracing her surgical scars, his touch making her feel things again. Desire. Hope.

She stared at Kiel, desperate to make the sensual memories stop unfurling. "Making love to me...was that one of your *options*, too?"

"Not—"

"Is that what Avenging Angels do?" she demanded. "Rescue damsels in distress to bed them?"

He never flinched. "Not exactly."

"Then what, exactly?"

"We right wrongs, Robyn. We fight injustice, we do what must be done to defeat tyranny—"

"Then I can think of half a dozen hot spots on earth where you're desperately needed." She glared at him. "This isn't one of them."

"Every injustice demands an answer, Robyn, whether that answer is ever obvious in the span of one human life or not. There is always justice, finally."

"Well, thank you very much, but I'm perfectly capable of fighting my own battles."

"Keller was, too, Robyn, but he's dead." He reached out to her and cupped her cheek as if he understood completely her fear of a man who knew more than he should. "Robyn, you can trust me. I know what I know because I am an angel. You suspect now that your husband was murdered, and you were on your way to Spyder Nielsen's house when you skidded off the road."

She straightened and turned away to rinse her mug in the sink. "If you can do all this, why didn't you intercept me before I got that far?"

He shook his beautiful, fiery golden head. "The point of avenging isn't to interfere with your free will, Robyn. You're human. You get to make your own choices. Your Guardian Angel created that traffic jam back in Denver, but the best he could hope was that while you waited it out, you would have time to reconsider your plan."

Her chin went up...again. "I still intend to confront those two. All I've lost is a little time." She wasn't backing down on that. "Do you know if Trudi Candelaria and Stuart Willetts conspired to murder my husband?"

"No." Kiel's golden brows pulled together. "I know how Keller died. I know the case against Candelaria ended in a mistrial because of Keller's death—and I know the reasoning that has made you suspect Candelaria and Willetts." He drained the coffee from his mug and set it in the sink beside Robyn's mug, then turned to look into her eyes. "What I don't know is what you hope to gain by confronting them."

She couldn't break off her eye contact with him. "I want to see their faces, Kiel. I want to suggest that they had to get rid of Keller before he sent Trudi to prison for life, and I want to see their faces when I do."

"Do you think they'll admit—"

"No. Of course I don't think they'll confess on the spot. Of course not! But if I go there and upset their plush little applecart, they'll react, and then I'll know what I'm dealing with." She took a deep breath and crossed her arms over her breasts. "Anyway, I thought you said you had come to prevent my death."

He nodded. "In part."

"You've done that." She had to move away, out of the aura that seemed to surround Kiel. She scooted past him and kept going. "I guess I should thank you," she said over her shoulder, "but—"

"Robyn, you're still in danger."

"Of what? I promise not to defy any more muggers."

His eyes fixed her. "Of you know what, Robyn," he said. "Suppose everything you believe may have happened, *did* happen. Suppose Willetts and Candelaria conspired to murder Keller. You have a dangerous reputation, you know. People tend to believe what an author of your caliber says. So if they killed Keller, and you tell them you're onto them, what's to stop them from killing again? They'll have to in order to keep you quiet."

Discounting the threat of being killed herself, she jerked the covers up on the feather bed, then tossed her belongings haphazardly into her suitcase.

The only thing she had ever willingly kept organized was her writing notes. Keller would have shot her a "fix that or die" look over the rumpled bedclothes, then she would have dared him to make her, and then they'd have made a worse mess of the covers than when she started. But Keller wasn't here anymore to make her do anything—or fall into bed as a consequence—and that was the point, wasn't it?

"I'm not going to let that stop me from exposing them," she announced, zipping shut her soft-cover tapestry suitcase. "Or let you stop me, either."

"Think again, Robyn." He straightened. The look he gave her from clear across the cabin said the threat of being murdered herself ought to be enough to give her pause. That after so many foolish decisions, she should reconsider her actions. And most clearly, that he was in charge of her.

She threw on a coat that wasn't hers and hauled the strap of her suitcase to her shoulder. "I'm out of here."

"In a while," he agreed.

"No, not in a while." She gathered her hair off her shoulder and adjusted the suitcase strap. "Now. There are things I have to do."

"Name it," he offered, "and I'll help you. But you're not going alone."

"You can't stop me, Kiel," she responded in the same even tone.

"I can, Robyn."

For a moment she believed he could stop her. And for another moment, however unforgivably disloyal it was to Keller, she didn't want to leave Kiel, or leave behind the feelings he had brought to life again in her. She didn't need to feel things anymore. It just made her life too complicated.

She shrugged. "Give it your best shot. Oh, and thanks for the rescue," she called out as she tugged at the door. The door swung open, but as she began to step out into drifts piled hip-high and the gently falling snow, she encountered a soft wall of nothingness.

Confused, and a tiny bit frightened, she tried again with the same result.

"Robyn—"

"No!" She glanced back over her shoulder at Kiel, clenched her teeth and threw herself against a force she couldn't see or feel or penetrate. She hadn't stubbed her toe, or banged her nose into anything, hadn't injured herself in any way, but she could not move into the outdoors.

She stood there a moment, snow falling inches from her face, drew a deep breath and let the shoulder strap fall. Her suitcase landed with a thud.

She felt caged. Worse than caged. Cold dread filled her, like the panic that seized her when she was inadvertently caught somewhere dark. This couldn't be happening. These feelings, this cold-sweat sensation, in the bright light of day...

Her throat shut down. She raised her fists and battered the solid, invisible barrier, which didn't even hurt her flailing hands, but it was useless. She lowered her clenched fists to her sides. Her shoulders drooped. She turned slowly around. Kiel stood watching her, his expression hard.

"You said I could trust you," she accused.

"Amend that," he said, his tone leaving her in no doubt that she was going nowhere except by his leave. "You *have* to trust me."

"How can I?" She slung her arm out behind her. Her hand neither hit nor bounced off anything, it only... stopped. "What happened to my free will, Kiel? What is this?"

He had no trouble meeting her eyes. No twinge of guilt or remorse for boxing her in. "It's only a force field, Robyn."

"Only a force field," she repeated inanely. She pushed her hair away from her face and back over her shoulder. "A force field. That explains it."

He frowned. "It doesn't explain anything, Robyn. It just is."

"I'm a prisoner here, isn't that right? In a cage crafted specially for me?" *A cage.* The irony was so thick it made a bubble of laughter rise in her throat.

A cage. As if her terror of the darkness wasn't enough, now she was caged. The perfect cosmic, metaphysical, New Age, create-your-own-reality mind-rot metaphor for the state her heart was in.

Imprisoned.

Locked up.

Well and truly sealed away, because her heart belonged to Keller Trueblood and he had departed life with the key. And Robyn Delaney's only excuse for taking the tumble into a feather bed with a perfect stranger was that she saw Keller in Kiel...where Keller couldn't be.

She stared at him. "Keller...Kiel, Keller, Kiel. How incredibly insensitive!" she jibed, on a roll now. His eyes seemed to fill with anguish. His chin strained. His hand clenched. "Wouldn't you think heaven could send me back Keller to be my angel?" she demanded. "Or at *least* someone whose name wasn't... But then maybe you're..."

Her tirade faded to nothing. Maybe heaven had sent her Keller. Maybe this man was the angel Keller had become.

And maybe she had just taken that final descent into undisputed madness.

Chapter Four

She backed up until her shoulder blades and back and bottom and thighs came up tight against the proof of her gilded cage and began to laugh. Her knees bent and her backside slid down the smooth, solid, invisible barrier until her fanny hit the floor. Her laughter was tinged with hysteria. Tears brightened her eyes.

He went to her then. He couldn't stand it any longer. In her tears he had all the proof he would ever need. His soul was the soul of Keller Trueblood, but he could never reveal the truth of her suspicions. Not without causing her a deeper despair than he was causing her now.

But he could ease her mind and mute the logic of her heart. He could distract her for the time it took to resolve the injustice of Keller's death. Maybe when his death was avenged, her heart would be at peace in her earthly life.

"Robyn." He reached down and took her hands. He used the physical contact to help ease her confusion. She allowed him to draw her to her feet. Her eyes were luminous, wide, frightened. He cupped her face and thumbed away her tears.

His cuff button tangled with her beautiful, shiny black hair and got caught. He felt suddenly trapped by her feminine and human nature, ambushed by desire no angel should ever feel. His body reacted swiftly, tightening violently.

At some higher level of awareness he recognized that his cuff button being caught was a warning, a cosmic clue, an alarm signaling the grim repercussions of tangling in this way with a human woman.

But he could not take the simplest recourse. He couldn't even manage that first step away from her.

Her eyes focused on his lips. He heard her swallow, saw her catch her lower lip between her teeth. Her breath, warm and coffee-scented, stirred the hairs at his throat. The exquisite tension flickering between them flared.

Her tongue dampened her parted lips. His gaze fixed on their glistening. She tilted her head up. He tilted his down. His need to kiss her was unlike anything Kiel had ever experienced . . . a tugging at senses and emotions he couldn't remember. An echo of familiarity only Keller's memory could have supplied.

Last night he had made love to her. Served her physical longing. Filled her emotional abyss to bring her back from the brink of death.

A groan escaped his throat.

This was not lust, for his soul and hers were mated into eternity. But he had not experienced for himself this yearning, this sweet anticipation pitched against the bitter insight that it would be better for her if they never so much as kissed again.

The regret nearly crippled his judgment.

He freed the button of his shirt cuff from her hair and drew back, planting in her mind the notion that it was she who chose to end the possibility of that kiss.

She swallowed and straightened. Disappointment sparked in her heart, then guilt. A year had passed. She missed Keller so much, craved his touch and his warmth and his love so badly, that she had tumbled to a total stranger and pretended it was Keller.

And as if that weren't enough, no matter how disloyal and wicked she ought to feel, her eyes still fixed greedily on the bronzed hairs at Kiel's throat. She admitted to herself that she had wanted that kiss.

She took a deep breath, reassuring herself that it didn't make her a despicable person, and that she still controlled her destiny. Whatever attraction she felt to this man, this . . . angel, she could handle. She looked up at him. "What now?"

"Let me help you, Robyn. I promise you we will get to the bottom of Keller's death."

"I make the calls?"

"So long as I'm with you," he agreed, an unruly lock of bronze hair falling over his brow, "you make the calls."

"Good." She angled her head toward the open door and the invisible barrier that blocked out the weather and shut her in. "You can start by opening the cage door."

Without the least outward sign that he was banishing the force field, he did so. When she could smell the snow and feel the cold, Robyn accepted the absurd. Kiel had supernatural powers.

Devil or angel?

She had no basis for a decision other than his word, which even with her deeply ingrained skepticism, she somehow, finally, believed.

Kiel must be an angel.

She could trust him. Together, they would avenge both Keller's death and that of Spyder Nielsen's, the man whose murder remained unsolved and unpunished because Keller had died before his time.

SHE WANTED TO DO THINGS the ordinary way. No angel tricks, and she made that clear. He donned shoes and socks and put the small piece of ivory carving in his sheepskin coat pocket. His boots, the Sorels, one of the true trademarks of a native of the Rockies, looked broken in, another trademark.

"Your car," he said, "is on the other side of that ridge. Are you sure you want to hike out of here?"

"I'm sure." The snow had stopped and the clouds parted. Sunlight glittered on the blanket of white snow, reducing it to drifts and patches where the late summer alpine flowers peeked through. Bedraggled as they were, the pretty blue wood asters, columbines and alpine gentian weren't ready to give up the ghost for winter.

Robyn took heart from their example and went through the door. "I could use the exercise. Besides—" she shot Kiel a look "—you can't be popping up with golden steeds and mountain hideaways all the time. Not if you're sticking with me."

"No more wish fulfillment?"

"None. Mitts off my fantasies, Kiel." She glared at him. "They're mine, and they're secret, and they won't be fantasies anymore if you make them come true. I'm serious."

His look said it was her seriousness that was the problem. "You've heard why angels can fly, haven't you?"

"Because they take themselves so lightly?" She rolled her eyes. Every angel book in a decidedly flooded angel-book market contained some variation on the theme. "Silly me. I thought it was the wings."

But without any wings of her own she was feeling incredibly light on her feet, and stronger than she had been even before the rotting mine shaft timbers had crushed her legs. Toting her own suitcase on principle, Robyn struck out in the direction Kiel had indicated.

He caught up with her, matching his much longer stride to hers. Dressed in jeans and the plaid flannel shirt, he let the gorgeous shin-length sheepskin coat flap open. They went along for several moments in silence. Robyn spent the time thinking about how striking the deal with Kiel had changed her own plans to confront Stuart Willetts and Trudi Candelaria.

After a while she also unzipped her parka—the one she hadn't packed, either—and put back the rabbit-fur-lined hood. The sun warmed everything in Colorado, melting off snowfall in a few hours everywhere but atop the fourteen-thousand-foot mountain peaks.

Rugged granite dominated the landscape. She picked her way across the rocky ground, choosing a path over damp layers of pine needles. It was easy to believe in back country like this that you might never find your way out. She should be thanking Kiel—without him she would have had no idea which way to go to get back to the road. On the other hand, she wouldn't be where she didn't know where she was if it weren't for him.

She spotted two squirrels chasing each other over a boulder jutting out of the ground. The bushy-tailed little guy in the lead must once have put up a hell of a fight—he had a raggedy ear and only one front leg. Kiel stopped and knelt to watch the pair of squirrels. Robyn finally asked herself the obvious question . . . why wasn't her own leg actively protesting the strenuous hike?

She gave Kiel a sideways glance. "Are you going to fix the squirrel's leg, too?"

"No leg to fix." He kept watching the pair of squirrels. "I didn't fix your leg, either. I just speeded up the progress you would have made yourself."

"Put it back. I'd rather do it myself."

Squinting against the sun, he gave her a quizzical look. "You really want it back the way it was?"

"No." She meant to say yes, but the truth popped out. How contrary would she have to be to wish her leg ached again? She had to clamp her jaw hard so her chin didn't start trembling. His question went to her heart, to the way she dealt with the world.

She put her suitcase down on a rock and sat down on the one next to that, folding her long legs up like a grasshopper and wrapping her arms around them. While everyone left in her life was busy encouraging her, telling her how well she was fighting back, coping and rehabilitating, she didn't much like herself anymore.

She didn't even like her plan to march in and get in Stuart Willetts's face about his affair with Trudi. The whole idea lacked any hint of the finesse she had prided herself on in her career.

"I didn't used to be like this," she said, resting her chin on her knees, watching a patch of snow melt away under the blazing sun. Kiel sat down beside her. "My dad was always making whatever happened that didn't suit him into this huge battle. There always had to be someone else at fault, something to be overcome, some evildoer to be defeated. *You 'n' me against the world, kid,* he'd say."

She didn't want to be against the world—with or without her father, she explained to Kiel. And she hadn't been, not since she'd figured it all out at the tender age of eight when Bobbie Cantwell stomped her 100 percent spelling paper into the mud on the playground and she decked him and her third-grade teacher made her come back inside the school room and write one hundred times on the blackboard *Fighting is never the answer.*

But this past year she had let everything in her life be reduced to fighting. She had to fight to live after Keller had died, fight the dark inside and out, fight to recover, fight to perform the grueling physical therapy work, fight her stubborn heart, fight a mugger, and now, fight her leg being better even though doing so made no sense at all.

Kiel cuffed her gently on the chin when she had spilled all that, letting his fist come to rest on her shoulder. "Some things are worth fighting for, Robyn." Her name sounded like an endearment on his lips. "You just have to be a little more discriminating."

Tears prickled at her eyelids. She nodded. "I know." She blinked back the pooling tears.

"This rule about angel tricks, for instance," he said, straight-faced, his smiling eyes goading her out of her pity party. He gestured toward the cabin, which still sat nestled at the low point of the valley. "I can't exactly leave a mountain hideaway where there isn't supposed to be one."

Robyn looked askance. "You remind me of Keller's five-year-old nephew, Nicholas."

"Me?" he croaked.

"Is that so surprising?"

"Well . . . I've never been a kid."

"Well, you're just like him. One more angel trick is the same thing as one more cookie or one last glass of water before bed. In a pinch he'll even go for another kiss." She smiled. "Though Nicholas isn't real big on kisses anymore."

Kiel laughed, but the sound faded in the thin mountain air. "Give him a few years."

Robyn broke off the look Kiel gave her. "Do your angel thing, Kiel."

He did the angel thing and made the mountain cabin where he had made love to her vanish into thin air. The human thing, kissing Nicholas Trueblood's auntie again, would have been a terrible mistake.

DESPITE HER UNHAPPINESS with her plan to confront Stuart Willetts and Trudi Candelaria, she knew it had to be done. If nothing else, Robyn thought, the respectful, *professional* approach was to allow them both to state their side of the story.

When Kiel led her back to her small coupe, the snow had melted, and the ease with which Kiel pushed her out of the mud made her shake her head.

She pulled a U-turn and headed back down the mountain. She needed a shower and fresh clothes. She drove to The Chandler House, a bed-and-breakfast in Aspen proper, checked in to her small Victorian-style bedroom, showered and lay down for a while. Later, alone in the four-poster bed, Robyn woke and got up, enormously reenergized.

Kiel had arranged a light supper to be brought in on trays. By seven that night, Robyn was prepared. Kiel stopped her only long enough to put around her neck the small ivory carving he had completed and strung on a fine strand of gold. Standing behind her at an elaborately framed mirror near the door, he showed her what it was.

Robyn stared at the intricate pair of angel's wings, joined in the middle, resting against her flesh. The ivory seemed to take on the radiance and sheen and warmth of the strand of gold. Centered in the deep V-neck of her mauve mohair sweater, the tiny wings were more beautiful than those of a butterfly.

"A reminder," he said.

She swallowed; the wings seemed to move. "Of what?"

"That an angel takes herself lightly."

THE HOME OF THE MURDERED Spyder Nielsen sat on the most coveted piece of residential property in all of Pitkin County, Colorado. The view, the sheer panorama, was unmatched anywhere in the Colorado Rockies.

The house itself was enormous, eleven thousand square feet, Robyn knew. Foreign nationals, princes with fabulous wealth, had built houses in the area nearing fifty-thousand square feet, so this house could only be called pretentious in a relative way.

As Robyn drove up the circle drive and parked near the garage, she thought this was the most stunning, natural use of granite and glass she had ever seen. The native landscaping hid the single-story house from the view of the road until the last possible second. Such was the power of very deep pockets.

Spyder Nielsen had parlayed his ski jumping into a reputation exceeded only by his fortune, and Trudi Candelaria, by escaping the conviction for his murder, had fallen heir to it all.

Robyn drew a deep breath and opened her door slowly, but Kiel bolted from the car. Accustomed as he was to flying to the stars, traveling the firmament, closed-in spaces smaller than a house this size made him crazy. Panicked by the dark, she knew what that kind of phobia was all about, but she was still smiling when Kiel punched the doorbell. Angels with egos and phobias amused her.

A sharp-faced middle-aged woman answered the door. "*Ja?*"

This was not a surprise. Frau Kautz had returned from her holiday, but Robyn's curiosity rose. Elsa Kautz had been Spyder Nielsen's housekeeper long before he ever brought Trudi Candelaria home. Robyn would have expected Trudi to get rid of her, or that the woman would not have wanted to stay on with the woman accused of murdering Elsa's beloved Spyder.

Robyn sucked in a quick breath and stepped forward. "Frau Kautz, my name is Robyn Delaney. This is my associate, Kiel..." She rushed on, not having thought to ask what he used for a last name. "We've come to see Ms. Trudi Candelaria, if we may, and Mr. Stuart Willetts. Are they—"

"Kiel?" she interrupted, looking right through Robyn. "Vaht kind of name—"

"Ezekiel, Frau Kautz." He turned on a thousand-candle smile, glided forward, took the daunting woman's hand and kissed her knuckles in a gesture reminiscent of a European count. "Kiel Alighieri. At your service." In spite of herself Elsa's stern visage cracked.

Kiel pressed his narrow advantage. "Ms. Delaney is a famous writer. She's considering a work on Spyder Nielsen."

It took all Robyn's mental resources not to go slack-jawed at Kiel's choice of a surname to use, or his approach. This wasn't the game plan—wasn't even close to the cover they had decided upon, but he was winging it blithely past a barrier Robyn hadn't prepared for, deftly turning the forbidding Frau Kautz from a harpy at the gates into a valuable ally.

With a few brilliantly conceived asides on how vital the old Frau would be to the success of the biography, Kiel had the woman leading them into the house, through the icy elegance of the stark and pristine white living room and the superlative ambience of a dining room done in shades of gray and mauve.

"Alighieri?" Robyn managed to whisper as they followed Frau Kautz.

"Yeah," he grinned without even looking at her, talking sideways. "You know, Dante's surname?"

"I know Dante," she whispered disgustedly, "I've just never seen such rank impudence!"

"Me, neither," he shrugged, still grinning. "Just a little spin on the inferno thing since I'm down—never mind. Show time."

In the massive entertainment room where they had arrived, Trudi Candelaria sat curled up on a chaise longue flipping indolently through a recent copy of *Town & Country*. Dressed in gray raw silk leggings and a pink cashmere sweater, she had kicked off a pair of gold sandals Robyn had recently seen on sale in Denver for three hundred dollars.

The room itself was enormous. Twenty-foot ceilings, three conversation pits, a fireplace at each end, floor-to-ceiling glass windows. A wall of glass, really, perfectly framing the Maroon Bells, the most famous and photographed mountain peaks in all of Colorado. An Enya CD played on a flawless acoustic system.

Facing the double French doors into the room, Stuart Willetts sat at the foot of the chaise, massaging Trudi Candelaria's feet.

Robyn's anger at Willetts, at this proof that he had in truth taken up with Trudi Candelaria, rose like bile in her throat. She exchanged glances with Kiel. She felt a calming aura swathe her. She could almost hear Kiel's sentiment. *Easy, Robyn.* Frau Kautz rapped softly on the doorframe.

"What is it, Elsa?" Trudi deigned to glance up from her fashion magazine. She seemed indifferent to visitors, and gave no hint of recognizing Robyn. Willetts ignored the interruption entirely until Trudi's interest sharpened when she saw Kiel.

"A Ms. Robyn Delaney to see you, ma'am, and Mr. Kiel Alighieri. Ms. Delaney is a famous author interested in interviewing you for Spyder's story."

"Robyn?" Willetts said, his head jerking up. In the split second between hearing her name and seeing her, his shoulders stiffened. In the next, he managed somehow to arrange his handsome, narrow face in an expression that might have passed for pleasant surprise. "My God! It's been . . . a year. How are you?"

His perfectly delivered solicitude galled her, all the more because she had expected to see guilt in his eyes, and there was none. She chided herself for being so artlessly naive. Michael Massie had warned her. Kiel had warned her.

She knew better.

She had interviewed more than a hundred murderers, several of them for days on end. Not one of them had guilt flashing over them like a bright neon sign. So why expect Stuart Willetts to roll over and give himself up?

Because she thought it should have been different with someone she had known before? It wasn't at all. If Stuart Willetts had been successful in concealing his early attraction to Trudi Candelaria, Keller had been deceived as well. But Robyn Delaney wasn't rolling over and giving up, either.

"I'm fine, Stuart. Physically." She left it to his guilty conscience to make whatever he wanted of that.

"Who is this woman, Stuart? Do you know her?" Trudi's beautiful plastic face creased as she dragged her gaze off Kiel.

"Don't you remember, darling," he said. "Robyn's husband was—"

"Never mind." Trudi's voice was whispery, childlike, but her tone matched the icy decor. "Send them away. I'm not interested."

Kiel stepped forward to shake hands with Willetts. "Kiel Alighieri. I'm an associate of Robyn." He turned to Trudi. "You may be interested. Robyn's husband was Keller Trueblood."

Trudi's enormous brown eyes narrowed as she turned her head slowly toward Robyn. She said nothing. One song after another played on the CD. Willetts seemed to hold his breath, waiting on Trudi's response. At last she spoke, her whispered voice tinged with melancholy.

"Did you love him very much?"

"Yes." Robyn's answer simply spilled out. She had been prepared for anything from this woman. Bitterness. Outrage. Contempt. Anything but that question framed in such sympathy. Robyn crumbled. She felt faintly nauseous. She wanted to turn and walk away. Or run.

She stood there and held her ground. Kiel sat in a deep-cushioned plum-velvet-covered chair. Stuart remained standing, his battleship gray eyes fixed on her. His uneasiness seemed to grow in tandem with hers, but that couldn't be.

It didn't even matter whether Trudi's sympathy was genuine or a calculated effort to knock Robyn off her pins. The only thing that mattered was her choice. Her response.

She couldn't stand up and fight for what needed to be done if she couldn't deal, a year after the fact, with having lost Keller. It was a question of deciding once and for all whether she would be defeated, crushed by her loss, or if she would rise up again and conquer her terrible, cold-sweat fear of darkness...and then find the grace and courage to be herself, alone.

"You're not in this alone, Robyn."

She turned to Kiel, grateful he could read her thoughts, for this sliver of time, at least. But she suddenly had the eerie sense that Trudi and Stuart were caught up in some kind of suspended animation, unhearing and unseeing. Neither moved. The expressions on their faces were static. Frozen.

Kiel explained. "I've slowed time for them, Robyn."

"You can do that?"

He nodded.

"They can't hear us?"

"No."

She shivered and rubbed her hands up and down the sleeves of her mohair sweater, accepting this minor miracle. "What just happened here, Kiel?"

"I'd say Trudi just took a stab at the gaping hole in your armor."

"Yes." Robyn exhaled sharply. "Maybe. But why wasn't her first instinct to come flying at me?"

Kiel shrugged. "Any number of reasons."

"Like what?"

"Maybe she's innocent."

"Or maybe she's been clued-in to the fact that it would be double jeopardy to retry her. That it would take an act of Congress to bring her up again on the charges of murdering Spyder Nielsen."

"She's cool, Robyn," Kiel agreed. "She was out on bail. She may even have seduced Stuart Willetts with the express intention of causing a mistrial."

"But if that was the purpose, why would it be necessary to murder Keller?"

"Maybe he saw what she was up to. Maybe he threatened to take Willetts off the prosecution team. The timing was critical. If Trudi already had Willetts wrapped around her little finger, Keller's dumping him would have been disastrous to his career and his reputation."

Robyn played unwittingly with the tiny pair of wings at her breast. "I don't even know for sure that she or Willetts had anything to do with that cave-in."

"You won't know, either, until you just plunge in and do what you do best. Ask the questions. Find the inconsistencies. Cross reference every answer with every other answer and every other witness." He smiled encouragingly. "You know your own drill, Robyn. You just have to trust yourself."

"I hardly recognize myself anymore, Kiel." She swallowed hard. "I let Trudi derail me with one simple question inside sixty seconds. How can that be? A year ago it wouldn't have happened."

"A year ago, you hadn't already lost Keller." He remained seated in the deep plum-colored chair. "Step back and make her play your game."

The advice sounded so much like something Keller would have said that it stole her breath away. No matter what Keller played at, he had made it into a mental game, a test of sticking power and wits.

"It's your move." He didn't offer to hold her or put an arm around her shoulders or bolster her in any physical way.

"I know." Did he know that's what she craved more than air, to be held? She thought he did know. She even thought he wanted to hold her too. Something stopped him, some greater strength than she possessed.

She would have to make do with her own resources now, and she was tired of waffling, tired of feeling needy. Needing to be rescued. "Okay. Let me at her."

Giving her a thumbs-up, Kiel sat back. Trudi's eyes darted to Stuart, then back up at Robyn.

She touched the wings at her throat once more and went on as if no time had intervened, this time without missing a beat. "I'll be straight with you Ms. Candelaria. I don't believe my husband's death was accidental."

Trudi blinked. "This has something to do with me?"

"I believe it does, yes."

"How utterly extraordinary!" Trudi raved. "Please, by all means, continue."

"Don't bother, Robyn," Stuart snapped. "Trudi didn't kill Spyder Nielsen, and she sure as hell didn't have anything to do with Keller's death."

"Did you, Stuart?" Robyn asked, sitting in the club chair opposite Kiel, turning her attention to Keller's former second chair and assistant.

"Look," he said, sinking back down onto the foot of Trudi's chaise longue. A low, three-foot-square beveled glass table sat between them. He and Trudi had already knocked back half a bottle of a wildly expensive rosé. He rapped on the gleaming surface of the table. "Let's cut to the chase. I know how this must look. 'Associate counsel blows away special prosecutor, drops charges, shacks up with wealthy murderess.' Am I doing the theory justice here?"

"It plays, Stuart."

"In Peoria, maybe." His attractive mouth shaped itself into a sneer. "An interesting Hollywood script idea, Robyn, but it didn't happen that way."

She sat back, ready to listen. "Then suppose you tell me how it did happen."

"Why should we talk to you at all?" Trudi asked, leaning into her cushions, still somehow amused.

"Because I want to know what happened, and I don't intend to stop looking for answers until I'm satisfied—and until my husband's death is avenged."

"Get a life instead, Robyn," Willetts advised, his voice edged with something not quite disdainful, not quite fearful. "My God, how self-destructive can you get? Keller died. It was tragic. But your reputation will drop like a stone if you try to make anything more of his death than a terrible accident. Do you seriously think that's what Keller would have wanted to become of you?"

Robyn exchanged glances with Kiel. She felt so in control of herself and her intentions that she wondered if Kiel had somehow kicked every endorphin-producing cell in her brain into hyperactivity.

"Keller isn't here, Stuart," she said. "And my reputation is my business. I don't intend to ruin my own credibility or libel anyone or make up wild-eyed stories or try to prove that someone succeeded in murdering Keller."

"Unless that is what happened," Kiel added.

Stuart scowled. "Who the hell are you, anyway? What's your interest in all of this?"

"Justice."

Kiel's body language looked about as angelic as Rambo's. She imagined if Willetts provoked him much further Kiel might fly off his heavenly handle and clap his mortal counterpart between a mighty pair of wings—if only to put the fear of God into him. She directed a quelling look at Kiel, then turned back to Stuart and Trudi. "Please. Talk to me."

"You already believe the worst, Robyn." Stuart shot Kiel another ugly look, as if what Robyn believed must be his fault.

"No one has ever dictated what I think, Stuart—not even Keller." Especially Keller. He'd been in love with her from the first because she was a woman with a mind of her own and the backbone to speak it. "All I want is the truth. Frankly," she said, "I won't settle for less. But I will listen."

"That's what your husband said, too." Trudi tossed her mane of blond hair and reached for the wine bottle. "He didn't believe a word I said." She sloshed the rosé into her wineglass, then swallowed two-thirds of it in one toss. "Tell them, darling."

Robyn got a spiral and pen from her bag and began running a tape player. Stuart stared at it a moment, then sighed and rubbed his eyes, ending by pinching the bridge of his nose. His features were ordinary by any standards, except for long, thick eyelashes most women couldn't contrive with mascara.

He began reciting the facts in the dry, emotionless fashion of attorneys. "Spyder Nielsen died on the night of October 12—almost two years ago—of a blow to the back of his head while he was sitting in the hot tub just outside those sliding doors. The case against Trudi was largely circumstantial. No eye witnesses. Elsa was gone that night.

"Trudi had been out to a party," he went on, stroking her hand. "Spyder refused to go. Trudi got home shortly after midnight, saw a shadowy figure slipping away, and then found Spyder dead—floating in the hot tub. She called the police immediately. Despite an alibi and the shadowy figure, the cops arrested Trudi the next morning. Her fingerprints were on the bronze statue—do you remember seeing it?''

Robyn shook her head. "I never saw any of the physical evidence.''

"Not in person, but Keller sketched it for you on a napkin at the pizza parlor, Robyn. The same night he was named special prosecutor and he hired me to be his second chair.''

She remembered that sketch. The murder weapon was a casting in bronze of a likeness of Spyder Nielsen hurtling through a racing course on skis. She'd seen the sketch again, not too long ago—on a night when she'd succumbed to loneliness and had been reduced to going through Keller's books trying to catch the scent of him.

She shoved the tattletale memory from her mind. Fingerprints on the murder weapon didn't prove anything conclusively. "I knew—everyone knew—that the case against you was circumstantial. But Keller would never have agreed to prosecute if the case wasn't airtight.''

"The air is very thin in Aspen," Trudi said. "My alibi didn't stand up because in the hot tub, Spyder's body temperature didn't drop as it might have otherwise. The time of death could not be established.''

"And motive?''

"I had motive to spare," she snapped. "I had very vocal, quite nasty scenes with the great and mighty Spyder Nielsen in public places. Yes. I had motive and opportunity and his precious bronze at my fingertips. My defense attorney tried to suggest to the jury that I am too small and fragile to have wielded that bronze hard enough or accurately enough to bash Spyder in the back of the head. I could have.

"But I didn't kill Spyder, Ms. Delaney—and your husband refused to believe me."

Chapter Five

Chapter Five

Kiel watched Robyn's response to the accusation Trudi made against Keller Trueblood. She had managed to re-group, to distance herself so that she wasn't kicked in the gut by Trudi Candelaria's recrimination. He was proud of her, touched by her. He let her handle the accusation her way.

"Most defendants on trial for murder protest their innocence," she said. "Tell me why Keller should have believed you."

"Because," she said, shrugging insolently, "I did not kill Spyder."

"Look, Robyn," Stuart interrupted. "This won't get us anywhere. Trudi maintains her innocence to this day. Keller believed otherwise until the day he died. He was capable of being wrong, you know."

Checking her tape player, Robyn straightened. She'd never known Keller not to own up to making a mistake or to *being* mistaken. "Was he wrong about this, Stuart? Was there any physical evidence inconsistent with Trudi's having committed the murder of Spyder Nielsen?"

Stuart shook his head. "No. There was no evidence implicating anyone else. There was a set of tire tracks in the snow that went unidentified, but that was all."

"Keller made every effort to have the authorities match those tracks?"

"Naturally. If you're serious about delving into this case, interview the police. Crandall. Ken Crandall. He's a real piece of work, Robyn. He has it in for anyone with two cents to rub together."

"That would include most people who live in Aspen. So anyone else with a motive could have killed Spyder, is that it?" Kiel asked. "Not only Trudi."

Stuart grimaced, refusing to look at Kiel. "Just talk to Crandall, Robyn."

"We will." She wrote the name on her notepad and circled it, but she didn't let Stuart get away with dismissing Kiel or his point. "It's true, isn't it, that if Crandall has a chip on his shoulder about wealthy Aspenites, he'd have been happy to nail any one of them."

"Maybe." Stuart's jaw tightened. "I'm just saying he has an attitude problem that you might want to keep in mind."

She nodded and looked at Trudi. "Ms. Candelaria, you said my husband wouldn't listen to a word you said. If the only thing you could say was that you didn't kill Spyder in the face of a great deal of circumstantial evidence, what was it you wanted him to hear?"

"I expected to be believed. I am many things, Ms. Delaney, but a liar isn't one of them."

Everything Robyn understood about body language lobbied on the side of believing Trudi, but in Robyn's experience, that wasn't unusual, either. Robyn shook her head. "Do you have any idea what percentage of defendants say exactly that? The 'I ain't no saint but you can trust this' routine is as old as the hills."

Trudi's eyes hardened. "I knew you wouldn't believe me, either." She flung an arm toward the door. Her twenty-four-karat gold bangles clinked together. "Get out of my house."

Robyn didn't move. "Give me something to go on. Anything. Any reason to believe you now."

"There is nothing, Robyn," Stuart answered. "If there had been, Keller would have been persuaded. But here's the bottom line. I believed Trudi on nothing more than instinct. Keller wasn't satisfied by that. In fact, he suggested I might have been thinking with some other part of my anatomy than my head. If you want something to go on, take my admission that was true. I was attracted to Trudi, she knew it, she fanned the flames—"

"Oh, stop it!" Trudi got up from the chaise longue in one lithe motion and sent her wineglass hurtling into the fireplace.

Robyn flinched at the crashing noise. Kiel's eyes narrowed in the direction of the fireplace. She guessed his energy prevented the splinters of glass from flying any further than the hearth.

"Don't say another word!" Trudi hissed.

Stuart quietly ordered her to sit down and shut up. In a million years Robyn would not have believed he would have had the nerve—especially if Trudi had turned him into a kept man, here in Spyder Nielsen's house and in her bed at her whim. Just as astonishingly, Trudi clapped her mouth shut and sat down without uttering another sound.

Stuart took her hand and went on. "I came perilously close to misconduct that would have caused the people's case to end in a mistrial."

"Isn't that the point?" Kiel asked. "That you were so enamored with Trudi you were willing to force the case into a mistrial?"

Trudi rolled her eyes but Stuart nodded. "That's the way it was, yes."

Robyn shivered. "Stuart, are you saying Keller knew about your affair with Trudi?"

"No. It wasn't a full-blown affair at the time, anyway.... But no. He never guessed how I felt about her," Stuart said, his features stark, even grimly composed. "Keller knew my work. He trusted me. He believed I was playing devil's advocate to the case—that's how we worked, how we'd always worked."

The betrayal struck at her composure. She felt a terrible anger rising in her. "You're telling me now that you were prepared to let the whole thing, your affair with the defendant, blow up in Keller's face."

He studied his hands a moment. "I'm not proud of it, Robyn, but yes. If he ever found out, the strategy would have backfired."

"Because Keller would have dropped you from the prosecution if he knew?"

"He'd have had me disbarred, Robyn. That, plus making a very compelling case before any magistrate that Trudi seduced me with the express intention of forcing a mistrial. In that event, the case would be brought to trial again. And I'd have been washed up."

"Stuart, that thinking was absolute madness! No matter when Keller found out, the results would have been the same. Why? Why would you do this? Don't you understand that everything you're saying tells me that you were the one desperate enough to kill Keller?"

Willetts literally shook. He rose and tried to ease a knot from the back of his neck, tried to get a grip on himself. "You have to understand, Robyn. We were just desperate enough to take the risk. Keller would have gotten Trudi convicted of a murder she didn't commit."

"Then you know I have to ask this question, Stuart. How far were you willing to go to prevent Keller getting that conviction or exposing your affair?"

"Don't answer that, Stuart," Trudi flared, turning her furious gaze on Robyn. "Neither one of us is on trial. Not anymore. It's *over*. You're powerless to hurt us or—"

"She's not powerless, Trudi," he interrupted her tiredly. "Judges have been known to allow charges to be reinstated on less than she already knows." He turned back to Robyn. "I would not have gone so far as to murder Keller, Robyn. You have to believe that."

She felt his strain. "You stood to lose everything, Stuart. Everything you'd worked for your entire life...your stature in the community. Trudi."

"I'm hoping that's the piece of all this you'll understand." He looked at Trudi, not with some calf-eyed, lovelorn expression, but with one of deeper, more complex emotions. "We're neither one of us kids, Robyn. We're as committed to each other and as much in love as you were with Keller."

Robyn put her pad and pen down on the glass table. Trudi seemed suddenly older, more solemn, silently agreeing, finally, with Stuart's statements and his reason for pasting his heart on his sleeve.

Robyn knew now why he had been willing to go on tape with this. He wanted to play on her emotions. He wanted her to have a reason to believe if he admitted to this much, he must be telling the truth. That Trudi hadn't murdered Spyder, and that together, they had not murdered Keller.

All of which turned inside out everything Robyn had walked in to Spyder Nielsen's house believing. Stuart's appeal to her to understand how much in love he was by comparing his relationship with Trudi to hers with Keller was a thundering shot across her emotional bow. But *was* he blinded by love?

If she believed him, then someone else had killed Spyder.

If she believed him, then if Keller had been murdered at all it must have been by someone else who feared Keller was onto them. Someone else who needed to make sure Keller was stopped.

Stuart Willetts made her stomach turn. He reminded her of the joke about California getting all the lawyers and New Jersey getting all the toxic waste dumps—because Jersey got to choose first among the available plagues.

What tore hardest at her was that despite the despicable things he'd done and wished and caused, despite his being the most reprehensible behavior she had ever seen, in her heart, she believed him.

She made herself set all that anger and resentment aside because she had to know what else he knew. "Are you certain Keller hadn't come upon information implicating anyone else?"

He gave a sigh. "You believe me, then?"

She wouldn't give him that. Not now, maybe never. "I don't know what I believe, Stuart. You're a self-acknowledged liar. How can anything you say be believed?"

"Robyn—"

"Let it go, Stuart," she warned. "It's not too late—it'll never be too late for me to go straight to the bar association. If you want to answer my questions, fine. Otherwise I'm out of here."

He sulked a moment, then met her look. "I can't be sure of what Keller knew. I just didn't care and I don't remember. I'd ask Crandall if I were you."

"Who else had motives to want to kill Spyder?" Kiel asked, sending Robyn a "well done" glance.

Trudi laughed bitterly. "Two-thirds of Aspen."

Robyn picked up her pad and pen again. "Was Spyder that unpopular?"

"Unpopular? No. He drew groupies like flies to honey. But sooner or later," Trudi said, her voice whispery again, her tone almost regretful, "Spyder managed to insult and alienate everyone he ever knew. Everyone who had ever cared about him."

"Can you narrow the field by remembering who was in Aspen at the time of his murder?" Kiel asked.

"God knows how many pathetic locals tumbled to his line. He didn't confine himself to Pitkin County, either. He strayed as far away as Steamboat Springs—for that matter, Gstaad. Spyder delighted in leading women on, Mr. Alighieri, and then spurning them. Humiliating them with their infatuation." She stared at her hands and turned her bracelets round and round. "The older he got, the worse he became, needing to know he could still attract young girls. But there are others who were far more likely."

She rattled off the shorter list of specific names, people closer to Spyder Nielsen. "Spyder's daughter Chloe had reason to want him dead. His sports marketing agent, Shad Petrie. Spyder was about to dump a major ski manufacturing endorsement that would cost Petrie dearly. Then there's my ex-husband, Pascal Candelaria. Spyder delighted in taunting Pascal, who, as you know, is yesterday's news himself. The sports network fired him last spring from his color commentator position."

Robyn recorded the names Trudi listed, then posed another question. "Ms. Candelaria, do you really believe one of those people killed Spyder?"

Trudi exhaled sharply. "They all had reason, believe me...but, no. All I know is that I didn't do it."

"Did any of them have reason to frame you for his murder?" Kiel asked. "Who had it in for you? Chloe?"

"Spyder's daughter and I have never gotten along well," Trudi said. "But of course, she stood to gain the most. If I had been convicted of the murder, Spyder's entire estate would have gone to her."

"Who knew you would be out and when you would return?"

"Elsa." Thoughtfully, Trudi turned the bangles on her wrist. "But she is the soul of discretion. Other than that, the people who were at the party I went to that evening."

"Was Chloe one of them?"

"No." Trudi frowned. "But if Chloe called that night and spoke to her father, she would know I was out of the house and that he was home."

"What about Elsa, Ms. Candelaria? Did she ever threaten to leave after Spyder was murdered?"

Trudi folded her arms. "Elsa is a very pragmatic woman, Ms. Delaney. This is her home. This is her territory, and she wouldn't leave it if the Ayatollah moved in."

Robyn closed the spiral notebook and twisted her pen to close off the ballpoint. "Kiel and I will look into all of this. We may need to come back."

Kiel rose from his chair. Stuart gave Trudi a hand up, then draped his arm around her shoulders, pulling her close. "This has to have been a tough year for you, Robyn—even getting back on your feet."

"You're right." She stood taller. Her leg usually ached deep inside. Tonight it didn't. "It has been a difficult year, Stuart. But if you're wondering whether I have the stamina or the heart to pursue Keller's death, don't. I won't rest until I get at the truth."

NEAR 2:00 A.M., long after she'd lit the old-fashioned glass lantern to sleep by and climbed into the luxurious four-poster bed in her room at The Chandler House, Robyn got up and wandered into the parlor. A fire crackled softly in the fireplace. Kiel sat slouched in the deep leather easy chair.

She curled up on the sofa. Tucking her nightgown up around her feet, she pulled a crocheted throw to cover her shoulders.

"Can't sleep?" he asked.

"No." She shook her head. "Usually when I wake up it's my leg bothering me." She looked straight at him, teasing. "I don't have that excuse anymore."

Despite the times he had held forth about taking one-self lightly, he wasn't easily humored this night. "What's on your mind, Robyn?"

"Keller. What a relief it is that my leg isn't aching. Why I can't sleep. Who killed Spyder. Why Keller had to die. How I'm going to get at the truth. And . . . Kell."

Kiel nodded. The lighthearted tone of her answer didn't wash. It wasn't as if he didn't already know the answer to his question. Keller was always on her mind, permeating her consciousness for all time.

The decision to keep from her the truth that his soul was Keller's rankled in his angel's heart. He felt something startlingly similar to the human equivalent of guilt. Again.

In all his time of service as an Avenging Angel, he had never suffered such indecisiveness, such self-doubt. These were not usually part of an angel's experience. Truth was truth, and justice, a clear and pristine proposition. Humans suffered with the gray areas, but in the place beyond temporal reality, no being harmed another and every soul was free to soar and expand and blossom into its fullness.

But in the here and now of Robyn Delaney's existence Kiel feared his presence harmed her more than helped. In his essence, Kiel *was* Keller Trueblood, so he must always remind her of Keller at deeply subconscious levels where she was defenseless.

He had taken the matter up with Angelo three hours ago, in earth time.

It took Kiel no real time at all to soar back to the offices of the Denver Branch of Avenging Angels. He found Angelo sitting on a stone bench in the garden that had passed its season. The night air was crisp. Moonlight filtered through fluttering oak leaves.

Kiel sat beside Angelo.

"You're in a dilemma," Angelo observed.

Kiel nodded. "I've never been on an assignment where I believed my presence as an Avenging Angel was doing more harm than good."

"Your perspective is alarmingly human, Ezekiel," Angelo agreed, invoking Kiel's full name to remind him his first obligation was to keep in place a larger picture than Robyn Delaney's emotional state. "Crimes against human beings have been committed—crimes that require your efforts to be set to rights. Avenged."

"Yeah," Kiel said. "I know. The thing is, Robyn will suffer. It's not fair to her to be kept in the dark. I may be an Avenging Angel, but I am also Keller in the truest sense. She knows. She recognizes me even though she has convinced herself that she was pretending, imagining I must be Keller.''

''Because you broke with rules and made love to her.'' Kiel felt divinely defensive. ''If I hadn't—''

''I'm well aware of the circumstances,'' Angelo interrupted. ''And I've taken this up with the highest councils. Robyn Delaney was teetering on the edge, heaven or earth, earth or heaven.'' He tilted his head one way and then the other. ''She had no way of knowing her destiny is far from fulfilled. You had no choice. To pull her back from the brink, she had to believe somewhere inside herself that she was coming back to Keller Trueblood.''

''But there are these complications now—''

''Exactly. The argument chases its tail. Robyn accepted you, and yours is the only help she would have accepted. You are the only reason she did not abandon her destiny—and there you have it. You must deal with the consequences, however heartrending.''

No argument could win. Kiel was stuck.

''Oh . . . and uh, about that 'Alighieri' business?''

Kiel groaned. This was the last time he'd get creative. Next time, Smith, he thought, or Dash's old standby, Divine. ''What about it?''

Angelo smirked. ''Got a laugh upstairs, kid.''

So HE WAS GETTING LAUGHS upstairs. He whisked back to the Aspen B and B, fed the flames in the fireplace and cooled his heels. The irony—wavering, stuck between hot and cold—filled him.

He was stuck, and the inferno joke was hardly a joke at all anymore.

Watching the firelight glint off Robyn's softly curling raven black hair now, he knew an awareness of Keller

Trueblood's feelings were slowly, inexorably coming to life inside him. He knew because he wanted to stroke her hair. He knew because his male parts throbbed, because the curve of her cheek begged his touch and because her own awareness of him heightened as surely as a doe in heat senses the stag.

Kiel cast a swathe of naiveté about her to protect her from her awareness of him. Momentarily disoriented, her brow puckered in a frown. Kiel cleared his throat. She had last spoken of Keller, so he began there. "According to Stuart, Keller knew what was up. Did he keep a journal?"

"Yes." Robyn gave a quick shake of her head. "But he doodled so much you could hardly make sense of what he wrote down. That didn't bother him, of course. He had a nearly photographic memory. But it drove his secretary and law clerks to distraction—when they weren't howling over his cartoon figures."

Kiel's consciousness quickened. "That's how he doodled? In cartoons?"

"Yes. Just quick sketches, but they were inspired, Kiel. He was really quite good. He paid his way through law school with freelance political cartoons. When I met him, he would sit in court and draw the little cartoon figures of the defense attorneys or the judge—even himself. What I remember best are the little beads of perspiration popping off the defense attorneys' heads when they couldn't get what they wanted out of a witness. Keller told me they were called plewds."

"The sweat drops you mean?"

"Yes." She spelled *plewds* for him. "He knew all the cartooning conventions, all the little squiggles and crosshatches and spirals—and what they were called. Like the little dust clouds Charles Schultz used to put all around Pigpen." She hesitated a moment. "Do you have the foggiest idea what I'm talking about? Being an angel, I mean."

"Sure. Charlie Brown. Beetle Bailey. Garfield." He tossed off names of famous cartoon characters, but the truth was, between one instant and the next, Kiel knew he could pick up a pen and re-create on the spot any drawing Keller had ever made, any doodle, any cartoon figures.

He could have told her those dust clouds were called briffits in a cartoonist's lingo. And the reason he could tell her was that everything Keller Trueblood had ever known about sketching and cartoons had just exploded into Kiel's consciousness.

But he could never actually tell her. The list of things Kiel had to keep from her got longer. Good thing old Gepetto wasn't his Creator.

"Remember," Robyn was saying, "that I told Stuart I hadn't seen the actual bronze statue that was used to kill Spyder? That Keller sketched it on a napkin for me?"

Kiel nodded, resigning himself to knowing about these things before she told him. He changed the subject. "So Keller had a near perfect memory?" He'd need to know because he would need one even more dependable—just to keep from screwing up somewhere along the way, betraying his possession of Keller Trueblood's consciousness. "Give me an example."

"Other than his law books? He remembered every case he ever read down to the footnotes." She didn't have to think hard to come up with many more. "Newspapers, magazines, cereal boxes. Keller could recite restaurant menus verbatim. It actually took a lot of effort to keep the minutiae of day-to-day living out of his head." She smiled at the fond memories that had come to mind. "I never ever saw him look at a menu. Information overload, he called it. He would just order a steak, medium rare, and fries. And a pitcher of iced tea to himself.''

''Would he have kept a record of what he was thinking when he knew Stuart Willetts was getting into bed with the enemy?'' The answers to these questions might become available to him as pieces of Keller's memories returned. Talking with Robyn might jog them. ''Any notes about what he planned to do about it or who he might have spoken to?''

''Yes.'' Robyn gnawed gently at her lower lip. ''He wanted everything down on paper, for the record, whether he ever had to refer to his notes again or not. I have his briefcase in the trunk of the car. He kept a Day-Timer, and he usually recorded his witness interviews on audiotape. His clerk typed them into transcripts that he rarely used again because his recall was so infallible.''

''How soon did you know that about him?''

''Everyone around him knew, so it was just out there, like everyone knows the sun's coming up in the morning. I can't say exactly when I knew it for myself.''

She settled deeper into the sofa cushions, hugging the comforter close. ''When I worked with him on the case that I wrote about in *Where Angels Fear to Tread,* I started out comparing what he told me with those records and transcripts as a matter of course—to double-check and confirm everything as I would in any other case.'' She gave a delicate shrug. The crocheted blanket touched her chin. ''I never caught him in a mistake, or even an inconsistency.''

Kiel grinned. ''You tried?''

''All the time—at first because it was so obnoxious that he was never wrong.'' She gave a faraway smile. ''Later... after we got to know each other a little better, it turned into a harmless game we played. A way to flirt and do business at the same time.''

Kiel flashed on a string of memories, Keller's memories, of ''harmless'' kisses and then less harmless ones, and then hotter, far less innocent, kisses he exacted over time as penalty from Robyn whenever his recall proved accurate.

He knew in those memories that there came a night in the spring when Keller had turned up the charm and the pressure and the heat, and Robyn had responded, challenging him on the accuracy of his recall not because she knew he was wrong, but for the opposite reason.

She knew he knew, and she knew perfectly well what would happen. Keller's penalties were Robyn's candy.

Kiel ''remembered'' how she had defied her attraction to Keller Trueblood at first. How she held up her professionalism like one of his force fields to fend off men, how she insisted she didn't want to be involved with anyone at the time.

She was fierce at first and for days on end, then her resistance caved in to her own affinity to an intelligent, quick-witted, daring, all-out man who made her laugh.

Keller's gradual seduction of her never felt carved in stone to her, like some routine he laid on anyone with breasts and a brain. He responded to her, not acting on whatever preconceived tactics he knew of in the battle of the sexes. He battered down her resistance by being willing to know her. To poking and prodding until he got at the truth about her. Truths that she would have had to spoon-feed to any other man she became interested in.

Finally knocking out her own defenses, she accepted his kisses, then liked them, craved them, invited them, returned them, deepened them, and came around for them again and again, until one night Keller took her on the desk in his office and they made love. Neither one of them was thinking at all or they would have thought to lower the shades and lock the doors.

No one had ever walked in on them, but Keller figured that was pure luck and poor planning. And they figured out soon that they *needed* a place of their own. A bed of their own...

This breech in Keller's far more intimate memories knocked Kiel for a loop. He dammed them up, but unlike the little Dutch boy sticking his finger in a hole in the dike, Kiel wasn't hopeful that stopping up the leak was going to be enough.

He made light of it all for Robyn, who could have no idea that her fairly tame revelation had triggered a stampede in him. "That kind of recall must be a pretty annoying habit in a husband."

"It was." She laughed softly. Her uncomplicated pleasure did a little, though not nearly enough, to ease his tension. She stared a moment into the flames. "Anyway, we could look at his Day-Timer and his clerk's records."

"Did he also have copies of the trial transcripts?"

"I would think so, yes. They are probably all in a vault in the county courthouse. His Day-Timer, though, is in his briefcase."

Kiel nodded. The book might well trigger further memories. He got up to put another pine log on the fire, then dropped back into the leather chair. The dry wood crackled and popped in the flames. The scent of burning pine got stronger. "Robyn, do you believe Stuart Willetts?"

Staring at the burst of fiery crackle rushing up the chimney, she looped a strand of her raven hair around her finger and twisted. "He desperately wanted us to believe him. A part of me is so incredibly offended by what he became—and that he would compare what Keller and I had with whatever kind of relationship he has with Trudi...but—'' She broke off. "I did. I believed him." She met Kiel's gaze. "Do you think he was manipulating me?''

Kiel held her look. "I think he knows you're vulnerable to that kind of emotional appeal—he's not above using it. But I had the sense he was sincere. That he believes what he said. There's no question, either, as to how good Trudi Candelaria was at manipulating him.''

"None," Robyn agreed. "Although, somehow she just comes off a lot less trustworthy than he is. Maybe if I'd lived for ten years with a womanizer like Spyder Nielsen, I'd be as brittle as she is, too. My problem with believing either one of them is that Keller wouldn't have been prosecuting her if he didn't believe she killed Spyder. I trusted Keller's judgment.''

"Do you know if he ever prosecuted a person who turned out to be innocent?''

Robyn nodded. "Once—that he knew of. A capital case. Murder in the first. A few years later, another man made a deathbed confession. The reason I trust his judgment so much is that he went to the mat with the system to free the man he'd convicted of the murder. Keller's career came to a screeching halt for a while, but he did what he had to do.''

Kiel's thoughts turned inward. He didn't know or remember the specifics of the case she was talking about, but Keller's emotional memory pulsed. The guilt connected with having sent up an innocent man, the internal battle between wanting to keep his own record of righteous prosecutions untainted and knowing better. Knowing his integrity was on the line.

"The tragedy of it all was that Willie Sandoval died three days before Keller thought he was going to get the appellate courts to release him."

A long, shuddering sigh escaped Kiel. He suddenly understood. "Willie Sandoval is the reason—" He stopped midsentence. He couldn't say to Robyn that the injustice Keller had caused Sandoval was the reason that *he* had been assigned to the Avenging Angels as Ezekiel. Those were the injustices that needed redeeming, so in the Hereafter, Keller was given that kind of responsibility.

"Willie Sandoval is the reason for what?" Robyn asked.

"For Avenging Angels," he answered, truthful if not totally forthcoming. "People like Sandoval, I mean, and the injustices that happen to them."

"Sort of like a karmic payback? If you cause injustice, you're condemned forever to fight it?"

"Like that, yes." Kiel couldn't restore Willie Sandoval's life, but he could make sure other injustices like that didn't go unavenged. He wondered what had become of Sandoval in the Hereafter.

Then there was the matter of Robyn's trust. She believed he'd said what he was going to say, but he hadn't. Sandoval was the reason Keller had become Kiel, but he'd generalized because if he hadn't, he'd have to tell her that he was in fact Keller. He had to wonder again how he was going to keep from blurting out the truth to Robyn. Every turn in their conversation seemed littered with the time bombs of Keller's awareness just waiting to explode into his consciousness.

"Do you know," she asked, her face solemn and interested, the firelight arranging a spectrum of light colors around her that his gifted, special sight saw as an aura, "what it was that you did, what injustice you caused?"

Chapter Six

Like the needle of a magnet pulling faithfully to true north, Robyn had honed in. He couldn't lie to her. This was a direct question, and very much against the rules to evade or lie about. "Yes."

She waited for him to elaborate.

His altogether human Adam's apple pitched like a shooting star through the night sky. "Maybe another time, Robyn."

Her lips pursed. He felt her disappointment like a tidal wave. Her life was an open book to him; his was slammed shut and locked tight against her. He watched her snatching a deep breath, repressing the emotion she felt. She shoved aside the comforter and arose quickly from the sofa. "I should try to sleep now."

She moved, wraithlike, jerkily, toward the bedroom door in the flickering orange-yellow light of the waning fire. Kiel didn't want her to go, especially like this, feeling so slighted, but he couldn't think of anything to say to stop her. "Sleep well, Robyn."

She turned back to look at him. A long, keen, somehow vaguely familiar moment stretched unbearably. A pocket of dry sap in the burning pine bough exploded.

The physical awareness between them that he had been so careful to tamp down flared. She stared at him.

Her pulse quickened. He knew it.

She turned and fled. Kiel's angel heart staggered. As an angel he had no need for tear ducts, but now he discovered how they worked.

THE HEART OF MODERN-DAY Aspen could be seen inside five blocks, between Main Street and Durant Avenue. The most renowned photo shots were of the iron-front Aspen Block in the foreground of Aspen Mountain, but the most famous landmark, the Hotel Jerome, where celebrities partied, and the county courthouse, sat on Main Street, the Park Avenue of the Rockies.

The courthouse hummed with activity. Even this, Robyn thought, was quintessentially Aspen. The building was a hundred-and-five years old, but cops also drove thirty-thousand-dollar Saabs.

Detective Crandall wasn't in, but the police here were friendly and helpful to a fare-thee-well. The police officer who took down Robyn's name to leave a message glanced up when she heard the name Trueblood.

"That's an unusual name. Are you any relation to Keller Trueblood?"

"Yes." She felt pleased for Keller's sake, that he was remembered here even now, more than a year later. "He was my husband."

Giving Robyn the once-over, the female officer nodded a bit forlornly. "We all *knew* he was married, of course, but . . . well. Don't get me wrong. I'm happily married, too—" She stopped herself from carrying on. "Let me see if I can track down Detective Crandall."

"If it's no trouble," Robyn said. "I just wanted to make a courtesy call. Otherwise, I can catch him later."

She gestured to Kiel. "This is my associate, Kell...um—"

"Kiel," he said, covering her near miss with his name, as smooth as butter. "Kiel Alighieri." Offering his hand, he turned on the thousand-candle smile.

The policewoman couldn't seem to take her eyes off him, or let go of his hand.

Subtly stepping on Kiel's toe, Robyn cleared her throat. His smile faded to maybe a hundred candles. A hundred bright ones.

"I'm...we're staying at The Chandler House. We'll be in town researching *Colorado v. Candelaria* for a few days, and we'd like to speak to Mr. Crandall. Do you know where we could find him?"

The woman checked a watch schedule. "Actually, he's off duty today. I'm afraid you'll have to wait and come back tomorrow."

Robyn didn't intend to wait. She'd find the policeman at his home if that's what it took. She thanked the woman and turned to go. On their way out of the suite of offices, Kiel blustered, "Why did you do that?"

"Step on your foot, you mean? Do angels experience pain?" she queried sweetly. "Dante?" she mocked, for good measure, still not over that one.

"Kiel," he corrected her snappishly, "and no, we don't feel physical pain, exactly, but—"

"Well, I did it to stop your egging on that poor defenseless cop," she answered primly, heading toward the exits. "Shame on you."

"Jealous, Robyn?" he teased her in a playful tone, but he couldn't leave it at that. He was an angel—friendly, sure, but nothing more. "I wasn't egging her on. You introduced me, I smiled and shook her hand."

"What*ever.*" She gave him a sideways glance. "I suppose it's not your fault that you're gorgeous."

His stunning bronze eyebrows pulled together. "Am I? Gorgeous?"

Robyn burst out laughing at his credulous tone, drawing curious glances from passersby in the old courthouse building. He really didn't know... or else, angels had no vanity. But surely it wasn't possible, was it, not to know, not to see, that redheaded, blue-eyed and as intensely male as he was freckled, he outshone the heartthrob Caruso a thousand times? "Don't tell me no one else has pointed this out to you, Kiel."

He shrugged in his loose-limbed way. "No one has, Robyn."

"That's ridiculous."

"It's the truth."

She turned suddenly, angry for reasons she couldn't even make come clear in her head. She backed him into a very small vestibule. "The *truth* is you must just have sprung out of the heavenly cabbage patch. Where did you come from, really? Mars, Mr. Call-Me-Dante?"

"Robyn—"

She held up a hand. "I don't want to hear it," she warned. "Not if you're going to tell me you're unaware of the effect you have on women. For heaven's sake, Kiel, the policewoman was all but drooling, and that little commandant Elsa Kautz melted. Even I—"

"You what, Robyn?" He felt that curious lack of oxygen afflicting his lungs again.

She clapped her mouth shut. This wasn't going anywhere, and what did it matter whether or not he admitted to knowing he had any effect at all on women? Because she was attracted to him and she wanted him to be—and admit it out loud—attracted to her?

Folly.

Complete, unadulterated folly. Angel or not, the absolute bar-none worst reason in the world to be attracted to him was that he reminded her of Keller. Refusing to be so horribly clichéd and predictably dysfunctional, she plucked up her shoulders, tossed him a devil-may-care glance and turned away. "I have a murder to solve."

She stalked to a telephone booth and checked the directory for the address of Ken Crandall. As she would have expected, had she been thinking instead of fuming, the police officer was not listed.

Kiel had followed. He took the book from her and let it fall on the chain that poked through a hole punched in the upper left corner. "Crandall lives at 0934 Carbondale, back down the valley a way."

She eyed him suspiciously. "How do you know that?"

"No tricks, Robyn." He stood slouched against a granite pillar and held up two fingers. Laughter played at his eyes. "Scout's honor."

"Oh, please." He was teasing her, and she couldn't stay mad at him for two minutes. Did an angel need to swear on Scout's honor? No. Well, maybe one conceited enough to call himself Alighieri and naive enough not to know a woman in the early stages of a swoon. But she shook her head. Deluded or not, she'd already bought in, lock, stock and barrel, to Kiel being an angel. "How do you know where Crandall lives?"

"I got Keller's Day-Timer out of his briefcase after you went to sleep last night. There's even a sketchy map. C'mon. I'll show you."

He took her hand and led her out into the bright mountain sunshine. Main Street looked deserted in this off-season time. Her car, like all the others, was parked on a slant to the curb. She unlocked the driver's door of her coupe and flicked the unlock button for Kiel. Once inside, he produced the Day Timer from the floor and flipped to the page where Keller had noted the address and drawn a rough map to Detective Ken Crandall's property.

Robyn studied the drawing. Keller obviously hadn't found anything to be amused about by Crandall. The sketch was perfunctory, a crude map and nothing more, with not even the likeness of a street sign anywhere.

"Okay. Let's go see what light Detective Crandall can shed on the story."

She drove to the outskirts of town, back down Main toward Killer 82. Crandall lived out in the country, northwest of Aspen near the town of Basalt. Bouncing down tracks of the ungraded road that Keller's map indicated, wincing when the underbelly of her car scraped against the hardened earth, Robyn pulled up between a small white Ford Escort and a '96 model four-wheel-drive import.

"Pricey vehicle," she murmured.

"How much?"

She shifted into park and switched off the engine. "Forty thousand, I'd bet."

Kiel looked at her, his amazing blue eyes clear as the Rocky Mountain skies.

She laughed. "You don't have a clue, do you."

He puffed up his chest and looked askance at her. "I can fly, Robyn. I don't need a clue."

"Well, for us mere mortals, forty thousand dollars is a hefty chunk of change. Maybe more than a police officer makes in a year." She would rather know what it was like to fly, but she didn't want to be shut out again as she had been in the middle of the night by asking questions Kiel couldn't—or wouldn't—answer.

She released her seat belt. "On the other hand, just FYI, not because you need a clue," she teased, "the house is boxy. Ordinary. As inexpensive as any property in Pitkin County gets." With its minuscule size, reddish brown aluminum siding and a sagging stoop, Crandall's house wouldn't have met design standards or covenants anywhere but back down these remote mountain roads.

Still, this was prime mountain property. The chilly air smelled fresh and clean. Blue skies stretched beyond the neighboring fourteen-thousand-foot peaks. She plucked up her shoulder bag from the center console, shut her car door and breathed deeply.

A woman opened the front door and came out onto the porch wrapped in an oversize sweatshirt. "Can I help you," she called out.

"Yes, thank you very much." Robyn crossed the small yard. "My name is Robyn Delaney. I'm looking for Detective Ken Crandall."

The woman folded her arms over her chest and tilted her head. She could have been no more than thirty and had a very pretty face, but she was way too thin. Her green eyeliner had run, giving her a bruised look around the eyes. "He's my father, but it's his day off."

"I understand. This is not police business, but personal. Is he around?"

She jerked her head in a direction behind the house. "He's fishing."

"Miss . . . Crandall?"

"Yes. Miss. Betsy."

Kiel introduced himself. "Would it be all right with you if we just walk down there and talk to your dad?"

She tucked her hair behind her ear in an embarrassed gesture. She smiled tentatively. "I don't think he'll mind."

Kiel nodded. "Thanks, Betsy." He tempered his smile. Crandall's daughter turned back into the house. Kiel took Robyn's elbow and guided her around the house.

The snow had all melted but the earth was still damp. Robyn followed in what would have been Kiel's footsteps, if he left any, which he didn't. They came to a steep decline. She could tell they were nearing a mountain stream.

She first saw a fly fishing line whipping through the air, then Crandall in hip waders, expertly casting the line. He pulled a trout from the stream as they came within shouting distance. He must have glimpsed them from the corner of his eye. He released the fish and tossed it back into the swirling stream, then waded back toward the shoreline.

Robyn picked her way nearer. "Detective Crandall?"

"Who's askin'?"

"Sir, my name is Robyn Delaney. This is my associate, Kiel Alighieri. I'm sorry to interrupt your day off."

A very fit man in his late forties or early fifties, suspicious by nature and profession, Crandall pulled the bill of his baseball cap lower against the intense sun and waited for information relevant to the interruption.

"My husband was Keller Trueblood," she offered.

Nodding, he strode to the bank of the glacial streambed. The flesh around his eyes relaxed. He glanced at Kiel, then trained his attention on her. "Keller was a stand-up guy in a world full of stand-down clowns. Cryin' ass shame, that cave-in. How are you doing?"

"I'm fine. Fully recovered." She tossed her hair back, annoyed now that she hadn't bound it up in a braid this morning. "But right now, my problem is that I'm not convinced that cave-in was an accident, Detective Crandall."

He tilted his head and his eyes narrowed again. The sun glinted off a small gold St. Christopher medal nestled in the graying hair at his collar. "Come again?"

"The cave-in," Kiel repeated. "Ms. Delaney has reason to believe that was no accident."

Crandall planted the hook on his line in the grip of his pole and leaned the fishing gear up against a tree stump. "What reason would that be?"

"I believe someone wanted Keller out of the picture."

"To bring Candelaria's trial to a screeching halt?"

"Exactly."

"Well, we know who that someone would be, now, don't we? Stuart Willetts was going to have to turn around and kiss his ass goodbye if your husband had his way."

Robyn exchanged glances with Kiel. "Over what, Detective Crandall?"

"Mr. Stuart Willetts had set himself on the do-not-pass-go path straight to hell."

Robyn lifted a brow. "How, specifically?"

"Professional misconduct, obstruction of justice at the low end. On the bright end, accessory to murder after the fact."

Robyn shivered. "Keller threatened that?"

Crandall shrugged. "My guess. Willetts was boinking the Candelaria dame. It doesn't take a rocket scientist to read the writing on the wall."

"All right. Stuart Willetts had a lot to lose," she granted. "Detective Crandall, did Keller ever ask you to follow up on any evidence that anyone else murdered Spyder Nielsen? The reason I ask is that if someone else did the murder, then whoever that was had to believe getting rid of Keller was the only way out."

Crandall began shaking his head the minute Robyn asked about anyone else. "Sorry. That don't wash."

"Why?"

Crandall spat in the direction of the streambed. "Two reasons." He held up his thumb. "One, the Candelaria woman committed that murder sure as I'm standing here in God's own country. And two," he added, holding up a soiled forefinger, "even if someone else did the deed, whacking your husband the prosecutor was in no way going to prevent *me* from bringing said make-believe perpetrator to justice."

Recoiling from the fishy smell of Crandall's fingers, Robyn nodded thoughtfully. "I see your point."

"'Course you do, because it makes logical sense. Because, for instance, you take Chloe Nielsen." He bent down and picked a weed from the ground and stuck it in his mouth like a toothpick.

"Who else had more to gain?" he went on. "Chloe gets every cent of Spyder's estate, with none bein' siphoned off to Candelaria, and it's bye-bye to the wicked stepmother in one fell swoop."

"Then she must have been a suspect," Kiel said. "Is it possible that Chloe killed her father and left Trudi Candelaria to find Spyder and take the blame?"

"Nope."

"Why not?" Robyn persisted.

Crandall started to say something, then his mouth slapped shut. "Let's just say her alibi was tight as a spinster's . . . well. Leave it to your imagination."

Robyn didn't need her imagination, or appreciate Crandall's crudeness. His language was far from the worst she'd heard. It had taken years of practice and a lot of mental steeling to let remarks like that go by for the sake of getting at the truth.

And the truth was, however crudely stated, Crandall was quite right. If Keller had come to believe, even in the middle of his prosecution of Trudi, that Chloe Nielsen or anyone else had really committed the murder, the problem would not be solved just by getting rid of Keller. Crandall would have had to be silenced as well.

"The problem here," Kiel said, taking on the doubting Thomas line, "is that Trudi Candelaria still claims she didn't kill Spyder."

"Yeah. I'll bet. Poor little rich girl, pure as the wind-driven snow." Crandall rolled his eyes. "Another cryin' shame, that dame being set free." He wiped his hands on his shirt and reached into a small cooler for a can of tomato juice. "Want one?"

Robyn declined. Crandall downed his in one guzzle.

"Detective Crandall, I need to get to the bottom of all of this for my own peace of mind. If that mine shaft collapsed because someone wanted to be rid of Keller, I intend to find out and bring whoever caused his death to justice. I know you must have spent a great deal of time—"

"You have any idea the hornet's nest you're messing with?" he interrupted.

"I believe I do."

"Well, missy, you may have been the prosecutor's wife, but it's highly unlikely you do. If someone made sure Keller bit the dust—and my chief candidate would be Willetts, you understand—then you're next if you come sniffing around."

"That's why I'm with her," Kiel said.

Crandall eyed Kiel, apparently judging him man enough to protect her. "All fine and good," he said, "and all due respect, ma'am. Bein' the widow, I understand why you'd want to get the bastards. But I seriously doubt you have the stomach or the inclination to get past square one.''

''You're wrong, Detective Crandall. I do.'' Robyn produced a résumé, a list of her credentials and writing credits, from her shoulder bag. Crandall crunched up the small empty can, tossed it to the ground beside his tackle box and took her sheaf of papers.

In the course of her research, people who had not read her work or heard of her often assumed she was a cop groupie or Hollywood-type looking for a quick and dirty TV movie-of-the-week idea.

Because he'd worked closely with Keller on the case against Trudi Candelaria, Crandall wouldn't have made those assumptions. But she wanted him to respect her for more than the fact she was Keller's widow. She let her extensive experience in follow-up criminal investigations speak for itself. Crandall should know up front that her own credentials demanded a high level of consideration for their own sake.

Crandall's brows rose as he flipped through her impressive but easily read papers. He flicked them shut at the end and looked at her. ''An authoress, huh?''

''Just 'author,''' she corrected him, smiling through her irritation. ''Detective Crandall, can you tell me where your investigation into the unidentified tire tracks was going?''

Crandall narrowed his eyes. ''You've already talked to Willetts.''

Kiel knelt and skipped a flat stone across the surface of the mountain stream. Shading his eyes, he looked up at Crandall. ''We're talking to everyone involved, Detective. Yes, we have spoken to both Trudi Candelaria and Stuart Willetts. We need a full record, and we need answers to the questions he raises.''

Crandall's brows drew together. "Even knowing he's more than likely the one who killed Trueblood, and damned near got his wife as well?"

"Especially knowing that, Detective," Robyn answered firmly. "According to Stuart Willetts, Keller was interested in the tire tracks. Willetts said they were never accounted for."

"That's right, and there's a reason. Willetts would like to pretend otherwise, but those tracks were leading us nowhere. And the only thing your husband was interested in was bringing in a guilty verdict on Trudi Candelaria."

Robyn swallowed. Crandall's characterization of Keller didn't sit well with her. She knew prosecutors who wouldn't get off their pet theories short of being blasted off with a stick of dynamite, but Keller? He would never in a hundred years have discounted real evidence.

"Why don't you tell us what you found out about the tread, anyway?" Kiel suggested, his tone of voice as lethal as an Avenging Angel's might well get.

Eyeing Kiel warily, Crandall pulled a pack of Marlboro's from his breast pocket and lit one, dragging heavily. "The tread pattern was as common as ditch water. Not new, not old."

He recalled the brand, the size, and that there were at least seven dealers in a hundred-mile radius who could have sold the tire. A list of buyers was unrevealing. No one even remotely connected with Spyder Nielsen drove a car that had those tires mounted on it at the time he'd conducted the investigation.

"So, one of two things happened," Robyn suggested. "Whoever had those tires replaced them right after the murder, or else there were people coming and going from the Nielsen residence that you knew nothing about."

"Sure," he acknowledged easily. "Or else," he went on in a sarcastic tone, "that tread print was meaningless—maybe from some coke-brain ski bum with too much money taking a spin around the neighborhood."

Crandall dragged on his cigarette one last time, flicked it into the stream, then reached for a beer. Kiel shot Robyn a glance. "Detective," he asked, "did you run a check to see who among Spyder's friends and enemies might have bought new tires after the murder?"

"Yes, sir, I did," Crandall snapped, twisting the cap off his beer. "But it was a freaking waste of time and energy, and everyone but Willetts knew it. We had our murderer dead to rights." He swigged the beer and exhaled sharply.

Robyn let him stew, waiting for her to say something.

"Look," he said at last, "I don't know what you're after here. Trudi Candelaria whacked Spyder. Period. Your husband was going to send her up for a very long time. Did she do Keller, too? Or cause him to be whacked? You want my opinion, it's possible. But for my money, Willetts stood to lose the most."

Detective Crandall's answers corroborated what Robyn had thought she wanted, but she found herself disliking Crandall. She wanted to ask why, if Keller's murder was such a clear possibility, if Willetts did in fact have so much to lose, or Trudi herself, *why* Crandall hadn't thought of it himself before now.

But as a matter of course the coroner had called Keller's death accidental, and she needed the cooperation of the police on the case too much to risk alienating this man with that kind of question.

She knew highly successful true-crime writers, peers and friends of hers who antagonized cops left and right as a matter of style. There were just too many roadblocks cops could throw up if they were crossed. She'd resorted to the tactic with cops she suspected were dirty, but it had never been her first choice of a way to deal with cops who were out there risking their own necks day in and day out to protect the community and keep the peace.

Crandall polished off his bottle of beer. "Anything else I can help you with?"

"The capacity," Kiel suggested.

She nodded. "Trudi would have had to have bought the expertise, someone who knew how to make a mine shaft collapse like it did. Stuart Willetts wouldn't have that kind of specialized knowledge, either. Any ideas?"

Picking up his fly rod, Crandall shook his head. "None. Explosives are out of my league. But you know what they say... follow the paper trail. Money talks."

"THE TROUBLE WITH following the money," Robyn mused, pulling back onto the two-lane road leading back to the resort town, "is that everyone in Aspen has plenty."

"Could you get to Trudi's bank records, anyway?"

She shook her head. "That would require a subpoena, and that would take convincing the D.A. in Aspen to look into the possibility that someone hired expert help to blow up the Hallelujah. How likely is that, based on no more than my suspicions?"

Kiel shrugged. "Not likely at all. Not unless you hire your own experts and they come up with evidence of explosives."

"Kiel, that's a great idea! Why didn't we think of that in the first place?"

He grinned. "Too obvious, maybe. But the trick is finding someone you trust to do the job."

"Actually, I do know someone. Lucinda Montbank. Keller and I leased a condo up here a month or so before the trial start date. I was fooling around, looking for some useful way to spend my time. About that time I was offered a chance to do a piece for the Smithsonian on historical murders and mayhem in mining towns."

"So Keller was here prosecuting a high-profile celebrity murder, and you were rooting around looking for some juicy historical scandal?"

"Not exactly," she protested drolly, snapping down her sun visor. "I'm a serious writer, Kiel, as opposed to a scandal-mongering one."

"Oops."

Good Lord, but his smile left her half witless. "Don't 'oops' me," she scolded. "This piece was pitched to me by one of the most venerable institutions in the country."

"But you were having fun."

"Okay. Sure. True-crime writing isn't your usual barrel of monkeys. The whole idea sounded like fun." She paused. Reality pitched in its two cents. Keller was dead because the idea sounded fun to her. "It didn't turn out that way... of course."

Kiel noticed, maybe more than Robyn did, that for the first time the memory of Keller's death hadn't slammed her on the spot for an emotional loss. "How did Lucinda Montbank fit into the picture?"

"She's an old flame of Mike Massie's. Mike and Keller were best friends. Old college roommates. When I mentioned my writing commission, he gave me Lucy's name. She's a mining engineer. Very wealthy. Her great-great-grandfather was one of the movers and shakers when the big legal battles over mining rights were going on in the 1880s. He was half owner of the Hallelujah."

"So that's why you and Keller were in the Hallelujah that day?"

"Yes. Lucinda still owns the rights."

"Where were you in the story, embroiled in the legal battles?"

"Yes. Not only that. There was a lot of skullduggery, claims jumped, frauds. Some of these guys would sell off a claim and be glad to get out with five hundred bucks and then want it back when a strike was made. But the big boys fought big battles. More than ten million dollars finally came out of the silver mines."

Kiel grinned. "Not exactly spitting contests, were they."

"Not hardly."

"So what was the big battle about?"

"It came down to this. When a strike was uncovered on the surface, what they called the apex, Colorado law held that the owners could follow a continuous vein as far as they could into the mountain."

"No matter if the vein led into the underground space of a dozen other surface claims?"

"Exactly. It was a classic battle of what's good for the few versus the good of the many. A couple of men would have outrageous fortunes at the expense of dozens of others with perfectly legitimate surface claims. The 'apexers' would have an unfair monopoly. The newspaper editor called the whole thing a racket, and local juries turned the statute on its head all the time. These surface claim guys would secretly build barricades. To retaliate, the apexers would force steam and sulfur fumes down the shaft to drive them out."

Kiel shook his head at the lengths humankind would go to for treasures that finally bankrupted their souls. "How did it all shake out?"

"When it came to one of the biggest claims of all, a Denver jury upheld the apex claim. Not long after, the guy who won the suit, a man named Jerome Clarke, was killed in an avalanche—or at least that's how the books have it."

"End of clash, then?"

"Yes. Lucy's great-grandfather, old Lucien Montbank, crafted the compromise. A new company was formed with everyone's holdings, then interest in the new company was doled out to both the apexers and the sideliners. Montbank made out like a bandit—but without the compromise, the mining operations were all shut down and idle, anyway. Lucy was a huge help in my research for the article."

"Lucien. Lucinda." Keller cocked a brow. "Any Lucifers in the family tree."

"Probably," Robyn said, laughing. "Lucy has gotten away like a bandit for a lot of years, too—she'd be the first to tell you about it. But she knocked herself out getting me access to records that are in temperature-and-humidity-controlled library collections. She also has an incredible collection of period pieces—weapons, telegraph stuff, flyers, wanted posters."

"And the Hallelujah."

"Yes. She gave me permission to explore the Hallelujah. She actually offered to go with me, but—" Robyn gripped the steering wheel and sighed. "We, that is, Keller and I . . . God help me. We were so much in love." She scraped a tear from the corner of her eye. "He'd done a lot of rock climbing and cave exploring—spelunking. I wanted him to go with me. Whenever we had a chance, we . . . took off and did things alone, so . . . I refused her offer."

Blindsided by her too-quick, unexpected flash of grief and the catch in her voice, Kiel felt himself sucked back into Keller Trueblood's memories, the fearsome dark hole lying in wait behind the boarded-up entrance to the old Hallelujah mine....

KELLER AND ROBYN had packed a lunch of sandwiches and Granny Smith apples, blue corn tortilla chips and a bottle of Cabernet Sauvignon.

Robyn wore a scoop-necked peach-colored tank top over her bare breasts, cutoffs and a bright red bandanna around her neck. Already aroused just from being around her on a braless day, which they had intended to squander, an already sunburned Keller wore jeans and a long-sleeved plaid shirt he had to go out and buy for the occasion.

Robyn had loaded her camera and bought four more rolls of film while Keller walked down the street to borrow a hammer and crowbar from a construction crew working two blocks from the condo they'd leased in Aspen. He left the crew with a couple of hundred dollar bills for a deposit. Piling into a Jeep, with only a roll bar and no roof, singing at the top of their lungs with a Jimmy Buffet oldie on the radio, they headed for the Hallelujah.

Chapter Seven

Keller and Robyn hiked in, guided by one of Lucy's detailed maps, spread out the picnic blanket at the entrance, ate their lunch and drank a little wine. Keller would have made love to her then and there and skipped the damned Hallelujah altogether, but Robyn put him off. One of them was always making the other wait. FPT, they called it.

Fever-pitch training.

There was no shaft house at this entrance. Robyn took up the crowbar and started trying to loosen the nailed-up boards. Even at ten thousand feet the early afternoon sun bore down relentlessly. The going was tougher than either of them expected even though Lucy had warned her this secondary entrance, while safest, would be tough getting into.

Keller stripped to the waist. Robyn's skin shone with perspiration. A stain of sweat soaked her tank top between her breasts.

At last they broke through. Keller grabbed her by the sweat-dampened bandanna around her neck, pulled her close enough to kiss her long and hard to celebrate . . . and then didn't.

Her turn at FPT.

She took a deep breath and blew off the rush of hormones that felt like adrenaline. "Do you think you can keep your hands to yourself for an hour now?"

He matched her stance. "Two hours."

"Three."

"Half an hour, then. Have it your way." He stuffed a bicycle helmet on her head and one on his, switched on the battery-powered lantern, took her by the hand and led the way, crouching low to clear the wooden slats remaining at the entrance.

Robyn was captivated. The dark, dank smell, the cool fifty degrees, the age of it all. The history lured her on. Creaking wooden rafters and stale air were no deterrents for her.

Keller didn't much care for it, but soon Robyn was leading and he wanted her to have this. He'd spent days, weeks on end, wrapping up his cases in Denver so he could take on this celebrity murder trial as special prosecutor.

He could give Robyn's interests a few hours, especially since he felt guilty that because they were married, she was steering clear of the highest-profile murder case to come along in the last few years. The Candelaria case was troubling him. He needed her insight. He no longer wanted himself cut off from her observations, as he had once thought. Their agreement to stay out of each other's work was, he thought, not liberating or even ethical, just truly misguided.

He intended, tonight, to spill his concerns, and get her take on the issues he faced regarding Candelaria. For now, he wanted to share what was consuming *her* interests.

For the sake of returning safely, they turned left at each of three forks in the shaft. An hour in, scribbling notes to capture every grubby, claustrophobic, magnificent detail, searching out tiny veins of ore, her imagination firing, Robyn went through five rolls of 1600 ASA film while Keller took out a penknife and started carving their initials in the bark of a tree trunk used for a beam to shore up the ceiling of the mine shaft.

Her eyes were lit up like moonbeams on mink. "Oh, Kell, what do you think?"

A menacing pop rang out, far back up the tunnel. What he thought was dust passing through the beam of their lantern he realized was really water vapor, but that was small comfort. In a cave created by nature, you could trust that the vast cavernous spaces down to the smallest crevasses weren't going to cave in, but he didn't have that kind of faith in the winding branches of some old silver mine. "The truth?" he asked.

She nodded.

He thought she knew what was coming because of her off-center grin. "I think this place scares the crap out of me."

"Come on, Kell. Can't you feel it?"

"Death and doom, you mean?" He owed her the truth of his feelings, didn't he?

"Well, that . . . but really, Kell, I mean, this is almost as good as time travel! Some of these tunnels go a mile-and-a-half in, right below a restaurant, and come out on the other side of the mountain. Think of Molly Gibson, the Smuggler. Can't you just imagine the lives of the men who slaved here, day in and day out, for their three bucks? Round the clock, hundreds of them, carving this tunnel out of the mountain?"

"The ones with murder in their hearts, you mean?" The work, the tons of rock and ore hauled out of here, boggled the mind, and the truth was, nothing about it fired his imagination, not even considering the vast fortunes made and lost.

"Well, you'd almost have expected more murders by far than there apparently were. When you consider what was at stake—"

"Silver crashed in '93," he reminded her.

"They couldn't know that then, though. And murder sure adds a touch of mystery and danger, doesn't it?"

She lined up another shot of a railcar track heading across a chasm where the earth had fallen down. "Do you think they could hear the avalanche down here?"

Keller hesitated halfway through her initials. He'd read through some of her research materials last night, and knew the death of Jerome Clarke in an avalanche at the Hallelujah had changed the course of local mining history. "I'd say that's a safe bet."

The thought of an avalanche, or a rock slide, or even a timber shifting, gave him the creeps again. "Remind me again," he cracked, "what we're doing down here."

"Something's not right, Kell. I can't put my finger on it, but I don't think Jerome Clarke was killed in that avalanche."

He cocked an eyebrow at her. "That's why we're down here? This hellhole is a place only Dante could really appreciate, Robyn."

"Well," she said, cocking a hip, planting her hand, "I had this sort of half-baked notion that someone used the avalanche for an excuse to toss Jerome Clarke down a mine shaft. I was so *sure,* Kell, that we'd stumble over Clarke's skeleton."

He blinked at her outrageousness, then finished the *T* standing for Trueblood, for *him,* in her initials. Smart alec, he thought. She hadn't expected to stumble over any skeletons at all. "Clarke died in the avalanche, Robyn. Didn't you read his wife's memoirs?"

She stopped clicking pictures and glared at him playfully. "Oh, Mr. Perfect Recall again, is it? Just because it's written down doesn't make it so, Kell. Was Mrs. Clarke there? No. Hearsay."

"History is hearsay, Robyn."

"But there weren't enough bodies found afterward for his to be one of them. Clarke wasn't one of them. *Res ipsa loquitur,* counselor," she quoted him.

"Yeah, yeah, yeah. 'The thing speaks for itself.' Trouble is, we're talking historical accounts here, *Mrs.* Counselor."

"Kell, Jerome Clarke lost a hand in a blasting accident years before. How likely is it that he died in the avalanche but his body was left unrecognizable?"

"Bodies can get pretty smashed up in avalanches, Robyn. Anyway, what's the point? The guy died. Lucien Montbank brought the opposite camps together, they got back to mining and everyone lived happily ever after."

"Everyone but Jerome Clarke," she muttered darkly.

"Sorry to rain on your parade, sweetheart, but no one cared one way or the other—which probably means he died in the avalanche and that was the end of everyone's troubles."

"Or someone did him in, and *that* was the end of everyone's troubles."

He stopped carving again and twirled a pretend handlebar mustache. "You wanna bet?" he dared her. "Costs you, you know."

"How are we going to prove it, one way or the other?"

He shrugged. "It's your baby, Robyn. I've got my hands full with putting Trudi Candelaria behind bars."

He frowned, just thinking of the case. Something was not right there, either, and he knew it.

"Okay, then sure. I'll bet you—darn straight. Clarke's death was just too neatly timed, Kell—and you know I don't believe in coincidence."

"Or neatness," he teased.

"Neatness is for little minds," she retorted, because she needed an excuse, he always thought, not because she really believed neatness precluded intelligence.

It *was* true that she didn't buy into easy coincidence, which basically spelled out the source of all their arguments, their biggest differences. Robyn was always looking for trouble. He wasn't naive, but he never went looking—he just dealt with trouble where he found it. Prosecuting the perps. Bringing justice, although he didn't believe for a second that justice was truly served in any sense when people had been murdered.

Between him and Robyn, the issue came up in different ways. Her darker suspicions sometimes made him mad, but he knew in his heart she was just trying to protect a more innocent core in her heart that really didn't want to believe people could turn out to be as rotten as they sometimes were.

He'd married her. Taken up protecting her heart. He loved her more than life, so he forgave her the way she forgave his obnoxious upbeat attitudes and perfect photographic memory.

When she started spouting off those dark suspicions, that's when he knew she was feeling threatened, and he knew it was time to make her feel less threatened. His best bet was always making love to her, and since he came away feeling less isolated and alone in the world himself, their relationship only got deeper. Richer.

"Proof, although forthcoming, will have to wait," she said, bringing his mind back to the moment. "Right now I'm occupied with my camera."

He just grinned and started hatching his collection process for the kisses she would owe him on her lost bet while he carved the heart around their initials and shot it through with an arrow.

She only stopped snapping photos when she ran out of the high-speed film. She put her camera away, and her notebook. Inspecting his work, she touched him in a breathtakingly intimate way and dropped a distracted kiss on his bare shoulder.

He put the lantern down on the floor by an old set of tracks for the ore carts, aiming its beam in the direction they would return. Beyond a cone of six or eight feet, pitch black resumed.

"Thanks for coming with me, Kell." She leaned in the shadows against a jagged wall of stone, facing him. The cold, he thought, had finally punched through her enthusiasm and she shivered. The dark stain of damp sweat at her breasts still remained. Her neck shimmered with the sweat of exertion and her nipples beaded in the cold, poking through the flimsy fabric. Keller ached.

He let his gaze travel the twisting, decaying beams. He couldn't touch her passion for this hellhole with a ten-foot pole, and he called himself a moron for resenting a hole in the ground sparking her like this. He stuck his fingers in his jeans pockets to ease the fit and shrugged. His voice dropped. Thickened. "Whatever turns you on, Robyn Jeanne Delaney Trueblood."

"This place interests me." She swallowed and blinked and swallowed again. Her nipples thrust harder. Keller ached worse. "You turn me on."

He let his head fall forward until his chin touched his chest. The pain of wanting her was such an exquisite buzz. The play of their shadows on the far wall caught his eyes. He pointed them out to Robyn, then reached for her. Eyes glued to the wall, they watched the shadow of his hand approach the peaking shadows of her breasts, his fingers hovering, straying, never quite touching her.

At last he hooked his fingers into the scoop neck between her breasts and pulled her to him. He took off her helmet, she took off his. They dropped them to the ground and the noise echoed.

Coming together, the shadows lost resolution. Keller lost his mind and flattened his hand to her breast and kissed her neck until she lost her mind, too.

His lips traversed her bare shoulder, past the bandanna, up her neck to her ear. He played with her nipple and stroked the curve of her breast, and he wanted her as much in that nasty, dank creepy place as he had ever wanted anything in his life, but his reverence for her finally swamped him.

She knew who he was, what he was about, and God knew, what he was about wasn't all hearts and flowers or perfect by anyone's standards. But Robyn Delaney brought him laughs and rare insight, peace and a place to hang his hat no matter where either of them were. His time with her was too precious and fleeting.

He whispered things in her ear he had never admitted before, even in his secret heart. He lifted her and tasted her, and she came to him open as a book, wrapping her legs around his waist, and when the earth began to move, neither one of them knew that the earth had in fact begun to shudder and collapse and disintegrate.

The horrible, twisting yawn of splintering beams rocked their dark and dank world. Robyn cried out and clung to him, trying to protect his head and body with hers, but the force of the rock-hard granite, heaving and collapsing, cleaved them apart.

He shoved her toward the solid rock wall and dove sideways to save the lantern, but above them the supporting beam, the one with their initials carved in a heart, crashed down.

His back was broken, his body crushed. Keller True-blood died with Robyn's name on his lips and her desperate, keening cry ringing in his head . . . but the last image Kiel beheld was one in which the devastation happened all over again, only it was Robyn, in his vision, whose body lay twisted and broken and lifeless beneath a splintered beam and deadly briffitts of dust.

"KIEL?"

He twisted in his seat. Pain roared through his head. "Dear God, how do you stand it?" he croaked.

"Stand what? Kiel, what's wrong? Are you all right?"

He wasn't. Even Robyn's car felt stiflingly small to him. Keller's memories faded and died, as his human form had died, but Kiel was left with the overwhelming sense of what it was to have the life crushed from his body. He recovered. Even Keller, from the instant of his death, had not suffered long.

The one left to suffer sat beside him. Kiel could not look at Robyn without knowing the scope of the battle she had waged to survive. The heart-pounding terror of any darkness after she was buried alive, unable to see her hand in front of her face. The physical trauma she had overcome in the face of memories of Keller dogging her every step of the way.

The torrent of Keller's memories lasted no more than a few seconds in real time, but Robyn knew something was wrong, that something had happened to Kiel.

She put her hand on his left forearm. "Kiel, what is it?"

"I just... I just witnessed the Hallelujah collapsing."

Struggling to stay on the road, Robyn shuddered. "How?"

He could not lie. "As if I had been Keller. Robyn, it's a miracle you survived at all."

"I didn't think so, Kiel. Not for a long time. Where was my Guardian Angel then? Where was Keller's?"

The question haunted Kiel, too. "Some things are destined, Robyn. I don't really know the answer. I had no sense of how hard it really is to be human."

He didn't know either how she coped from day to day with such devastating memories lurking below the surface, ready to spring on her at the slightest crack in her guard.

"It's easier, being an angel?"

He gave her a sideways smile. "We aren't usually troubled by painful emotions or memories. Every time you turn around, Keller is there, isn't he."

"Yes." She sniffed. "Not only Keller, though. I still remember the shame when my dad cracked my knuckles for not using a knife. I remember my great-grandma brushing my hair. I loved that brush. It was this amber color with a cameo lady on its back. I don't know what became of her brush, but in my memory it's still the most beautiful thing I have ever seen. She made all my little-girl problems feel like fairy dust I could gather up in my hand and blow away."

"You loved her very much."

Again, filled with complicated emotions, she nodded. "Grandmama Marie was old country right down to her Bible. Austrian. She had this thing she used to say—I'd almost forgotten. I guess it's like the Austrian national theme. 'Vell, my deeer,' she'd say to me," Robyn quoted, mimicking her grandmother's accent, "'ze situation iss hopeless, but not so serious.'"

Robyn took her eyes off the road and glanced at him. Her eyes, *moonbeams on mink,* Kiel thought, glittered. She took a deep breath and expelled it. "Guess that about says it for the human condition, doesn't it? Everyone of us is a hopeless pit of emotions, but it isn't so serious after all. Life goes on. We get over it or we don't. Either way, life does go on."

Kiel smiled for her. "You've come a long way, Robyn."

She smiled. "I have, haven't I. Anyway. What do you think of going to Lucy?"

"You like her?"

Robyn nodded. "I do. She's very down-to-earth for a woman who owns whole chunks of Aspen real estate. We spent a lot of time together. I'm sure she could turn us onto explosives experts."

"So how do you handle it? Alone? Together?"

"Do you want to meet her?"

"Sure. But I'd like to spend some time going through Keller's trial transcript notes."

"Not to mention interviewing Chloe Nielsen, Shad Petrie and Pascal Candelaria." Robyn came to a stop at the intersection of the county roads. She waited on a couple of high-end, pricey four-by-fours, then turned back to Aspen. "We've got two things going here. One, was it really Trudi who murdered Spyder? and two, was she or whoever did kill Spyder threatened enough by

Keller to want him dead? Did you think Crandall was telling us the truth?''

"The truth according to him. But he made the case against Trudi Candelaria. Why would he play devil's advocate to his own work?''

"For the sake of the truth?'' Robyn suggested.

"The truth is set in concrete for guys like him.''

"Mmm. A 'don't confuse me with the facts' kind of guy.''

Kiel laughed. "That's a good one. But to be fair, the weight of facts had to be on Crandall's side, or Keller would never have signed on as special prosecutor.''

"I don't agree with you, Kiel. Keller—er, Kiel—'' The juxtaposition and similarity of the two names had her tongue tied in knots. Laughing at herself, she started again. "*Keller* said it often enough. A prosecutor's case is only as good as the weakest link. Crandall was the crucial link, and I think, after listening to him today, that he had his mind made up. Once the grand jury indicted Trudi Candelaria, the die was cast.'' She darted through a yellow light and pulled into a slanted parking place in front of a popular cappuccino bar.

Ready to lambaste her theory, Kiel rolled up the window to prevent any passersby from overhearing him. "Think about what you're saying now, Robyn. Based on one interview with Ken Crandall, you're saying Keller Trueblood, your husband, a man whose instincts and integrity you trusted to the nth degree, caught and ran with the ball of a man whose instincts turn you off and whose integrity is yet to be proven.''

"That's not—'' Robyn broke off. Propping her hands over the steering wheel, she gave a weary sigh. "You're right. What can I say? I guess, deep down inside, Kiel, I believed Trudi Candelaria.''

"You *want* to believe her, or you *do?*"

"I don't think she killed Spyder. I think the evidence must have been compelling. I can't imagine how Crandall could have slanted it so much in her direction if it wasn't already pointing that way. Enter Stuart Willetts. Keller had to have been caught between a rock and a hard place with her story, because his co-counsel was already embroiled in an affair—or at least an infatuation—with her."

Kiel watched the pedestrians passing by. All of them seemed to be wearing designer clothes. A town for the very rich. "So where does that leave you? If you believe Trudi didn't kill Spyder, can you believe she would buy someone to make sure Keller was stopped?"

"I can't, Kiel. I don't know where this is coming from, or if I'm losing my mind. I know she's lived in Aspen a long time and she has connections out the wazoo, but I just can't see her getting so desperate, when she didn't do the murder, that she'd murder the prosecutor, instead. And no matter how much was at stake for Stuart Willett, I can't see him plotting Keller's murder, either."

Kiel ran his fingers back and forth over the fine leather grain of Keller's Day-Timer, thinking, saying nothing.

"Am I wrong, Kiel?"

He gave a quick shake of his head. "Your instincts are always clean, Robyn." He reached for her hand. "I'm just concerned that you're second-guessing yourself."

"Just adjusting theory to fact. But even if I am, Kiel, it's because even though I may believe her, I don't like Trudi Candelaria. She knew she could wrap Stuart Willetts around her little finger." She turned her hand in Kiel's and held tight to him. "And that's exactly what she set out to do."

"I'm not sure I get the connection."

"Michael Massie told me the only thing Trudi Candelaria cared about was Trudi Candelaria. Is that enough to suggest she would murder Keller?"

"Not necessarily...but—" he looked askance at her, teasing her "—I'm still not following this tortured piece of reasoning, Robyn."

Her own brows raised. "If the logic seems tortured," she said, "it's because things didn't stay simple for Trudi. She actually fell in love with Stuart, and that had to come as a surprise to her. If they are in love, bully for them. But she used him first. I think she absolutely *was* prepared to let Stuart sacrifice his credibility and his career and flush his reputation trying to save her bacon. That's not what I call love."

"Me, either."

"The problem is, all of this leads us back to square one—and I could be dead wrong." She pulled a moue at her choice of words there, but went on. "Stuart had so much to lose that it makes sense, if anyone killed Keller, if anyone had to kill him, it would be Stuart Willetts."

"And the problem with that," Kiel said, still holding her hand, still stroking his thumb along the life line carved in her palm, "is that with all Trudi's money, what did he have to lose, really? With that kind of backing, he didn't need his credibility or his career—and the risk was minimal. Who was ever going to uncover all this?"

Robyn sighed in frustration and let her head fall back against the headrest. "I keep thinking it's all too paranoid by half to believe Kell was murdered, anyway."

Kiel understood her frustration, which paralleled his own. Angelo's answer to his questions had never really satisfied Kiel.

If, as Angelo stated, he had been the mortal Keller Trueblood, and there seemed little doubt of that as Keller's memories kept surfacing, then why didn't Kiel know he'd been murdered, why didn't he have a sense of evil having been perpetrated against him, why couldn't he come into the Hereafter like Agatha Orben demanding that her death be avenged—all remained unanswered questions.

So while Robyn was dealing with the lingering doubts and fearing herself paranoid, he knew she had reason, if only because this case had been brought to the Denver Branch of Avenging Angels. There must be something to avenge.

He just couldn't tell her why, and that constraint was wearing very thin.

Chapter Eight

The only thing to do was plunge ahead. He turned to look at Robyn. "Are we going to find Lucinda Montbank at this cappuccino bar?"

She laughed, relieved, he supposed, for any excuse to stop the ruminating and get on with what lay before them. "Maybe. Since she owns the building, her cappuccino is free, which is exactly the way she likes everything." Robyn pointed across the street to a renovated structure from the 1890s. "But Lucinda Montbank's engineering firm has the entire second floor of that building. That's why we're parked here."

As it turned out, Lucinda Montbank was in the cappuccino bar sipping a rare blend of beans and holding court in her inimitable manner on the state of the complex interactions between the precious metal and commodities market, real estate and skiing tourism.

A natural blonde, Lucy wore her hair in an elegant French roll. Her violet eyes, enhanced by colored contact lenses, widened with surprise bordering on consternation when she spotted Robyn waving from behind the back of one of Lucy's faithful followers.

Caught off guard by her friend's brief flash of dismay, Robyn laughed uneasily. "Lucy, you look like you've seen a ghost!"

Lucy gave a sigh. "Well, it's just shame on me not to have kept in touch with you. I heard you were in town, but I didn't believe it." She stepped off the stool wearing expensive leather pumps and an exquisite dove gray pinstriped suit. At a negligent wave of her hand, the crowd dispersed, all of them, even the twenty-fiveish young man Robyn recognized as Lucy's leading minion.

Lucy reached for her and touched both Robyn's cheeks with hers, then held her at arm's length. "Robyn, you look absolutely... well!"

"I only just ended my therapy, but I am much better these days. No limp, no cane." Her eyes flicked to Kiel. None of that had been true before he came along. "Michael said to tell you hello. Says you're still the best."

"Ah, Michael. Of course he let me know how you were doing from time to time. I understand it's been a terrible year for you. Come. Sit down and catch me up. I thought your memories of Aspen might be so vile as to keep you away forever—and I feel responsible, of course. I should've provided expert guidance for you in the Hallelujah. The accident might never have happened if I had just done that one thing."

"Lucy, you did offer. Keller and I refused. Please don't give it another thought." Throughout their exchange, Lucy was eyeing Kiel. "I'd like you to meet a friend of mine. Lucinda Montbank, Kiel Alighieri. Kiel is working with me now, and you're right. I should have called you the minute we got into town."

Lucy offered her hand. Kiel's made-up surname seemed to go right by her, as well. "You're working with Robyn?" she asked. "In what capacity?"

"An investigator." He took Lucy's hand in both of his but saved the winning thousand-candle smile. Robyn wanted instinctively to leap into the silent standoff between them—they reminded her of wild cats circling and snarling, but she also knew it was Lucy's style to get a man's measure through sheer force of will and intimidation.

The first time Keller met Lucy, he backed off the handshake and blew on his fingers with a rueful smile, acknowledging her as a high-powered woman. Keller's dry wit had won her over, losing the battle but ultimately winning the war.

Lucinda Montbank lived for such metaphorical spitting contests.

Kiel, however, was not backing off.

Tension crackled between Kiel and Lucinda like electricity firing down high-voltage transmission lines. He'd left the word *investigator* out there like a gauntlet Lucy could only take up at her peril. If she cared, if investigating anything intersected with anything she cared about.

Robyn held her breath.

The force of Kiel's will, the dominance of his compelling eyes, the sheer magnetism of his strength and character, held her spellbound. She had rarely seen anyone, man or woman, hold their own when Lucinda Montbank chose to prevail. In Kiel, Lucy had met her match, and to see him go toe-to-toe with her made Robyn's flesh tingle as it had not done in all the months since Keller had died. Or, until Kiel had made love to her and she pretended it was Keller.

The threat of feeling again made her throat close tight.

The reminder of what it was to be so deeply attracted to a man as she was to Kiel, to an angel, now, left her mind numb and her body utterly tuned to his every nuance.

She fought to focus on the confrontation. Choosing to sidestep his gauntlet, Lucy blinked first. Robyn sucked in her first breath in several long seconds. She'd never seen her friend, this formidable woman, come away so empty-handed.

"Well." Lucy was the one to offer the dazzling smile first. "A real man. What a pleasure."

Kiel answered with a sardonic grin. Robyn thought she understood its meaning. A *real* man he wasn't, no more than Pinocchio was a real boy. Her thinking intruded into his mind, startling him, triggering amusement. He turned to Robyn, surprise and mock fire lighting his eyes.

Time stopped in a spell he cast, like the one he had created the night before. Robyn's thinking of Pinocchio made him realize the connection between their souls was intact because, less than thirty-six hours before, he'd thought to himself how lucky it was that old Gepetto was not his creator.

Coincidence? No. Not between Keller and Robyn, not between Kiel and Robyn. The awareness that sizzled between them was sexual, and more. Far more. Lucy's smile remained unchanged, comical in its persistence in the time warp Kiel had created.

"Pinocchio?" His expression bespoke sharp irritation, but his eyes smiled.

"Yes. Pinocchio." They squared off over the nonsense issue, as lovers square off for the heat of the battle and the thrill of the dare. A wave of pure, intense pleasure moved through her. She lifted her chin. "You know, the little wooden puppet boy who wanted more than anything to be a . . . a real boy."

He could have no reason to wish to be a real man, except that he did. He wished to kiss her like a man, to silence her smart mouth with his, to answer her, to cross her battle lines and take her.

His eyes fixed on her lips. His throat tightened, his mostly human angel heart sped. They got no closer than arms's length, but he could feel the heat of her desire and she could smell the need in him to throw off his angel cloak and be a man.

The moment stretched. The sizzle in the air invoked a smell only lightning leaves behind. He broke off his gaze and instinctively reached to cradle her cheek in his hand. When he touched her, he satisfied her desire, and then he hid it from her, and then he left her smiling at Pinocchio images. In physical pain just like a real man, a frustrated man, Kiel ended his folly and closed the time warp.

Lucy's smile faded naturally, and Robyn's broadened. It was as if he and Robyn had only shared a private joke, but never throbbed at each other like a real and needy woman and a real and needy man.

He'd fooled this shark of a woman, this harridan and friend of Robyn's, with a stand she was unused to facing. But that didn't lessen his respect. Lucinda Montbank on their side was a far better thing than Lucinda Montbank opposing them.

But his body still throbbed. *A real man,* she'd said. *A pleasure.* "A pleasure," he agreed.

Robyn let her belated smile fade. Disoriented a moment, and confused at all the times in Kiel's presence that she'd become so hazy, she shook her head to clear it. "Lucy, could I...could we impose on your time? If we could talk privately in your office..."

"Of course you can, Robyn." Turning to the cappuccino bar owner, Lucy ordered up a carafe of coffee and a selection of pastries, then led the way out, one arm looped through Robyn's, the other through Kiel's. Robyn had no opportunity even to exchange glances with Kiel while they crossed the street and went up via an antique cage elevator to Lucy's offices.

Done in silver and brown, the decor was as upscale as any New York firm. Lucy's display of artifacts added to the ambience. Roaring Fork Valley historical mining heritage.

Rather than sitting behind her expansive glass desk, which rested on pillars of locally mined marble, Lucy chose to sit in a conversation grouping with her back to the window. Kiel took the deep burgundy leather chair to her left, and Robyn sat across.

She poured the hot beverage, offered the plate of pastries around, then sank back into her chair. "So. What can I do for you? Are you interested in getting back to your story for the Smithsonian?"

"The historical murders?" Robyn shook her head. "I'm not even sure they're still interested, so I can't rule it out, but this is something much closer to home, Lucy." She frowned. Even though she had only talked to Trudi Candelaria and Stuart Willetts last night, Robyn would almost have expected Lucy to have caught wind of it. Her connections and ties in Aspen were just that sophisticated—and that simple. "I checked into The Chandler House yesterday—"

"As I said," Lucy interrupted, "I heard that you were here, but . . . without a clue as to why."

"Where did you hear?" Kiel asked, sitting back, crossing an ankle over the opposite knee. His voice was soft as warm butter, sharp-edged as a knife.

Lucy blinked at him. "I don't remember, Mr. Alighieri. I hear a lot of things."

Robyn's friend still looked no older than thirty-five, but the concern creasing her features betrayed her pampered skin by at least ten years. Robyn sent Kiel a look. She could see these two were going to be at each other's throats all the time.

Lucy turned away from Kiel. "Robyn, I am surprised you could come back to Aspen for any reason."

"I'm not sure I would ever have returned, Lucy. You're right about the memories. If I had never come back here again, it wouldn't have been a great loss to me."

"Believe me, everyone here understands that—at least those of us who knew you and Keller. So what was important enough to you to overcome all that?"

Robyn took a deep breath and plunged ahead. "Lucy, I have serious questions about the timing of Keller's death. The truth is, I don't think the cave-in at the Hallelujah was an accident."

Lucy paled. "Dear God, Robyn, you can't be serious! Are you?"

"I am. I think someone set out to cause that collapse. Massie and I were talking about it a few nights ago. I think someone had very good reason to want Keller out of the way. I think someone knew we were going to the Hallelujah that morning and took the opportunity to make certain Keller never made it out alive."

Lucy's eyes widened in horror and disbelief. "Who could be so twisted? So cruel? So...so *evil?*"

"Someone who had everything to lose," Kiel suggested softly. "If your life was at stake, like, say, Trudi Candelaria must have believed hers was," he went on, "wouldn't you go to just about any lengths?"

"Including murdering the prosecutor?" Lucy asked. "I'm a hard woman, Mr. Alighieri. You'll find those who swear I breakfast on nails. I might even have entertained—for a moment—some similar notion had I been in such circumstances." She leaned back, daring to be judged. "I never discard avenues of attack or of escape out of hand. But even I would have been hard-pressed to come up with such an inelegant solution as to murder Keller Trueblood. Wouldn't it have been a thousand times easier, and more certain, to…well, you know, just attack him in some dark alley?"

Robyn understood Lucy's aversion to suggesting other ways Keller was more likely to be killed. "The thing is, I don't think it would have been easier."

"Why not?"

"Aspen isn't exactly your usual site of drive-by shootings or dark alley stabbings."

"Amen to that," Lucy put in.

"But I don't think Keller would have been easy or reliably easy, at least, to catch alone. He was always either working on the case with someone over dinner, at least in public, or he was at home with me."

"Come on, Robyn," Lucy answered skeptically. "He went home alone every night for eight or nine weeks."

"That's just it, Lucy," Robyn argued. "He didn't. I could count on one hand the times he came home without an entourage—including Stuart Willetts and a minimum of two or three law clerks, not to mention—"

"All right." Lucy held up a hand. "Still, the Hallelujah would seem to me to be even more unreliable. As a way of making sure Keller was put out of the picture, I mean."

"It's possible," Kiel said, "that if someone did cause the mine shaft to collapse, it didn't really matter what the outcome was. Keller was not going to escape unscathed. Maybe the reasoning went, even if Trueblood survived, there was no way he was going to wind up his prosecution, either. Effectively, he was stopped.''

Lucy grimaced. "It makes me sick to admit it, but it's possible. It's all entirely possible. How can I help you? What do you need?''

"Three things, just off the top of my head," Robyn said, going on with the train of thought she and Kiel had followed. "One, we would like you to come up with a list of people with the expertise to pull this off, and two, a list of experts in the detection and identification of explosives residue.''

"The second coming first, most logically," Kiel said. "We have to know if the Hallelujah was sabotaged in the first place.''

"And the third thing, Lucy, is your opinion. Kiel and I talked to Ken Crandall this morning. He believes that Stuart Willetts had the most to lose." Briefly, Robyn related Crandall's theory about Willetts's career and blind passion. "I keep second-guessing myself. I can't see Trudi doing this stuff. You have such a keen insight into people—''

"No more than you, Robyn.''

"Maybe, but I'm not exactly a disinterested, objective party. If Keller had never come here, or if I hadn't wanted to go see the Hallelujah for myself... You see what flaming hoops I put myself through." She sat forward, her hands clasped around her knees. "Please. You hear things. You know as much or more about what goes on in this town as anyone. I value your judgment. Do you believe Trudi Candelaria killed Spyder? And if you do, is it a logical extension to think she or Willetts would have the stomach for taking Keller out like that?''

"Logic is pretty useless in a situation like this. I tend to think of murder as a crime of passion." Lucy's eyes slid to Kiel.

He nodded. "Motivated by passions, of course. At least one like Spyder's murder. But it would have to take a lot more reasoned thinking to have murdered Keller by the collapse of a hundred-year-old mine shaft."

"True enough." Tapping her lips with her forefinger, Lucy sighed. "But honestly, I don't know if Trudi killed Spyder or not. She had reason, she had all the opportunity in the world, and she had that bronze statue at her fingertips."

Robyn nodded. "Even Stuart Willetts admits all the evidence pointed to Trudi. He swears she didn't do it, of course, but his vouching for her doesn't count for much."

"No, it doesn't. If you want my opinion, I'll give it to you. Yes. I personally believe she did knock old Spyder off, and again, personally, I wouldn't blame her. He was a world-class jerk. I never heard anything less than completely self-serving coming out of his mouth. So...if she whacked him over the head with his own bronze, then again...yes. She'd have the moxie to hire out the so-called accident that ended Keller's life. Since she and Willetts are so cozy—I assume you know that?"

Robyn nodded.

"Then you have a case of one hand washing the other. Is Trudi smart enough to hoodwink the prosecution second chair? Or just sexy enough to short-circuit his real brain?" Lucy smiled coldly. "You bet she is. Crazy like a fox. Even I would think twice before tangling with her."

"So if she said to me that she didn't kill Spyder, and I believed her, I would be a fool?"

"Not at all, Robyn," Lucy argued. "No one knows who killed Spyder. You're right. I do hear a great deal, though nothing ever to exonerate her. It's highly unlikely we'll ever know for sure. But if she didn't kill Spyder, she had an even stronger motive to get rid of Keller. Don't you see? If she was going to be sent up the river for something she didn't do, she might have been just desperate enough to get the trial derailed—whatever it took."

"We've thought of that, too." Kiel got up and began pacing around, idly examining mining memorabilia, antiques set in glass cases that were discreetly and expertly spotlighted along one wall of Lucy's office. "Is it possible for you to come up with a list of people in the area with the expertise to have caused the mine to collapse?"

"Almost impossible, I'm afraid. Aspen isn't a very eclectic place. Filthy rich or dirt poor about covers the territory, because in between, you just can't afford to live here. But in those two, you have two very distinct populations. The rich and very rich, who live here in summer, jet in and out, and take only the most cursory interest in the heritage and history—and their polar opposites. The descendants of the ones who came here a hundred years ago, hacked their way through granite to precious metals or marble, and made it big only to lose it, or didn't ever quite make it to begin with. Robyn, Kiel, you have to understand. It wouldn't take a scientist or engineer to blast the Hallelujah to kingdom come."

Her bubble pricked, Robyn nodded. "Basically, what you're saying is that all it would take is one person with the nerve to light a stick of dynamite and run."

"Yes. High school kids could do it."

Kiel's brows drew together. "Did anyone ever make any effort to find out if that's what happened the day Keller was killed and Robyn's leg was crushed, or was it just assumed that the Hallelujah collapsed on its own?"

For a moment Lucy stared blankly at him. "I doubt any attempt was made. There was no reason to think anyone would do such a thing. And there weren't that many of us who even knew Robyn and Keller would be there."

"Who knew?" Robyn asked softly.

"I knew. I'm sure Stuart Willetts did as well, which meant Trudi knew." Lucy shook her head in disbelief. "If Trudi knew, or Stuart, either one, that's pretty telling, isn't it? But I believe the hikers who reported that the mine had collapsed never told the rescue parties or authorities that they heard a blast that might have caused the collapse first."

"We'll check those records," Kiel said, "but in the end, it all comes back to whether or not someone set charges that caused the Hallelujah to collapse." He shrugged. "Unless we find proof of that, all the rest is sheer speculation."

Lucy warmed her cappuccino from the carafe, then pressed an invisible buzzer concealed in the arm of her chair. The twenty-fiveish young minion poked his head in the door in about two seconds. "See if you can get hold of Adelmeyer or Palmer for me."

When Lucy's young aide left, Robyn looked at her for an explanation.

"They're both mining engineers. Gene Adelmeyer is ex-FBI, and an explosives residue expert, in addition. Tee Palmer is just an old miner with an instinct that won't quit. He's a cousin of mine, actually. Lives like a busted-down hermit, but he has several hundred thousand dollars salted away—and that's only what he trusts the bank to hold." She smiled fondly. "I'd bet there is a million more in ore he's stashed beneath his cabin in leather pouches."

Robyn felt encouraged. "They both sound perfect for the job."

Lucy shook her head. "They are, Robyn, but I hate to hold up such hope of proving anything."

Staring at an 1880s vintage cabinet displaying rock picks, axes, blasting caps and a couple of six-shooters behind authentic period glass panels, Kiel turned back. "Why is that?"

Lucy smiled, her expression somewhere between seductive, admiring and regretful. "Because it wouldn't necessarily even take a stick of dynamite to cause a collapse. I could show you stopes—the spaces left after the ore has been taken out—where huge slabs of rock have separated from the ceiling and fallen down all by themselves. It doesn't take much."

"Are you saying it's impossible, Lucy?"

"Not at all, Robyn. Don't get me wrong. I'll go to the ends of the earth if necessary to find the top men—but the Hallelujah is an old mine. All I'm saying is that in the realm of possibilities, even you or Keller could have inadvertently caused the collapse."

"Lucy," Robyn protested, "when the mine began collapsing Keller and I were standing in the middle of the end of a small tunnel—"

"It doesn't matter, Robyn. Even if we discount the possibility that your being there somehow upset the balance, a lot of blasting took place down in those shafts. Every hundred feet, a new level, new blasting. There'll be trace evidence of powder and dynamite all over creation that could be well over a century old."

"How does that keep us from identifying new blasting activity?" Robyn asked. "Granted, it's a year old now, but—"

"If I were going to try to make an old mine shaft collapse in an attempted murder," Kiel interrupted, catching Lucy's implication, "and if I wanted to cover my tracks, I'd use plain old-fashioned dynamite." He looked to Lucy. "Isn't that right?"

"Exactly." Lucy blinked slowly. "You sure as *hell* wouldn't use signature materials, or even anything remotely modern."

Chapter Nine

Robyn and Kiel met with Gene Adelmeyer at Planet Hollywood that night. He promised to take surface and core samples, based on Lucy's computer graphics representations of the Hallelujah. The samples would be tested in his Denver labs for explosives residues, but as Lucy had suggested, if dynamite had been used and not any modern-day explosives, dating the blast residues would likely prove impossible.

Tee Palmer proved more elusive. If he kept a cell phone, Robyn thought, he wasn't particularly slavish about keeping a functional battery. If he'd gone prospecting, there was no telling when he could be reached.

In the meantime, Lucinda Montbank provided Robyn and Kiel with underutilized office space in her building. Cartons of records were checked out of the county courthouse vaults, with nothing more than a Montbank personal guarantee, and transported the three blocks down Main Street to the building her company occupied.

Robyn put in calls to the Savannah Beach, Georgia, couple and the University of Colorado students who had been hiking independently in the vicinity of the Hallelujah the day of the accident.

Lucinda's memory was accurate. Neither group, upon reporting the collapse, had mentioned hearing a blast that could have created the cave-in, and when Robyn finally got through to them, they all repeated that they hadn't heard a blast.

"Which doesn't mean it didn't happen, Robyn," Kiel said.

She sat at a desk in an office Lucinda had provided, layers deep in files and court records. Tossing her pen down, she leaped up and began to pace.

"Kiel, this is all feeling like a wild-goose chase to me. Like some ridiculous notion I latched onto as if it were a lifesaver, when really it's an anchor pulling me down!"

Kiel exhaled sharply and put aside the notes of interviews Keller had conducted with Detective Crandall. "Robyn, look. I know this has to be frustrating. *I'm* frustrated. But there is something screwy in all this. Maybe Candelaria didn't murder Spyder—or even Keller. Maybe Willetts is getting the short end of the stick here. But I was sent because some injustice was done. I think we just have to be patient and work through what we have until something turns up."

Rubbing her hands up and down her arms to dispel the chill, Robyn nodded. "I know. But it sure feels like we're going in circles. Have you come across anything useful in Kell's notes?"

"One thing. A sort of recurring theme in his cartoon figures. Come look."

He showed her the first several pages of notes Keller had taken in interviewing the witnesses he had thought were going to be key to the presentation of the prosecution case. There were drawings all over the place, quick impressions Keller had recorded in that fashion. Then

Kiel narrowed what he showed her to the pages devoted to discussions with Ken Crandall.

Keller had perfectly captured the square shape of Detective Crandall's body, and a more triangular head—aspects he caricatured that Robyn had not noticed but recognized immediately as Crandall.

"Look. This is the first time." The doodle was just a caricature. "The second." Beside Crandall, a heap had been sketched in, like a pile of smelly manure.

Robyn laughed. "Look at how you can tell this pile of doo-doo stinks."

Kiel smiled. Keller had used what cartoonists call a *waftarom* to indicate the stench, but Kiel had the presence of mind not to name it, not to reveal he knew what Keller knew.

He flipped between pages as if he had Keller's perfect recall to several more. Beginning with the third one, the cartoon figure of Detective Ken Crandall was wielding a shovel.

"What do you think Keller was indicating here?"

"One of two things, I guess," Robyn said. "Either Crandall was digging through piles of manure to get at the truth, or he was shoveling manure at Kell. Stuff he couldn't believe. Is that what you were thinking, too?"

"Yeah. And it would seem to me that by the time Keller signed on as special prosecutor, digging for the truth of the matter should have been a done deal." He pulled another notebook full of Keller's scribbling, from later dates. "This is how it changes."

Looking at the next one of Keller's sketches that Kiel showed her, Robyn frowned. The pile in the margin, sketched at the edge of Keller's notes, had been reduced now, half behind Crandall's blocky figure and triangular head, half still before him. A tire lay submerged in the remaining half.

"This must mean Crandall was looking for the tire that left that tread mark in the snow at Spyder's estate."

"Looks like it. And now this." In the next one Kiel showed her, the tire was barely visible in the smelly heap behind Crandall's caricature, only the *waftaroms* had gotten thicker. Kiel turned pages once more. "We're almost to the end. See here?"

It was difficult to pick out in the margin, but she could see the outlines Kiel traced with his freckled finger.

"The smelly part is behind him, and Crandall is now digging a hole in the ground."

Robyn rubbed her forehead with her knuckles. "Why a hole in the ground?"

"Just what I wanted to know. A few minutes ago I came upon this one—and you can see we're right up to a day or so before you two went to the Hallelujah."

The final cartoon piece Keller had sketched during his interviews with Detective Crandall was chilling. The hole Crandall's caricature had dug had consumed him, and the county courthouse, accurate in every detail from its distinctive roofline to the central tower with the United States and Colorado flags flying over it, was distorted. From its base the building was being pulled, dragged in the direction of the hole.

"It's as if," Robyn said, "Crandall had dug himself into a hole and was pulling the halls of justice down with him." Cold seized her shoulders, and she began to pace again. "This is too creepy, Kiel. I was *here*. We'd rented that condo. I was living with Kell. If he thought anything like this, why wouldn't he have said something to me? Anything?"

Kiel shook his head. "Didn't you agree it would be better, professionally and ethically, to steer clear of Keller's cases when you married?"

She thumped the pile of Keller's notebooks. "There's a big difference, Kiel, between knowing every little thing that was going on as Keller recorded them like this, and telling me the case was taking a dive. I mean, *look* at this, Kiel. This is the county courthouse getting dragged down into a bottomless pit! It would not have been any ethical blunder to say to me, 'Robyn, there are big problems here.' I didn't have a clue!"

"This isn't much to go on, Robyn. Maybe Keller thought there were problems, and maybe he thought cops like Crandall would finally drag the judicial system down. We don't know."

She breathed out and crossed her arms over her chest. "But why wouldn't he have said something to me?"

Kiel flashed on a moment when he was experiencing himself as Keller going down into the Hallelujah with Robyn. Keller *had* been thinking that there were serious problems with the Candelaria case, and he'd intended to tell her about them the night he died. "I have a feeling," Kiel said, "that Keller would have told you everything if he'd lived."

"I suppose. But it doesn't feel right, Kiel. We should never have made such a stupid agreement. I could have dealt with knowing what was going on without writing about it."

"I'd bet Keller was arriving at the same conclusion himself."

She stared at Kiel, at his bronze coloring and bright, intense blue eyes, at the freckles that made him so stunningly attractive and as different from Keller as he could possibly be—and deep doubts assailed her. Doubts over things Kiel knew that only Keller should have known, and things he said, such as, *Keller had come to the same conclusion.*

How did he know?

Was he only the most brilliant of Avenging Angels, to guess so often and so well what Keller knew and wanted and thought? Or was it all a savvy manipulation worse than Stuart Willetts had ever dreamed of, a creepily intuitive ability to discern what she most wanted or needed to hear?

A part of her mistrusted him so much that she wanted to run. A part of her believed so much in his integrity and truthfulness that she doubted herself more than she doubted him. And there was the lesson Great-grandmama Marie would say her soul had invited.

To trust herself.

If she wasn't still so afraid of the darkness, the void Keller had left, as well as the real, profound, *literal* fear of being in the dark, she could begin. For now, she had to believe, to trust that an angel of God would not lead her into an even more terrifying darkness.

Kiel had stuck a pencil behind his ear. Now he sat back and planted his feet up on the desk he'd been using. "Do you want to talk to Crandall again?"

She plunked down in her own chair. "I think that would be a useless drill. He will only say what he's already told us. And why not? Why should he tell us anything now?"

"Come on, Robyn. You've interviewed plenty of people who have absolutely no reason to want to tell you the truth. You just keep hammering away until they crack, isn't that the way it goes?"

"Yes," she granted. He was quoting her now, straight out of *Where Angels Fear to Tread*. Every person involved in that case had a secret, and a hidden agenda. But she'd tried to find the truth. Hammered away until, finally, one person cracked, and then another and another.

"The thing is, I don't want to spend weeks on end if the whole process can be short-circuited. What if we were to go see Judge Ybarra?" The Honorable Vincent J. Ybarra had occupied the bench in *Colorado v. Candelaria*. "Maybe Keller went to him."

"There's no record of it here."

"Off the record, then. Maybe there were sidebar discussions or in-chamber meetings with Keller that didn't show up in the record."

"It's worth a try."

Robyn nodded. "I think so." She reached for the final notebook where Keller's distorted sketch of the courthouse being dragged into Crandall's hole appeared. "If only he'd been a little less cryptic!" Nothing in Keller's written notes helped to interpret his thinking on the issue.

"He wasn't expecting to die, Robyn. He knew what they meant, and at the time, that was all that mattered."

Lucy chose that moment to check in with them. "Robyn, Kiel. Hi. What are you up to?"

"Our eyeballs—in Keller's paperwork, trial transcripts, case notes. We're almost done."

"In only two days!" Lucy exclaimed. "How very diligent of you."

It wasn't so much a matter of diligence, though. It was true that between midday on Wednesday and now, at midday on Friday, she and Kiel had made their way through seven weeks of Keller's time spent interviewing witnesses, cops, Detective Crandall, Chloe Nielsen, Spyder Nielsen's agent Shad Petrie, even Trudi's ex, Pascal

Candelaria. But mostly their speediness had to do with Kiel's being an angel who required no sleep, who could focus his concentration in a way mortals could not.

And on Robyn's part, it had a lot to do with avoidance. Better to pick up one more file than sit there looking at Kiel through her lashes trying to figure out why he had captured her interest when Keller would never vacate her heart. Better to comb through another volume of courtroom transcripts than look up, and notice him noticing her and feeling that totally inappropriate zing . . . the tug of distant memories, the insistent rapping of more recent ones.

Of making love with Kiel Alighieri.

So it wasn't diligence. What it was was avoidance.

"Come have lunch with me." Lucy gave Kiel a desultory look. "Just us . . . girls."

Another avoidance mechanism. "Kiel? Would you mind?"

He glanced at the ivory charm hanging around her neck. She wondered again whether the intricate subtle wings were supposed to be some kind of high, heavenly voodoo amulet to protect her outside his presence. The notion seemed too whimsical altogether. Heaven and voodoo didn't quite go together in the same breath, but who knew?

The small charm brought her comfort in the night when her confusion about Kiel, and what went on between them that she couldn't quite remember, began to loom before her. She had even wondered if he was taking deliberate swipes at her conscious mind to erase her recall.

The wings reminded her through the day that she was not in this dangerous situation by herself.

Sometimes she needed the reminder. Sometimes her stomach pitched and twisted with how vulnerable she was making herself doing what she was doing here, virtually daring Keller's murderer to silence her, too. She needed Kiel's ivory charm when she remembered that leaving sleeping dogs to lie made much more sense than stirring them to snarl and snap and do to her what they'd done to Keller.

And yes. She needed to go let her hair down with Lucy and forget that she even needed the small wings. "Kiel?"

He tossed a pencil down in the open binding of court records and jerked his bronze-haired head toward the door. "Take your time. We'll follow up on this other stuff later this afternoon."

"Thanks." Robyn put a bookmark in the next page of Keller's accumulated notes and stood.

Lucy had a table reserved at a private club. She walked arm in arm with Robyn, remarking on the shame it was that a fungus of some sort had attacked all the aspen leaves. "No gold this fall. Sort of sad, sort of telling."

"Telling?"

Lucy shrugged. "Sure. Like the old Casey striking out at bat story. No joy in Mudville tonight." She hugged Robyn's arm to her side. "Robyn, I can't tell you how sick I am that Keller died here, how it pains me to think of what you've been through in the last year."

"Life goes on, though, doesn't it?" How many times would she have to reassure herself and everyone around her of that before she knew in her heart that life *would* go on?

Lucy understood that. "The world goes on. Aspen goes on. Spyder was murdered, and then Keller died— possibly murdered. But nothing is ever the same. So, yes. The dismal fate of the aspen leaves reminds me that things aren't what they're supposed to be. And they might never be again, for you.''

Robyn wanted to protest that *dismal* was too harsh, and that if she couldn't see her way past the ruined leaves this season, she would again—but they had arrived at the entrance to Lucy's club and turned in.

The foyer was paneled in dark mahogany. The patina must have been acquired for well over a century. An Oriental carpet runner graced the hardwood floor, and an enormous bouquet of exotic hothouse flowers, birds of paradise, orchids, lilies of the valley and hybrid roses, sat in a four-foot-high fluted crystal vase on the floor at the maître d' station.

The staff fawned over Lucy in as discreet a fashion as they could manage. She greeted each of them by name, ordered vintage wine and a cold cucumber soup for an appetizer, then turned to Robyn. ''Where were we?''

Robyn smiled, sipping at her ice water. The slice of lemon touched her lip. ''About to sink,'' she said, using the raw linen napkin, ''into a pity party. I may never get over losing Keller, Lucy, but I've...I've come to think I'll survive it. Be a little stronger. Find a way to be happy on my own.''

Lucy covered her hand encouragingly. ''I know you will. I won't see nearly enough of you because you'll find some new case to write about that will take you off to some exotic locale.''

Robyn laughed, interrupting. ''Aspen is about as exotic as the locales get, Lucy. I mean, think about it. For my first book I got to spend eight stellar, fun-filled months in and out of Ryker's Island.''

''Ah, New York's finest place. But you eventually got to come to Denver.'' The chilled cucumber soup arrived. Lucy picked up her spoon, but went on. ''Are you going to attend my birthday party tomorrow evening? It will be quite the occasion.''

Lucy's black-tie parties always were occasions. ''I wouldn't miss it. I talked to Jessie yesterday, since I knew you'd asked her to come.'' Jessie wasn't really thrilled to be coming. Covering VIP birthday parties for the TV audience wasn't what she'd prefer to be doing with her broadcast expertise, but station management wanted it, anyway. ''She's going to bring up one of my evening gowns and shoes and jewelry.''

''Is she coming with Mike and Scott, or with her camera crew?''

''The guys.'' Michael Massie, of course, had grown up around Aspen. Scott Kline, Robyn's friend on the Denver *Post,* was trailing along for the hell of it. ''Kiel has rented a tux.''

Lucy's features hardened. ''That concerns me, Robyn. Do you think it's wise, jumping into a relationship with someone else when you haven't really laid Keller to rest in your heart?''

Kiel. Robyn's heart thumped. ''Not Kiel,'' she said.

''Well, yes. Kiel.''

Robyn shook her head and took her time with a few spoonfuls of the chilled soup. ''Lucy, correct me if I'm wrong here, but wasn't I just saying I thought I would eventually find a way to be happy on my own?''

''It's the eventually that troubles me, Robyn. You may never get there. You need space. Time. I'd hate to think you were being pressured out of the time you need to...you know, get over Keller.''

''I've had space and time, Lucy.'' Besides which, all the space and time left her weren't going to be enough. Not to mention that Kiel, if she believed him, was not going to be around after Keller's murder, and Spyder Nielsen's, were avenged.

They had no future, and she had no chance of falling in love with a real man, anyway, so long as every other thing about Kiel plucked at her memories of Keller. But these weren't protests she could possibly lodge aloud.

The waiter came and went, taking their order, bringing their food. Robyn guided the conversation on to other topics—the rest of the guest list for Lucy's birthday, the local gossip, the latest celebrity DUI's and contretemps.

But Robyn's own thoughts scattered, fragmenting and flowing like iron filings to a magnet, back to Kiel. When her frozen dessert had melted and lost its exquisite swan shape before she took so much as one bite, Lucy touched her arm.

"What, Robyn? What are you thinking?"

She snapped out of her unintended reverie, put down the spoon and pushed the now unappetizing, drooping confection away. "Lucy, you wouldn't believe me if I could tell you."

"Try me, Robyn."

"No, really. I . . . my mind is just off in some crazy mixed-up place."

"Robyn, don't be ridiculous. We came to lunch to let down our hair and . . . just *be*," Lucy urged, sitting forward. "We haven't been friends such a long time, but I thought we grew very close very quickly—like fate. Like we were meant to meet."

She felt inexplicably crowded by Lucy's concern. A year ago Robyn had felt that way, too. Some people presumed too quickly on acquaintances, sticking like glue too fast, calling too soon, too often, making too many invitations, asking and offering too much. Until this moment, that hadn't seemed true of Lucy, but Robyn wanted her friend to understand.

The real truth was, she needed someone who would understand when she confessed to having fallen into bed with an Avenging Angel, but that wasn't an option.

"I was just thinking," she said, "that everywhere I turn, I see Keller—or maybe I just keep looking for him. It's like this trick my mind is playing that I'll see a gesture that was Keller's or hear a tone of voice he used, or see a light in someone's eyes like the twinkle in Keller's eyes was. Sometimes I even feel this eerie sense of recognition."

"With Kiel."

Robyn sucked in a breath and nodded. She'd gone too far, been too obvious, said too much, but the milk was spilt, and Lucy, despite her shock at this admission, was a friend. "I know. How looney tunes is it to think Keller could be lurking in someone else's body pulling off this elaborate twilight zone stunt?"

Lucy shook her head slowly, meeting Robyn's eyes. "I had no idea, Robyn. How awful for you. I always thought that memory must fade. That by now maybe you would even be grieving that you couldn't remember the sound of his voice." She lifted her brows, her eyes filled with pity, or something too much like it. "Your memory hasn't dimmed one iota, has it?"

"No." She cleared her throat to knock back the dull throb.

"Have you thought, perhaps, that you need to get away from Kiel?"

Robyn's heart twisted. She broke off the eye contact. "I can't, Lucy—"

"Of course you *can*," Lucy chided gently. "I wouldn't say this to you if we weren't friends, Robyn, but we are.

If he keeps you so in mind of Keller, get rid of him. You don't owe it to anyone to put yourself through this, Robyn, least of all some man.''

But that wasn't fair, and Robyn knew it. "Lucy, it's my fault, not Kiel's, that I see Keller in him. It isn't fair to blame Kiel.'' Together, she and Keller had each been whole, larger than life. One.

One.

She was like the jam on his toast. He was as essential to her as the cream in her coffee. It was only that she couldn't get used to being "jam" without purpose or place. "I've been drinking my coffee black for a while now,'' she mused.

"Is that something I'm supposed to understand, Robyn?''

She shook her head and gave a smile. "No. Lucy, I'm not going to curl up and die. I'm not a shadow of my former self, and . . . even if I thought I could get rid of Kiel, he won't be dispensed with.''

"I would help you,'' Lucy offered. "I have staff I can turn over to your use this minute—''

"Lucy,'' she interrupted, touching her friend's hand, "I can't. I've never run away from anything in my life, and if I start now, how will that make me better? Is there some other reason you believe I should get rid of Kiel?''

Lucy straightened and set aside her napkin with a thump. "I've said too much, haven't I, even between friends? Of course you must do what will finally make you better. If I overstepped, Robyn, please forgive me, but it's because by your own admission, he's making you crazy.''

"Or...maybe he's making me well.'' *Like flypaper,* her great-grandmama Marie used to say. *Flypaper traps flies;*

so your soul captures what it must learn, and the people to learn from.

Or in this case, Robyn thought, the angel.

AFTER ROBYN LEFT with Lucinda Montbank, Kiel sat staring into space for a long time. Every bit as troubled as Robyn by their lack of real progress in resolving the murders of Spyder Nielsen and Keller, he knew they must be edging closer. And he knew it was the nature of the beast, of investigating, that a certain amount of time was likely to be spent chasing leads that went nowhere. But his own frustration had more to do with Robyn, with keeping her in the dark as to his true self, than anything else.

His eyes fixed on the lighted display cabinets along the wall of the office and the collection of Wild West lore, everything from old decks of cards to bullets, recovered doorsills and pictures of dead bodies from drunken, brawling shoot-'em-ups in the mining camp saloons. Old Lucien Montbank, Lucy's great-grandfather, had owned one of the brothel-saloons, and must have had an unexpectedly forward-looking bent of mind to save such things for posterity. For instance, the bullet that killed BlackJack Turner, the notorious gambler.

Just for exercise Kiel split his consciousness, focusing both inward, on thoughts of Robyn, and outward, on that bullet. His eyes trained on the misshapen metal bullet, focused sharply and zoomed in until a part of his being and awareness shrank and actually entered into the molecules of the lead itself.

This was truly what Kiel would consider an angel trick. David Copperfield could make the Great Wall of China appear to disappear, so it wasn't so amazing, to Kiel at least, that he himself had the power to both materialize, and then make disappear, that mountain cabin—or anything else, for that matter. But this...this ability to be in consciousness in two different places, this was a feat befitting an angel. He could at once explore the inner contours of the spent and deadly bullet, and at the same precise time, be sitting in a chair in an office as would any mortal being, thinking.

He knew there were times when Robyn believed she had taken a startling left-hand-turn into madness. He would either have to resolve this case quickly and get out of her mortal life, or finally explain to her who he was.

The deception was sanctioned as the most humane and compassionate choice, but every minor piece contributing to it now corroded his angelic sense of fairness and truth. And with or without the memories of Keller Trueblood, Kiel's human manifestation was falling deeper in love with Robyn's earthbound one.

He couldn't handle it much longer. Since the last thing he wanted to do was to deal with a look of betrayal in Robyn's eyes, he had to do something—and fast. He ended his little exercise with the bullet in the display cabinet and sealed the division in his consciousness to get on with the business of resolving the murders.

He cloaked himself in invisibility and followed the path Robyn and Lucy had taken, then sat in for a moment on their conversation in the dining club.

He didn't like Lucinda much. He had the sense that despite all her obvious help, she was hanging around to throw roadblocks in their way. She manufactured disputes with him where there were none, and goaded him every time Robyn went out of earshot. He was tired of messing with her, and he would have loved to flare up into his fearsome angelic visage just to put her in her place. He couldn't see what it was that Robyn admired in

Lucinda Montbank, but instead of taking her on, he went out of his way for Robyn's sake not to get into power struggles with Lucy.

He didn't like her and didn't like the tone of her lunch conversation, but he left the restaurant telling himself he had to have faith that for the next hour, Robyn would be fine without him.

And if she wasn't, by the carving of ivory wings he had made for her, he would know it. He soared in his invisible state of being around the mountains surrounding Aspen in search of Tee Palmer, the crusty old miner Lucy had promised but so far had been unable to deliver.

Kiel traveled in ever-widening circles, searching for the consciousness of the old man. He found him taking a smoke break from his labors in an obscure old mining shaft that would have been closed down cold inside a week had government safety inspectors ever seen it.

Kiel materialized out of sight in clothes the old man would not automatically mistrust—which were ones about as filthy as those Tee Palmer wore.

He walked up the hillside for about fifty feet so as not to surprise the old man, either. "Tee Palmer?" he called out from a distance of thirty feet.

"Depends." The old guy squinted hard though the sun was at his back. "Who in the billy hell are you?"

"Name's Ezekiel. A friend of Lucinda Montbank."

"She didn't say you could find me up here, 'cuz she don't know what I'm doin'," he answered suspiciously. "So how'd you find me?"

"Lucky break, I reckon. Need some help. Mind if I sit awhile with you?" Kiel asked, tailoring his words to the old man's speech patterns.

They sat and talked awhile. Palmer smoked another cigarette, then another, while he listened to Kiel explaining what it was Tee could help him with.

The old man sat soaking up the sunshine for a moment, dozing. He startled awake when a bird screeched at a squirrel, still in mind of what Kiel had been talking about.

He settled his backside differently on the hard, downward-sloping ground. "That old Hallelujah cavin' in like it did that day set me t'thinking. Came a runnin' m'self when I heard it go. In that bunged up ol' Jeep, anyway," he said, jerking his head in the direction of a vehicle Kiel would bet had seen thirty years on some army base, and another thirty in Tee's possession.

"Were you at the Hallelujah when they rescued that woman and her husband?"

"Dead-as-a-doornail husband, yep. Can't figure it. Dumb-ass people get theirselves killed all the time going where they oughtn't oughta go, but I had a sense about this not being a case of dumb asses," he went on, "but somethin' nefarious goin' on instead."

Amused as he was by Tee Palmer's mix of quaint and sophisticated words, the sentiment, the skepticism, shook Kiel. "Why is that, Tee?"

"Just a feelin'. About as much logic as fits in a pinhead, but the feelin'..." Tee shook his head. "That lack o' serious reasoning don't change the feelin'. Only times in a long life I've ever been in real trouble was when I ignored m'gut and went with logic."

"Is it possible that someone set off charges?"

"More'n possible. Likely. Had to set off a few more to rescue them kids, too—that lawyer fella 'n' his wife."

Kiel had a powerful sense of himself being one of the kids Tee was talking about, only the mortal body of

Keller Trueblood had been stone-cold dead. But the point the old man had made was an important one.

More blasting had been necessary to clear a path into the tunnel where Robyn and he, or rather Keller, had been found—which meant new traces of explosives residue were to be expected.

"So there'd be no way of telling, would there? No way to prove someone intended for the Hallelujah to collapse on those two?"

"No way on God's little green earth I know of," Tee said. "You know anybody had it in for that mouthpiece fella?"

Kiel nodded. "There were some. Nobody such as yourself, though, who'd know how to do the dirty work."

Tee shook his head. "Wish I'd been around, maybe I'd a seen who done it. I mighta been in the gen'ral vicinity," he reflected, "'cept I was five miles away chasin' off after some damn-blamed fool New Age hippies gettin' naked in my hot springs."

Kiel grinned. It was too bad Tee Palmer had not been in the vicinity to see who'd been anywhere near the Hallelujah planting explosives. He stood up when Tee shoved himself up to his feet, and shook hands with the old miner. "Thanks for your help."

"Ain't much, come to that."

"Did you get rid of the hippies?"

"I fixed their wagon good," Tee said, cackling a bit. "Filled in the springs with boulders, that's what."

Chapter Ten

Judge Vincent J. Ybarra kept a dark courtroom every Friday afternoon. Robyn and Kiel checked in with his clerk, and he had, in fact, gone home for the weekend. She told them it was the Judge's habit to go soak in the mineral hot springs at the back of his property. That was where they found him.

His aging housekeeper had taken their names, and he'd sent her back to invite them in.

The trek out had to be a quarter mile over a footpath just worn through the weeds. Covered to his bare neck in a pool cut out by the natural springs, Judge Ybarra smiled broadly and waved an arm at the two of them. He had a full mustache, head of snowy white hair and distinctive Hispanic features. He was one of the most respected magistrates on the Western slope. "Robyn Delaney," he said. "I'm quite a fan of yours, young lady, I've read all your books. Found them quite good, in fact. And you're not a trained attorney, are you?"

"No, sir, I'm not," she answered. "Thank you. It's always nice to hear that someone enjoyed my work, but doubly so, coming from you." She turned to Kiel. "You've not met Judge Ybarra." Kiel introduced himself.

"An alias, or a descendant of the great Italian poet?" the old judge asked, his eyes sparkling with the devil.

"I chose it, sir," Kiel answered. *Smith,* he swore, next time. Smith.

"Well, if you're going to choose a name, why not?" Ybarra asked. "A dear friend of mine, a civil rights attorney, went from Ken to Sebastian. Quite fitting, I believe now, though in my younger days, I thought changing one's name a bit on the side of overweening. Take off your shoes, both of you, and dip your feet while we talk. You'll find it really very therapeutic."

Robyn peeled out of her light knee-highs and loafers inside thirty seconds. Kiel took a few seconds longer.

Ybarra's expressive face went solemn. "Your husband was a very fine young man, Robyn. His loss must be very difficult for you, as it is to all of us who respected his work so highly."

"Thank you so much for that. Keller held you in the highest regard, too."

"As he should, as he should," Ybarra joked. "You'll find I am not a falsely modest man."

Kiel finally stuck his feet in the hot springs. "Judge Ybarra, I'm working with Robyn, going through Keller's files. We think there may be reasons to doubt the integrity of one of the investigating officers in *Colorado v. Candelaria.*"

The old gentleman sat up, spreading his thin arms on the rock behind him. "What reasons?"

"That's really what we came to see if you could help us with," Robyn answered. "In Keller's notes . . . I don't know if you were familiar with Keller's cartoon sketches—"

"Oh, quite," Ybarra interrupted. "I found him in contempt twice for scrawling cartoons when he should

have been paying attention." The skin around his old
brown eyes crinkled nearly shut when he laughed at her
startled expression. "I confiscated his drawings as pay-
ment." Ybarra leaned forward, whispering, "I framed
them. They're of me. Quite good." He sat back, laughing, roaring for his housekeeper to bring him a cigar.
"But you were saying?"

Robyn smiled and shook her head at the sly, funny old
magistrate. "I was saying, that in Keller's notes are several caricatures of Detective Crandall—all quite recog-
nizable." She described the series of drawings, ending
with the courthouse being pulled into the hole Crandall
had dug. "My question, Judge Ybarra, is this. Did Keller
come to you privately and suggest that he mistrusted
anything Crandall had done, or anything he'd testified to
in court?"

The housemaid was in the midst of lighting Ybarra's
cigar. He puffed on it several times, making smoke rings
sail into the steamy vapor over the hot springs. The
smoke rings didn't last in the humid air like they might
have in the crisp autumn air above.

"Keller did, in fact, indicate a certain level of mistrust," Ybarra stated.

"Over the unidentified tire track?"

Ybarra nodded.

"Did he think the charges against Ms. Candelaria
should have been dropped?"

"No." He sank back down again in the hot springs
until the water rose to his neck. "Keller was troubled over
that issue—but, and I tell you this now in confidence—
even the defense investigators failed to come up with any
specific identification on that tread."

Planting her hands behind her on moist rock, Robyn
massaged the instep of one foot with the toes of her

other. She exchanged looks with Kiel. "Judge Ybarra, were you also aware of the problem with Stuart Willetts?"

"That, my dear, I was not. Not at the time, I should say. Mr. Willetts behaved with the utmost decorum in my courtroom, and as you may well know, I do everything in my power to absent myself from the social scene in this town."

"But now you know?"

Ybarra nodded. "It's my understanding, at least, that Mr. Willetts has moved into the house of the late Spyder Nielsen. I now know as well, although it's purely hearsay, that they were...involved all the while Ms. Candelaria was on trial." Ybarra frowned. "Very troubling," he concluded softly.

An understatement, Robyn thought, if she'd ever heard one. Though Ybarra was speaking frankly, she sensed his feelings were much, much stronger than his words would indicate. Known to be a very religious man whose strengths all sprang from his ability to separate his personal feelings from the law, his emotions from the facts, *troubling* was probably the least onerous word he could find for behavior he must find deeply offensive.

Kiel rolled up his pant legs and let his feet drag the bottom of the pool. "The reason we ask, Judge Ybarra," he said, "is that Stuart Willetts told us himself a couple of nights ago that Keller would have dismissed him from the special prosecutor's staff. Keller's own staff, of course."

"As well he should, had he known. I have never before seen misconduct of this nature—not unless you count the dish running away with the spoon." He waited for the requisite laughter, the twinkle in his eyes acknowledging the absurdity. "In any case, I find it highly

unlikely—no, *prohibitively* unlikely—that Keller Trueblood would jeopardize the prosecution by not coming
forward with such information had he known. Which
means he can only have learned of the affair sometime
after Friday at noon the day before he died."

A glimmer of realization lit the old man's nut brown
eyes. The timing of Keller's death, stated as he just had,
boded very ill. He shook his head slowly. "The death of
your husband was very fortuitous for Mr. Willetts, was
it not?"

Robyn nodded. "Only fortuitous, do you think?"

Judge Ybarra let his head fall back. His eyes closed.
For a long time he appeared to have fallen asleep. Robyn
said no more, only exchanged glances with Kiel.

Their feet accidentally brushed together below the
surface of the hot, churning, sulfur-smelling spring.
Their eyes clashed. The slick, intimate sensation went on
as neither of them moved. For a pleasurable, intense few
moments before Ybarra spoke again, Robyn's heart
pounded.

"I cannot think," Ybarra said at last, in the moment
Robyn made herself move her foot, "that Stuart Willetts could have done what the timing implies."

Robyn nodded her agreement. "I have thought that as
well. But then the question about Detective Crandall remains. What do you think Keller could have meant by his
cartoons?"

The judge's features drew together in concentration.
"Is it possible Crandall was the one who brought Keller's attention to the affair between Willetts and Candelaria?"

"It's possible, sir," Kiel answered. "But it doesn't explain the tire in the muck."

"But you indicated the tire appeared in later drawings in the pile behind the Crandall caricature. Wouldn't that indicate a discarded possibility?"

"Or," Kiel suggested, pulling his feet from the hot bubbling spring, "one that Crandall dug up and succeeded in burying again."

"Then, the only remaining possibility, to my way of thinking, is that Keller became aware of some other damning piece of evidence as to the credibility of Detective Crandall."

ON THE DRIVE BACK to town, uncertain as to whether their interview with Judge Ybarra had been at all productive, Kiel reminded Robyn it was Stuart Willetts who had suggested Crandall's attitude should be looked into. "Remember what he said? That Crandall had it in for anyone with two cents to rub together?"

"Are you thinking his attitude can't have been much of a secret?"

"Not a secret at all." Kiel slumped deeper in the leather passenger seat. "Do you remember Chloe Nielsen had an airtight alibi for the murder?"

Robyn frowned. "I remember hearing that, but I don't know what it was."

"Well, get this. Chloe was in the county jail house overnight for driving under the influence. What do you want to bet Crandall was the arresting officer?"

As soon as they got back to the offices where the files were kept, Robyn looked up the telephone number for Spyder's daughter. Robyn kicked off her shoes and leaned against the desk because the seat of her jeans was still wet from sitting on the rocks at Ybarra's hot spring. Kiel plunked down into his chair while she dialed the number.

Spyder's daughter answered on the fifth ring. Robyn got no further than to introduce herself and ask if they could meet somewhere to talk about the murder of her father when Chloe cut her off.

"You people never give up, do you? Is this some sick excuse to get a rise out of me for that DUI? Or print that picture of me behind bars in the tabloids again?"

"Actually, Chloe," Robyn said firmly, calmly, "I want to know if Ken Crandall is the one who put you there."

After a long silence, Chloe said simply, "Don't call me again," and then hung up. But her silence told Robyn their conjecture must be true—and that if she hadn't feared some retaliation on Crandall's part, Chloe would have said quite a lot more.

THEY WENT TO DINNER that night in a Victorian-style restaurant tucked away on Durant Street where sepia photos of historical Aspen adorned the walls and lush green plants separated the bar from the eating area.

After dinner Robyn left their table to go to the washroom. A woman younger than Robyn slipped in behind her, and went directly to one of the four sinks in the marble counter. Examining her hair and lipstick in the mirror, she never made direct eye contact with Robyn at all. It didn't matter.

"Do you know me?" the young woman asked, as if speaking to the mirror.

"Yes." Robyn only recognized her from an old newspaper clipping she had seen of the funeralgoers at the burial of her father, Spyder Nielsen. "Chloe Nielsen."

Chloe's long dark hair fell past her narrow shoulders, and an aloof expression reflected in her sculpted, almost anorexic features. Her clothes and hair smelled of smoke, as if she'd been waiting in the bar for the chance to catch Robyn alone.

"Yes. I've changed my mind about talking to you. I've been checking around. You're digging into what happened to my father. Who killed him." Her eyes, a murky gray, flicked to Robyn's in the mirror.

"That's true." Robyn put her shoulder bag down on the marble counter and turned on the faucet to run warm water over her hands. "Is there...someplace we can meet to talk?"

Chloe took out a brush and began fussing with her hair, still not looking at Robyn. "It's not really me you need to talk to."

"Then who? Where?"

Chloe grimaced and put away her brush. "I'm not sure he'll talk to you. He's tending bar at Lucinda's party tomorrow night. He's agreed to meet me later in the evening in the storeroom at the bar. He doesn't know why." She refreshed her lipstick. "Be there. Eleven-fifteen." Before Robyn could double-check the time with her, Chloe had slipped back out the door.

Thoughtfully, Robyn dried her hands and ran her finger through her own shining black hair. She dashed on a bit of lipstick, though for the first time in as long as she could remember, she had a little natural color without the sleepless bags under her eyes.

She walked back and sat again at the table where Kiel waited. He'd ordered her a dessert—chocolate *gâteau* with fresh raspberries. "You must be cheating again."

He looked aggrieved. "Angel tricks, you mean?"

"Yes. Angel tricks. How else do you know the combination of chocolate and raspberries is my complete undoing?"

Kiel looked down at his hands. He didn't even have to make some verbal slip, to slip big time. He wouldn't know. Keller would. Especially the undoing part. Keller would order them for the express purpose of undoing his wife.

Kiel fended off whatever memories of Keller's were hovering with a supreme effort. "Come on, Robyn. Everybody loves chocolate and raspberries."

She looked steadily into his eyes. She knew something was up, she just didn't know what. She had to chalk it up to angel tricks. He'd promised to leave her fantasies alone, but she was being paranoid again. A lot of people like chocolate and raspberries.

"Guess who I just ran into in the ladies' room?"

"Trudi?" he grinned. "Elsa?"

"Oh, sure." She shot him a look. "No. Chloe Nielsen."

"Really. Was she lying in wait for you?"

"No, but she slipped in and out, staying only long enough to tell me that if I could slip away from the party tomorrow night to the liquor storeroom of the hotel, there would be someone there I should talk to."

He knew without asking that she didn't intend to keep the assignment alone. "Any idea who or why?"

Robyn shook her head, savoring a bite of the *gâteau* and berries. "She just said she'd changed her mind about talking to me. She apparently did some checking around and heard I was investigating who killed her father." Robyn put down her fork, determined to make the dessert last more than thirty seconds.

"Did she seem nervous?"

"No—at least, I didn't get that impression. It was more on the order of a command that I be there."

Kiel watched her enjoying the rest of her dessert, jabbering between bites to extend the experience about meeting Chloe Nielsen and the mystery man at eleven-fifteen on the night of Lucinda Montbank's birthday bash.

When the waitress brought the tab, Kiel pulled a wad of cash from his pocket. Cash he'd materialized right out of thin air a few days ago when he needed to pay for the dinner trays at The Chandler House.

He worried about it a minute, freshly stung for having pulled more angel tricks, but then, it hadn't occurred to Robyn to think about asking where an angel laid his hands on money, so this stunt, at least, she couldn't hold against him.

He dropped four twenties on the table—dinner in Aspen came dearly—and hustled her out of the restaurant so she could forget that by now, post-*gâteau,* she must be undone.

It was ten o'clock when they walked back along the park in the quarter moon and Kiel spotted the empty swings. Plenty of time, he thought, and the perfect opportunity.

He knew how they worked, but only because he'd seen kids stretching out their legs going forward and tucking them under on the backward arc. "Come on. I've never been in these things."

"You're kidding—no. You're not. You really haven't been, have you?"

"Nope."

But he took to them naturally; body physics and flying were among those things he understood on an innate basis.

He sat sideways on his for a while, straddling the swing seat, watching Robyn pumping back and forth, her braid catching in the air vacuum behind her like a little girl's pigtail each time she leaned way back and pumped higher.

After a few minutes she let the swing slow. The night air was cold. He sensed her shivering.

"Do you want to go?" he asked.

She wrapped her arms around the chain links and shook her head. "I was just wondering if this is what it feels like to have wings. To fly."

It didn't compare. Didn't even come close. "A little bit," he said.

She turned her head to look at him. "But it's not really, is it?"

He swallowed. Shook his head. "Only in the way that you don't feel . . . earthbound, I guess."

"Could you show me? Could you take me with you?"

"You are undone, aren't you," he teased. "High as a kite on chocolate and berries."

"Is that a no, Kiel?"

He cleared his throat. "It's an 'I don't think it's a good idea,' Robyn."

She gave a petulant sort of sigh. He knew in a heartbeat, in Keller-memory, that she was not giving up, but turning up the heat, the way Keller had never been able to refuse. "Are you always such a killjoy, Kiel?"

He should have shut her down then. No doubt. But he couldn't. He knew before he even answered her where this was going, and where they would go if he didn't stop it. Though he could have let Keller's memories feed his hunger, he wanted the original experience for himself.

He recognized the seeds of emotional greed, the threat of lust, but the glimpse of hellfire and damnation wasn't enough. He was, after all, the soulmate of this earthbound woman, and nothing that went on between them could be construed to send him down that path. And so, instead of shutting her down, he fed her fire.

"You have a real mouth on you, woman."

Her stomach felt as if it had dropped, the way it feels in a dream when you've missed a step and you feel you're going to fall. "Kell said that, too."

"Then it must be true."

"And is it true that you're a killjoy? That you never cut loose?"

"I cut loose plenty, in my own way."

She slowed and got out of her swing and took the three steps to his swing. Her leg no longer ached, her hands were healed, and so was her face where that mugger had knocked her nearly senseless. Kiel had even made love to her. It was true he had declined to tell her what he'd done to be cast into the role of Avenging Angel, but maybe he would do this for her.

Maybe he would take her to the stars.

"Show me, Kiel. Show me what it is to have wings. Fly me to the stars. Show me where Keller is."

His angel heart was on fire. He took her hand and laid it on his chest. Too much to hope, he knew, that that small gesture would tell her where Keller was. He turned straight on in the swing, then helped her climb on him, her legs around his hips, and he kicked the earth with his foot, setting the swing into a gentle back-and-forth motion.

She didn't know if he would take her where she wanted to go, but she knew he wanted to kiss her.

She raised her eyes and looked into his. She could only see the moon shining, reflecting, nothing of their color. His gaze fell to her lips.

Her pulse raced. Between her legs, his hard masculine body shifted. His elbow caught around the chain, he let his hand cup the back of her neck, beneath her braid, and he pulled her closer.

His breath touched her lips, and then it was his lips touching her lips, pressing, slanting. The *gâteau* was sweet and wonderful, but as an aphrodisiac, it paled beside Kiel's kisses.

She felt the swing begin to move higher, felt lighter, safer against his body, and not so safe. His kisses deepened. Her heart thundered. The swing went higher up, higher back, higher up again.

Deep in his embrace, deeper still in his kisses, she felt as if the earth had fallen away, and it had. He let her fall away from him, too, but held her hand and somehow they were soaring.

Soaring, like Superman and Lois, only that could have been only a slick cinematic trick, and this…this was real.

Far away, she saw with her own eyes the blue-green ball that was earth, the land masses, the seas. She should not have been able to breathe. Here with Kiel, she didn't need to breathe. She should not have been able to slip the bonds of earth, to escape gravity, but she had.

Joy flooded every part of her being. The perspective lightened her heavy heart. From here she could see into eternity.

This was where Keller must be. Out here, somewhere, Keller must be.

She laughed and cried, and when she looked at Kiel's dazzling bright form she could see his halo, see how his thousand-candle smile outshone the sun without blinding her, and that his human form had wings attached— enormous, beautiful, shining golden white wings.

He showed her the moon and the stars and the North Pole and the South. He showed her K-2 and the Angel Falls, Old Faithful and Sri Lanka, Jupiter's moons, Saturn's rings and nebulas never seen from earth or its most far-ranging satellite probes.

She thought they spent a night and a day and another night, but after a while she felt herself pulled back into his embrace and into his kiss, and then she felt the incredible drag of gravity pulling at them.

She was again in Kiel's lap, in the swing in the park in Aspen. Back on Earth, her watch said it was 10:52 on the twentieth of September.

With what he had given her in that hour, with what he had shared with her and where he had taken her, knowing now what it was to fly, she knew when he left, her heart would be broken all over again. But she would not trade it back.

Not for anything.

Chapter Eleven

Jessie Blahnik, Mike Massie and Scott Kline drove up from Denver for Lucy's party. Kiel had been so much a part of Robyn's life in the past week that it seemed impossible her friends had not met him. The shock on Jessie's face, to find a man in Robyn's suite at The Chandler House, made Robyn laugh out loud. Scott's brows went up, too. Mike managed to keep the shock off his face, but he was schooled in impassive poker faces where Jessie was not.

"Jess, really. You should see yourself!" Robyn turned to introduce Kiel one more time. In a tux, he looked incredibly handsome...sexy. She put her arm through his. "Kiel Alighieri, local investigator helping me sort through Keller's records, these are my friends, and Keller's, from Denver. Jessie Blahnik, TV news producer extraordinaire, Michael Massie, Denver defense counsel of choice, and one of my fellow writers, Scott Kline of the Denver *Post*."

Kiel shook hands with Jessie, and then Mike and Scott. Jessie turned to Robyn, pretending to fan herself from a swoon over Kiel's good looks.

Massie launched into a discussion with Kiel and Scott over what progress Robyn had made in trying to uncover the truth about Keller's and Spyder Nielsen's deaths.

Robyn took Jessie back to the bedroom suite. Jessie presented her the dress bag and small suitcase she had brought up containing the backless bra, earrings, purse and shoes Robyn needed to go to the party. Jessie had only to slip into her gown and shoes, but dressing together gave them their first chance to talk in the week Robyn had been gone.

Taking Robyn's gown from the garment bag, Jessie demanded the scoop. "I absolutely cannot believe that you didn't tell me about this guy when you called!"

Robyn took the dress on its hanger from Jessie and shed her robe. "He's a little hard to explain, Jess, but I didn't mean to be holding out on you."

"What does that mean, 'a little hard to explain'?"

"He's...different, he's not—" Robyn broke off, confronted again with the difficulty of accounting for an Avenging Angel dropping into her life. "What can I say, Jess?"

"Indeed!" Jessie cracked. "A week ago, you were still in the thick of a lot of pain over Keller. Now you're not? Now you've suddenly got a hot date for a ritzy party in the middle of—"

"That's what I mean, Jess. He's not a hot date." She put on the backless bra and then stepped into a glittering, sequined midnight blue gown. "He's not going to be any part of my life. I will always be in the thick of my feelings for Keller. Kiel is just...helping me." She pulled the bodice of the gown up over her breasts and turned her side to Jessie. "Look," she said, sticking her hand out, waiting for Jess to help with the zipper. "I haven't even taken Keller's wedding ring off."

Her friend stuck the straight pins that had been holding her own dress on its hanger into her mouth and
reached for the zipper placket, talking around the pins.
"Meaningless, Robyn. Have you kissed him?"

In the mirror, Robyn watched her own china doll
complexion go prettily, shamefully pink.

Jessie glanced up into the mirror, too, to see the dress,
then did a double-take at Robyn's expression. She
snatched the pins from between her lips. "Omigod.
Robyn, you've slept with him, haven't you?"

"Jess, you don't understand."

"Are you crazy? What's to understand? What do you
know about him? Did you use a condom? For heaven's
sake, Robyn, in this day and age, you can't just go out
and get yourself—"

"Give me a little credit, Jess." Her tone silencing her
best friend's tirade, Robyn turned away and sank onto
the bench in front of the old-fashioned dressing table.
She began fashioning her hair up into a high, elegant
chignon. "It wasn't like that."

Jessie sat down on the bench beside her, facing away
from the mirror. "How was it, then?"

Robyn stuck in bobby pins here and there. "He...I was
caught in that snowstorm and my car got stuck off the
road. I got out and started to walk—"

"Oh, Robyn! I knew I shouldn't have let Massie goad
you into running off on a wild-goose chase—"

"I had to come, Jess. You know that. I *know* it was
way beyond the pale to get out of my car in the middle of
a blizzard. It was stupid. I was on this deserted road on
my way to Nielsen's estate, and I thought I could make
it. I was wrong. I fell a couple of times but...do you
know what?" She picked up the hot curling iron and began working at stray tendrils of hair. "Jess, I didn't care

if I died! That's how bad it was. I remember thinking I could be with Keller again if I just let go."

"Robyn, no. You don't mean—"

"I did, Jess." Her throat locked for a moment. "I couldn't take it anymore." She skipped over the worst of it. "Anyway, I was about dead from hypothermia when Kiel found me. He saved my life, we made love, I...he volunteered to help me avenge—I mean *resolve*—Keller's murder. End of story."

"Well, thank *God* he saved your life, Robyn—" she broke off and took the curling iron. "Let me help you with this one. You have to know it sounds like he took advantage of the situation."

"He didn't, Jess." She tried to keep her mouth shut, but the truth wasn't going to stay buried, not with Jess. "The truth is, I took advantage of my own stupor to take advantage of Kiel."

"Robyn, that's positively daft!" Jessie protested.

But it wasn't. It was exactly what she'd done. She was the one who saw Keller where Keller wasn't. "Isn't it taking advantage of a man," an *angel,* she thought, "to make love with him and pretend he's someone else?"

Jessie's soft brown eyes, shades lighter than Robyn's own, misted. "I don't understand. Are you saying you were...pretending he was Keller?"

Robyn's jaw clamped tight; her chin wouldn't quit puckering. She couldn't keep the tears back.

"Oh, Robyn." Jessie reached for a tissue. "Don't cry. You'll ruin your mascara."

Jessie always made her laugh. That's the way this had all started—with Jessie making her laugh about the decadent rich and famous of Aspen. But this was too hard. "It hasn't happened again. It won't. He..." *He's an angel.* Not to be confused with a real man. "It just won't."

Jessie offered a quick hug. "I'm sorry to scold. If it does happen again, maybe that's a good thing. Maybe it should, Robyn. Maybe he's perfect for you. Maybe this is what God intended when he took Keller."

"Jessie, you don't believe that!"

"Well—" she stood quickly and peeled out of her jeans so she could get dressed, too "—maybe I'm starting to." She took off her sweater and put on a slip, then reached for her dress. "Fix your left eye, girlfriend." She gave a savvy grin. "Otherwise, you know, the whole effect of a twelve-hundred-dollar dress is sorta wasted."

Massie started pounding on the door. "You women coming out, or what?"

Robyn opened the door. He almost knocked her on the nose, but he backed off. The effect of the dress wasn't wasted. Kiel's eyes told her so. Jess nagged at Mike for being so impatient, but she smiled like a fellow conspirator at Kiel's look.

Robyn sighed happily, knowing all the while what Jessie *didn't* know, what heartbreak she was setting herself up for all over again.

The limousine Mike had rented was still waiting outside. "Sparing no expense," he crowed, handing Jessie and then Robyn inside the luxurious interior.

They arrived by nine-thirty, half an hour after the start time on the invitation. The ballroom at the historic hotel was only moderately filled. Unlike the celebrity Christmas parties of years gone by, this was off-season, and the guest list for Lucy's party was even more exclusive.

Jessie had to break off to spend a few minutes with the Denver TV station camera crew that had driven up separately, arriving before them. Lucy's big bash would get a couple of minutes airtime on the ten o'clock news. It wasn't hard to draw top performers to Aspen. The band was well known but loud.

Scott hung out with Jessie, and Massie was having an old home week. Kiel and Robyn began to circulate. Kiel was getting a lot of interested looks, enough to irritate her. "So what do you think of Mike?"

Oblivious as usual to the feminine interest, he grinned. "Quite a spendthrift, isn't he?"

She decided to relax and bask in being the reason Kiel was so oblivious. "Michael Massie is one of the most generous people I've ever known, actually. Not just with his money, either. He spends probably twenty hours a week helping kids in juvenile detention centers."

"I wouldn't have guessed," Kiel admitted.

"Not many people do at first blush." She looked up at Kiel. "I thought angels had instant insight."

A waiter stopped to offer them champagne and mushroom caps stuffed with steak tartare. "We don't. We're not mind readers, Robyn.... Well, sometimes." He adjusted his statement at her skeptical look.

He thought about his mentors in the ranks of the DBAA. Only little Ariel was more a rookie at this in all the DBAA than Kiel, but between them, Sam and Dashiell had centuries' worth of experience. Kiel gave Robyn Dash's take on darkness lurking. "Evil exists. No way around it. The thing is, even with our powers, even with *higher* powers than all the angels, there are these dark crevasses in the human heart no one can see into."

Balancing her cocktail plate and glass, Robyn polished off a mushroom. "All that free will stuff?"

Kiel nodded solemnly, drinking champagne from his crystal stem. "That's what makes you human, you know? The ability to choose for yourself, to decide right from wrong."

"The absolute right to screw our lives up all by ourselves, you mean."

He laughed. "Yeah. Anyway, Mike grilled me the whole time you and Jessie were getting dressed. Scott pretty much let him do the honors."

Robyn polished off a mushroom. "Jessie was dying of curiosity, too. What did they want to know?"

"Everything. Whether or not you were closer to proving his theory that Keller was killed to scuttle the trial. Where I came from. Massie wanted to know what my intentions toward you are."

She choked on a sip of champagne. Kiel had to pat her on the back, and she drew lots of concerned looks. It was funny on one hand, Kiel being an angel being questioned about his intentions, and not funny on the other. She wanted Kiel to have intentions an angel could never have.

"What did you tell him?"

"To mind his own business." Kiel grinned, but the look in his eyes told her he knew what was funny and what was not.

"Good for you," she managed to say. "Although, if I were to guess, I'd say that only made him more nosy."

"I just went on telling him what we'd been doing. He had to settle for that, or be an ass. He might get there yet." He touched a tendril of the softly curling hairs at her nape. "If he does, it's because he cares about you, Robyn. You—" He broke off and took his hand away from her hair, away from the heat of her. "You have good, caring friends. That's important."

"For when you leave, you mean."

Small muscles at his jaw tightened. "Yeah. For when I have to go. But for all time, Robyn. Good friends, in the end, are the best testament to one's life."

Her chest tightened. In the end, Keller had been as much her best friend as her lover, the one who brought her back to earth when she went off on some tangent, the one who strung her Christmas lights and brought her flowers and drew her funny little cartoons.

Keller was the best testament to her life in that sense, but he was gone. She had to go on alone being the testament to his life, the better person she had become because of him.

She drew a deep breath and drank down all her champagne. The fizz, the warmth, emboldened her, and she kissed Kiel, bold and naughty, with tongue and teeth.

He growled deep in his throat at her, took her by the elbow and propelled her along until someone he didn't know she knew might stop them and say hello.

The local newspaper editor, talking shop with Scott Kline, proved to be the one. Margaret, an older woman, born and raised in the valley, a woman Robyn knew to be absolutely allergic to exploiting celebrity in her paper, threw her arms around Robyn. "Robyn Delaney, how wonderful to see you! You look positively stunning!"

"Thanks, Margaret," she answered warmly. "I am fine. I'd like you to meet a friend of mine, Kiel Alighieri."

Out came the thousand-candle smile Robyn knew to be totally sincere. Margaret, like all the women before her, tumbled to it. Kiel spent a couple of minutes talking about what a relief it was to have such a fine party in the off-season. As if Kiel would know...but he made a great listener, which was all Margaret ever really wanted, second only to an avid reader of her newspaper.

Margaret turned back to her. "Robyn, I'm sorry we never got the chance to keep our appointment. I was just telling Scott that I wished I'd thought to send him those papers I copied for you. The Hallelujah caved in, and then naturally, you were not here."

"I don't remember now if we were just going to meet to talk shop, or—"

"Oh, no! Well," she amended, "that, too, but you had a very specific agenda. Something to do with Jerome Clarke. The day he died. About the avalanche, that sort of thing—at least, that's what I understood you to mean. I went through rolls of film from the newspaper accounts and made printouts for you."

Robyn gnawed gently at her lip, trying to think back. "I haven't even looked at my notes for the Smithsonian article since the . . . accident." She didn't want to get into her theories about the collapse not being an accident. Not tonight, especially. It was looking less and less as if they could ever prove someone had intentionally caused the cave-in.

"Are you thinking about picking up the threads of your story?" Margaret asked.

"I don't know, Margaret. It's hard to get passionate about the story idea again when you've been buried alive and excavated out."

The old newswoman laughed because Robyn had made a joke of it. "But of course, it must be really hard to marshal any enthusiasm."

Her last word came out loud as a shot when the band abruptly ended a set. Everyone standing around the three of them laughed, teasing Margaret.

Kiel went back to the subject of the article. "I don't think you've given up the idea of returning to your article altogether, though, have you, Robyn?"

She didn't know where he was going with his question, but his pointed tone cued her to go along. "Not entirely."

He turned to Margaret. "Robyn was just telling me the other day about her research before the accident. Weren't you thinking, Robyn, that Jerome Clarke couldn't have been killed in that avalanche?"

Where was he getting this stuff? "I had some questions, yes."

"That day was one to go down in history," Margaret admitted, raising the level of her voice when the band started another set. "My father was a small boy at the time. Grew up, as you know, to write several history texts and to teach at the university."

"What was his opinion?"

"Oh, there was never any doubt about Mr. Clarke's demise. The whole town was in an uproar, all the rescue teams and such. I believe there's even a photo of the volunteer fire department. They had a wagon on which they could interchange wheels and sled runners."

"And Jerome Clarke? Was he in any of the photos?"

Margaret frowned. "None that I can remember. I believe it was said Mr. Clarke went up the mountain to see how he could facilitate the rescue, and was then killed in the second wave of the avalanche."

"Where was this all going, Robyn?" Scott asked, trading his empty goblet of champagne for another as a waiter passed by.

"I barely remember anymore. I think... yes. I saw something in the Denver newspapers about Clarke falling ill at the conclusion of the apexer's lawsuit."

A small clutch of more rowdy guests crowded their way through to the dance floor. "I do believe Mr. Clarke was stricken with some pneumonia or other," Margaret said.

"Then would he have been out and about in the middle of an avalanche?" Robyn put her arm through Kiel's.

"I remember also thinking it was pretty odd that his body was never found."

"That wouldn't have been uncommon, unfortunately," Lucy said, sailing into the group, her spirits high. She laughed. "Shame on me for eavesdropping—but really! This is a party!" She threaded her arm through Robyn's other arm. "I know the concept is not entirely lost on you. Come. I want you to meet a few friends I don't think you know."

Kiel gave Robyn's hand a squeeze to indicate she should go on without him. It was ten-thirty by then, forty-five minutes until he and Robyn would find their way to the liquor storeroom to meet Chloe Nielsen and the mystery man. Kiel wanted to become invisible and move among Lucy's guests just to see if Robyn's presence in town had set someone on edge.

He moved around in his physical form for a while, finding it unnecessary to use his powers to become invisible because so few people knew him. By a few minutes before eleven o'clock he'd taken up a position and cloaked himself in invisibility near the door, just in time to see the arrival of Trudi Candelaria and Stuart Willetts.

Fascinated to see what would happen, he followed them from the time they arrived to the time they left. Despite their formal clothes and the fact that the party would go on for at least another two or three hours, the couple stayed less than ten minutes, having been snubbed at nearly every encounter.

Kiel had never seen anything quite like the silent drubbing doled out to Candelaria and Willetts. He hoped he never would again. He hadn't understood what social pariahs this glitzy fickle town had made them into, but it was clear the high rollers and VIPs in this town believed she had murdered their most famous and infamous celebrity, and gotten away with it.

If Candelaria and Willetts had come thinking, or even hoping, that the fickle winds would have started blowing their way by now, they were terribly mistaken. All it took to seal their painfully short appearance was the bitchy behavior of Spyder's spoiled and self-righteous daughter.

The whole incident left an indelible impression in Kiel's mind. If they were in fact innocent of the murder, of covering it up and of killing Keller Trueblood, and Kiel was not convinced they were innocent, then they had been pretty badly persecuted. The impression in his mind as he sought out Robyn to go meet with Chloe Nielsen was that this was a piece, perhaps a major part, of the injustice he had been sent to set right.

CHLOE NIELSEN'S mystery man had turned up in Aspen four years before, bored with life in the small Nebraska town where he grew up and disappointed in the pedestrian New Age fare he found in Boulder. He drifted to Aspen looking for something more real. What he found was Crystal Star Rhapsody and her former chiropractor husband, Divine Light Rhapsody.

"You create your own reality" was their message, but after Curt Wilson coughed up every cent he had buying into their message and still got plowed into on his bike at the corner of Main and Third, he tossed out the notion he'd created that reality. Busted and broke, he had to take a job driving for Mellow Yellow. He'd taken what he thought was at least one step up since then to tend bar.

The liquor storeroom where they met was one floor below the grand ballroom of the hotel. The ceiling above them reverberated with the music. Shelves ten feet high lined every wall, and a dim, bare light bulb hung from the floor joists.

Chloe stood with her elbow resting lightly on a tube of paper towels she had found, trying not to touch anything. Disliking her condescending attitude as much as he had her behavior, Kiel sat on a crate of unpackaged wine, and Robyn stood beside the closed door. Curt sat straddling a shipment of pricey liqueurs.

He was an attractive-enough guy, but he was never going to amount to anything. If Chloe Nielsen hadn't known that before she took up with him, she clearly knew it now. Her disdain for Curt was almost palpable; his resentment toward her just as thick. When her father was murdered and Chloe had no one left to rebel against, Robyn thought, she must have dropped Curt like a hot and essentially rancid potato.

He didn't want to talk to Robyn, and even less to Kiel, but when Chloe made it clear he had no choice, he began to tell his story.

"After I got run down by that clown, I was in the hospital for three weeks. I hooked up with this physical therapist chick."

"You were cheating on me," Chloe put in, goading him. "Go on."

He gave her a look that said *die*. "Yeah, I was cheating and, yeah, you were paying the bills. None of which has a damn thing to do with anything, Chloe, so shut the hell up or get the hell out of my face."

Chloe closed her mouth and folded her arms over her exquisite cream jersey gown.

"Curt, what does this have to do with anything?" Robyn asked.

"Well, I wasn't the only one cheating, see. This chick was having a fling with Chloe's old man. So you see, we had this twisted little ménage, a foursome, whatever. Me and Chloe, me and this chick, this chick and Chloe's old man." Curt looked from Robyn to Kiel and back. "I know what you're thinking. If this chick had a thing going with the high and mighty Spyder Nielsen, why'd she shack up with me? Likewise, why'd I screw around on someone like Chloe?"

"People do things for a lot of different reasons, Curt," Kiel said quietly. "Nobody's judging you here."

"Well, the truth is, this chick and I, we knew the score. There was no way we were ever going to be invited into the bosom of the family.

"But then, this chick turns up pregnant. She tries this number on old Spyder, but Chloe here blows the whole thing wide open, saying it's probably my kid, anyway. Spyder and Chloe have this knockdown drag-out father-daughter fight, and meanwhile Trudi Candelaria coughs up five grand on the spot to buy off this chick."

Robyn's heart clinched. "Did she use it to get rid of the baby?"

"No. She would have never done that.... Her old man woulda gone nuts. But she got so drunk that night she fell and lost the baby, anyway."

Robyn and Kiel exchanged glances. Someone's father had a powerful motive to have murdered Spyder Nielsen and frame Trudi Candelaria.

"Did this girl have a name, Curt?" Kiel asked in the same quiet tone.

"Yeah." He cleared his throat and shuddered. "Betsy Crandall."

Chapter Twelve

"Oh, my God," Robyn whispered. "Detective Ken Crandall's daughter?"

"That's the one." He stood and slung a case of beer up to his hip. "See yourselves out. I gotta get back to work."

"Curt, please," Robyn said, jumping to her feet. "Didn't you go to the police with this?"

He snorted. "Once. I showed my face in that county courthouse once. Guess what? Crandall walked me outside and offered to make me buzzard bait if I didn't keep my mouth shut."

"So why are you telling us now?"

He jerked his head toward Chloe. "Ask her. I'm out of here."

After he'd gone, Chloe closed the door again in case anyone else should happen down to the cellar.

Robyn drew a deep breath, waiting for Chloe to talk. For a few moments she only paced, holding the skirt of her gown up off the floor.

"What's up, Chloe? Did you know this stuff?"

She shook her head. "I never knew this Betsy's last name." Chloe even spoke the first name as if it made her physically ill. "You know, I despised my father. He threw me out and took me in and gave me things and took them away. I finally just wanted to deserve some of that treatment for once, so I took up with Curt and threw it in Spyder's face every chance I got.''

''But you didn't kill him,'' Robyn said.

''No. I might have. I wished he'd die often enough, but I didn't kill him. You know where I was.''

''In jail,'' Kiel answered.

''Yeah. Driving under the influence. And you were right. Crandall was the one who nailed me. Spyder refused to bail me out. I never saw my father alive again.''

''Did Crandall already have reason to be picking on your family?''

''Other than being a prick, you mean?''

''Chloe, did Crandall know at the time he arrested you that your father had been hitting on his daughter?''

Still pacing, Chloe shook her head. ''I don't know. I didn't put any of this together until I ran into Curt a year later. He spilled the whole thing, but of course, he wouldn't come forward—and I really couldn't make him do it. For all I knew, Crandall would kill him.''

''And now?''

She gave a bitter smile. ''Now? Curt is ready to go home to Nebraska, anyway. This town finally does that to people who really can't afford to live here. I still wish Trudi had done it and been convicted. But Crandall did this, and Spyder was my father. He can't get away with it.''

KIEL SAT WATCHING while Robyn danced with Massie and Kline and then Massie again. She had looked forward to dancing again, to the sheer joy of moving with a modicum of grace, but her heart wasn't in it. Curt Wilson's tale had all but ruined the party for her.

Kiel cut into Massie's third dance with her. "You should try to enjoy yourself a little, Robyn. Cut loose, you know?"

"I do. And I know it's too late to really do anything about Crandall tonight, but I can't stop thinking about it. Do you think it's possible he killed Spyder Nielsen?"

Kiel led Robyn more toward the center of the dance floor where people standing around were less likely to hear them. "If what Curt told us was true, Crandall had a powerful motive. But the missing piece is that we don't know if Betsy Crandall told her father anything, or even if she told him who was the father of her baby."

"We have to talk to Crandall tomorrow, Kiel."

"Or take what we know to the chief of police."

She didn't argue, for once. He didn't trust her silence but he let it go. The band segued into a set of oldies. *Something in the way she moves...* Kiel pulled her closer. His hand settled in the small of her back. The music, the scent of her hair, the feel of her, the warmth between them seeped into him.

It had occurred to him when he heard Curt Wilson's story that they had come very near now to resolving the murder of Spyder Nielsen, so near that his time with Robyn might be very short.

It was clear to both of them that Detective Ken Crandall was dirty, one way or another. That he had either murdered Spyder Nielsen himself, and as his retribution against Trudi, made her the chief suspect in the largely circumstantial case—or else he had hired the dirty work to be done, and again, let Trudi take the fall.

What wasn't clear to Kiel, and had never been, was whether or not his mission was in fact one to avenge his own death. Keller Trueblood's death. Neither he nor Robyn believed Trudi Candelaria or Stuart Willetts capable of instigating Keller's death. Perhaps that crime was Crandall's, as well. But Kiel had never been able to discern an aura of evil intent surrounding his own death.

He would have given anything to be able to share these doubts with Robyn. It wasn't so much that he thought her mortal insight might prove more telling than his own, given his angelic prowess, but talking things over with her made him ask different questions.

These were not thoughts he could reveal to Robyn, but he knew that uncovering Crandall's involvement came very close to cracking the case, and if that were true, Kiel's time with her was nearly spent.

He would never dance with her again. He wanted to give her something to remember him by, and so he cloaked her in an enchanted space. For a time, no one existed in that ballroom but the two of them.

"Something in the Way She Moves" segued into "Country Road" into "You've Got a Friend," then into "Don't Let Me Be Lonely Tonight." Every song was theirs, every sentiment, but the set came to an end.

The glittering ball overhead cast sparkles around the ballroom, but none so bright as the sparkle in Robyn's eyes. When the music began again, a vibrant, pounding Latin beat, Kiel danced the tango with her like no one had since Pacino in *Scent of a Woman*.

The floor cleared and the crowd watched, dazzled by them. His spell had created a sliver in time in which Robyn Delaney Trueblood, the soulmate of a man now an angel, was more fully alive, more herself, more heightened and vital and uninhibited than she had ever been in her entire buttoned-down life.

When the Latin music ended, and she clapped for herself, her friends gathered round and added their congratulations. Kiel stood back a moment and let them crowd around her, let them welcome her with their hugs back to the land of the fully living.

He ached with deep pleasure for her. He wanted to hold her, but they were her friends who would remain when he must go. He couldn't prevent himself from moving in again to claim her, anyway. Talking animatedly, Lucy tried to ease Robyn outside her circle of friends. Kiel put his arm possessively around Robyn's shoulders and stood firm.

Lucy grew annoyed. "Dear God, Mr. Alighieri! One would think you'd single-handedly reinvented Robyn. Let her go."

Turned into Kiel, touching his chest, Robyn cajoled her friend. "Don't be silly, Lucy. Kiel is only—"

"Only what?"

"Showing me a good time, Lucy!" The music resumed, but no one around them moved. Massie and Kline exchanged looks. Jessie could only stare dumbfounded at Lucinda's sudden, inexplicable tantrum. "I don't understand what you're getting so upset about!"

"He rarely lets you out of his sight," she snapped. "He controls your every waking moment. He behaves as if you're able to dance again solely because of him. I've quite had it up to my gills."

"Gills?" Kiel knew discretion, and he should have used it, but she'd goaded him one too many times. He was done pulling the punches where Lucinda Montbank was concerned. "An apt description."

"Kiel, don't," Robyn cried softly. "It's not worth it!"

"*Res ipsa loquitur,* Robyn," he said, eyes clashing with Lucy's. "If a thing has gills, it must..."

But in the same instant, in the way he had of dividing his consciousness, he sensed the color draining from Robyn's face, all the pleasure emptying from her body.

She pulled away and turned on him. "What did you say?"

Res ipsa loquitur. An odd term Keller had used. Often. He looked at her stricken face, at her breasts heaving, at the pulse pounding in the thin, delicate column of her neck, and he knew what the slip had cost him. What it had cost her.

Heat streaked down his belly. He tried to cover the mistake. "'The thing speaks for itself'.... Gills and ill-tempered creatures—"

"That's not what you said. You said—" *Res ipsa loquitur.*

He heard it as surely as if she had uttered the words only Keller would have said. "Robyn—"

"Keller. You are Keller, aren't you? That's your real name, isn't it? Not Kiel!" Her heart slammed and her head throbbed. Her friends were looking at her as if she'd lost her mind, when the truth was she'd just found it. She thumped his chest. "Aren't you? You've been lying to me...you said angels couldn't lie. You said, oh God, I can't even *believe* this. You—"

Massie moved in from behind her, and Jessie, who interrupted her and took hold of her arm and tried to reason with her. "Robyn, sweetie, no! What are you talking about? This is Kiel— "

She jerked her arm away from Jessie. Reason told her the truth no one else could guess. "Don't tell me this isn't Keller, Jessie...can't you see it, don't you see?"

Her whole world seemed to collapse and go silent. The music continued, but she stopped hearing it. The air never stirred. She was making a spectacle, but she couldn't stop herself. Kiel's eyes were shuttered, his face closed to her. "Don't you see that's why I went to bed with him, because I sure as hell wasn't—"

"Oh, for God's sake, look what you've done now," Lucy railed angrily. "You've pushed her right over the edge, babbling about going to bed with you in public. Are you satisfied? Now will you finally leave her alone?"

"Leave me?" Robyn cried, despising the hysteria climbing in her own voice. "Leave me? He's already done that, and come back pretending—no, *lying*—"

"Robyn, stop," Kiel commanded, stepping forward, slowing time so that everyone and everything around them in the grand ballroom of the fanciest hotel in Aspen all but stopped. The music persisted in a constant, nerve-racking hum, every note drawn painfully long.

She looked around her at the frozen expressions of confusion and pity plastered on the faces of her friends who believed she'd snapped.

A deadly calm rose in her when she looked at Keller in the disguise of Kiel. A furious and deadly calm. "How could you? How could you do this to me? How could you lie? Keller never lied to me."

"Robyn, you needed me."

"I needed Keller."

"I knew that."

She backed up. "I made love to my husband."

He stepped forward. "I am your husband."

The throb in her head darted clear to her bare, chilled shoulder. "You lied to me, Kiel."

"Robyn, it's not so simple."

"Keller believed the truth is simple."

"*I* believed that." He hung his head. He jerked loose the white tie around his neck. "This wasn't so simple. Do you think for one minute that I wanted to hurt you?"

"Do you think it matters at all to me what you wanted? What should I think?" she cried. "Should I believe you could possibly have thought so little of me? Or should I just accept that in heaven they think every mere mortal must be too simpleminded to guess the truth. Is that it?''

"No. There is no—''

"And even when I knew, even when I said that if they could send me an Avenging Angel, surely they could have sent back my Keller, that maybe you *were* Keller, even then you stood there and let me believe I was losing my mind. What am I supposed to think, Kiel? Or is it Keller? Kiel. You tell me.''

He lowered his head. The terrible silence mocked him, the still-frozen faces of her friends, *his* friends, shamed him. He had denied her time and time again so he would never be confronted with her loss or this anger.

He had never felt so heavy, so laden, so much less a being not subject to gravity and space and time. He had to get out of here, had to get her away from here.

He stilled her with his angel tricks and touched her so that together they could be transported away, and then he sealed the rift in the continuum of time on earth and moved with her in the blink of an eye back to her suite at the bed and breakfast. He thought it, and a fire to warm her began to blaze in the hearth.

She blinked and looked around the now familiar surroundings. Clamping her mouth shut, she turned away from him. The irony clawed at her heart. Heaven had sent her Keller and tried to make her believe he was not.

She swallowed her tears. "Why, Kell?''

"You needed me, Robyn, but no one wanted to see you go through losing me twice in one lifetime.'' He stripped out of the tux coat and slumped into the easy chair behind her. "Seemed like a good idea at the time. Seems monumentally wrong now—but...that's not true. I knew it was wrong a long time ago.''

She sank down on the hearth to the fire. The supple fabric of her sparkling blue dress gave easily enough. In another life, another time, no matter that neatness had never been her strong suit, she would never have risked so expensive a dress so close to the fire, or on a hearth where soot could so easily spoil the gown.

The dress didn't matter. She couldn't think what mattered.

"Your life matters, Robyn."

"So now the cat's out of the bag, you might as well pull all the angel tricks, even mind-reading? Or should I call it eavesdropping?"

"Robyn, could you look just once," he said wearily, "just this one time, for the good intentions?"

Tears made her throat feel tight and on fire. "Yep, that's my Kell." The fault Keller always found with her. But that was when he was human and alive and more honest than an angel. "Haven't you heard? Good intentions pave the way to hell."

He looked away, suddenly deeply angry. "You think you're the only one who suffered? I'm the one who died in that godforsaken mine shaft, Robyn. I was the one trapped and broken, listening to your cries and knowing there was not one blessed thing I could do to break free and hold you." He shoved himself out of the chair, too wound up, too filled with grief and anger, to sit there any longer.

"If you think it was easy to watch you making such self-destructive decisions, and then to pick you up from that snowdrift and know that you wanted nothing so much as to die, then think again, Robyn. How do you think I felt, confronted with those scars all over your legs, and your hands bleeding and raw, and your battered face? If you—" His voice cracked. He had to start over. "If you think it was an easy decision to let you believe in your heart it was me making love to you, you're wrong. I did what I had to do to make you step back from that decision, and I would do it all over again because saving your ungrateful little neck was what I was given to do."

"I'm not ungrateful—"

"You can't have it both ways, Robyn. Either you're grateful to be alive because I let you believe I was Keller, or you're not."

Her face felt tight and hot, swollen with tears she fought back. "I wanted it to be you so much." He couldn't say anything. "Didn't you know?"

"Robyn, dear God, of course I knew. Yes. God help me, I knew. But there was nothing else I could do. When I became an Avenging Angel, I possessed the same soul as Keller but I had no memory of *being* Keller. But after a while, things—memories—started coming to me. I told you how I flashed back to the cave-in as if I were Keller."

She nodded, waiting for him to go on.

"Well, it wasn't only the mine caving in. I was Keller. I was with you there. I carved our initials in the support beam." He swallowed. "I was the one pointing out our shadows on the wall." He stopped. "Should I go on?"

She was numb, must have been numb not to stop him.

His eyes bore into her. "I was the one...I lived it again. I was the one with his hands all over you. I was the one getting hard, right there in your car, right in the thick of Keller's memories."

Her heart thumped beneath her ribs.

"Think about it, Robyn."

The air was locked in her lungs. "Kiel...Keller. I can't think of anything else. Was it . . . is it a sin? Is it so terrible?"

He met her weepy gaze, then had to break it off. "This was no sin. This was the love and the lust of a man for his wife, only this body is Kiel, not Keller." He looked steadily at her again. "I'm an angel, Robyn. What am I supposed to do? How am I supposed to deal with carnal feelings of a mortal man for his mortal wife?"

The inescapability of it hit her hard, the tension, the need he had denied. She finally understood it must be one thing for him to make love to her when she was intent upon letting her life slip away, and quite another thing for him to have such feelings, such desire, out of a life-and-death context.

At last she understood what it was all about, the times he had touched her and filled her needs, denying his own. She finally grasped the nuances of all the times he had been forced to cloud her mind and memory so she would not see Keller's need in him, or the answering instincts in herself.

She understood that it had to be Keller they sent to her, because she would never have come back for any reason other than Keller himself calling her back.

"Kiel, I'm so sorry. What are we going to do? How is this ever going to turn out all right?"

"I don't know." He shook his head. He had no reason to believe that it could all possibly be made right, none but faith. He sank down again into the chair. "It might all end very soon, Robyn."

She rose from the hearth and went to kneel at his feet. "Then, make love to me, Kiel." She spread her hands on his thighs. "Now. Make love with me now. It can't be wrong between us."

Heat spread through his physical body "Robyn—"

"Shhh." Her hands stroked higher. "Don't say anything, just . . . kiss me."

Frantically he sought the dispensation he had been granted when it was her life at stake, but the awesome silence in his head granted no such surcease. Her hands were very close now to the throbbing in his groin, and he gave up the desperation. He cradled her face in his hands.

"Robyn." Her name was a prayer on his lips. A surrender to a calling more primal and urgent and sacred. He leaned forward. His lips approached hers. His body hummed. The space between their lips was alight, charged, alive. Sparkling.

"Kiel."

He thrust his hands into her hair and pulled her closer, closer, until the heat of their flesh melded, until the flesh of their lips touched.

It was a kiss, he believed, more glorious, more sacrosanct, more pure, than any kiss anywhere, in all time, had ever been. He turned his head in the smallest possible degree, back and forth, so that their lips brushed ever so lightly, the stroke like his own angel wings against the vast firmament of the heavens.

But her body was mortal and was on fire and she wanted more than the chaste and pure, more than heaven. She reached for his hands and dragged them to her breasts. She tore at her bodice and ruined the dress, but the beautiful midnight blue gown had long since ceased to matter. His hands cupped her fullness and stroked. His thumbs drew across her beaded nipples.

Her cry of stabbing pleasure filled him. Her eyelids fluttered closed but he saw beyond them into the eyes of her soul, and he saw heaven there.

And he saw in her eyes the faces of his unborn children.

Agony ripped through him and he began, literally, physically, to disassemble. He wanted her children to be his so powerfully that he had caused a rift between heaven and earth.

He felt his physical body dispersing, fragmenting like a holographic image slowly exploding into points of light until he was no more than a specter. He focused every bit of his will and power into their kiss, but too quickly the instant of his disappearance came and she knew.

She opened her eyes. But for the barest specter of light in the shape of the hands of Kiel Alighieri at her breast, he was gone. Sparkles of light, the last of his physical energy, went out.

To Robyn, it was as if the stars had gone out that night, and if that was true, the sun must also have died.

She sank to the floor. Changed in ways she could not have described with all the power of her pen, she knew she was still Robyn Delaney Trueblood, skeptical to her bones, believing in what she could see and hear and touch.

Heaven had taken Keller away from her again. She had no way of knowing whether or not he would be back. Hell, she remembered the saying went, hath no fury like a woman scorned.

She shed her dress and panties and nylons and dragged a blanket and pillow from her bedroom to sleep in front of the fire so she wouldn't have to wake in some wretched sweat when the darkness finally got to her.

Left to her own puny mortal devices or not, she would continue seeking justice where Kiel had left off. Maybe then they would let her have Kiel back. Or Keller. Then she would believe in more than what she could see and hear and touch.

But she doubted, as she doubted most things, that such a thing would ever come true in her lifetime.

Chapter Thirteen

In the morning, she rose stiff and sore from sleeping curled like a rag doll in the chair. She knew instantly that Kiel was not there, that he had not returned in the night. Resigned, she showered and washed her hair, dressed in jeans and a sweatshirt, put on her shoes and went looking for Detective Crandall.

She would not think about anything but the task before her. Confronting Crandall.

He had called in sick, she learned, but, driving up and down the streets of Aspen, she spotted his four-wheel-drive vehicle parked, very nearly hidden from view, alongside a garage in a fenced enclosure. The sign on the fence forbidding unofficial entry clued her in. Unless she was very much mistaken, this was a police storage facility.

She drove around the block and parked her car on the street perpendicular so that it faced the garage and would be less identifiable. Studying the layout and surrounding properties, she guessed that the updated garage had once been a carriage house for the much larger Victorian mansion adjoining the fence.

She had two options, and neither was all that much to her liking. She was a writer, not a sleuth or a detective, but if she was going to take Crandall by surprise and get from him what she needed to know, she had to get onto that property. So she could either dart into the yard to the side of the Victorian house, climb the tree, maneuver herself out onto a limb stretching out over the police yard and hurl herself down . . . or she could grow her own set of wings.

Quick, hot tears stung her eyes. She dashed them away and started to get out and cross the street when another police vehicle, this one marked, cruised by. The female officer didn't notice Crandall's vehicle until her car had passed the gate. She backed up and pulled into the drive at the gate. Looking annoyed, she got out of her vehicle and sorted through a ring of keys for the one to the padlock.

Robyn decided this was as good an opportunity as she was ever going to get. There were no windows on the street side of the old carriage house, and once the police-woman had entered the building to see what was going on, Robyn could slip through the gate and hide along-side the garage on the opposite side of the outbuilding from the door.

The policewoman snapped open the padlock and left it hanging on the latch as she shoved the gate open far enough to walk through.

Her heart pounding, Robyn got out of her car and forced herself to wait until the officer opened the door and went inside.

Tamping down her fear of getting caught, Robyn stood and walked across the street as if nothing in the world mattered, but once she was inside, she ran for cover. Making her way along evergreen shrubs to the north side of the carriage house, she went to the back, then across the back to the southwest corner.

She waited what seemed forever, straining to listen, hearing nothing, but in what was really less than two minutes she heard the door open again. Peeking around the corner, she watched the female officer walking back to her car, apparently satisfied that whether Crandall had called in sick or not, he had reason to be in a locked storage facility.

A small, cranky terrier in the yard of the adjacent Victorian house caught sight of Robyn and started barking and snarling. The policewoman looked back. Robyn held her breath and flattened herself up against the back of the building until she heard the gate clanging shut and the police car drive off. The dog's owner called her snapping, angry pet into the house.

Robyn took a few deep breaths to calm her frayed nerves. Was this worth it? But she was in now. Locked in, to be accurate, so she might as well do what she had started out to do.

She plucked up her very righteous anger and walked calmly around the corner, slipping inside the dark, dank entrance to the outbuilding. She could hear Crandall's grunts as he shifted boxes about, somewhere to her right. She moved along the south wall.

She'd been inside police property rooms before. This one, although evidently housing older items and not current evidence, was set up similarly, with removable metal shelving in rows like library stacks. Looking through them toward the lighted end of the old carriage house, she spotted a figure in a larger area with a table.

She went silently down the side aisle until she came to the place where Crandall stood at a table pulling archival computer tapes from a carton.

She leaned against the end of the metal storage racks. "What are you looking for, Detective Crandall?" she asked softly.

Startled, he dropped a canister of digital tape. He jerked his head around in her direction. "How in the hell did you get in here?"

"Through the door."

"Well you can just take yourself right back out the door, Miz Delaney," he mocked. "This is a restricted area on police property."

"I assumed it was. And since you're just like any other private citizen when not on duty, why are you here when you called in sick?"

He scowled at her, but he clearly wasn't at all that concerned. "I'm a cop, I have matters to research. This is where that gets done. You, on the other hand, are not a cop, but a broad sticking her nose in business she'd be better off leaving alone. Now, I'll do you a favor and look the other way while you get your butt out of here."

"I don't want your favors, Detective Crandall, but if asked, I'll be sure to tell your supervisors you were willing to be very accommodating about a civilian trespassing on police property."

Sighing heavily, he picked up the canister he'd dropped and flung it back into the carton. "What do you want?"

"I want to know where you were, Detective Crandall, when Spyder Nielsen was murdered."

"Oh, for chrissake, spare me your candy-assed theories! Candelaria whacked Nielsen. Period, end of discussion. Where I was has about as much to do with that as nothin'."

"Except Trudi Candelaria did not kill Spyder, and I think you know it. I think my husband knew it."

"You know what? What you think or what your husband thought or what Howdy Doody mighta thunk doesn't interest me in the least."

Her anger pitched higher. Struck by Crandall's resemblance to Keller's caricatures of him, she made herself stay collected. "How many people knew your daughter, Betsy, was pregnant with Spyder Nielsen's baby?"

"That he'd screwed her and then dumped her, you mean? That his freaking doxy threw money at my little girl? Is that what you mean?" Crandall's face registered such anguish for a split second that she felt a stab of sympathy for him. The anguish dissolved to a sneer. "Well, lady, you're undoubtedly somebody's little girl, too, but you've just bought and paid for a one-way ticket to hell. You get my meaning?"

Her chest tightened. Her ticket had better be to heaven after all of this, or hell would see the fury of a woman done truly wrong. "Did you kill him, Detective? Did you go there and pick up that bronze and murder Spyder Nielsen?"

He swore vilely. "No. Somebody beat me to it."

"Somebody? Not Trudi Candelaria?"

"You just don't know when to give up, do you." He slammed the four sides of the top of the crate together and hurled the box back onto the metal shelf only four or five feet away from her. He closed the distance in three steps of his squared body and grabbed her by the wrist, twisting her arm behind her back.

Pain shot clear to her shoulder. She struggled, knowing she had no chance against Crandall's bulk and power, but in the instant she pulled loose, Crandall went flying backward. He crashed into the table and fell on his butt to the floor.

Robyn stared at her arm, where there was no more pain, and then at Crandall, whose rank confusion screwed up his face, and she knew.

It wasn't any native strength of her own that had broken free and thrown Crandall to the floor, but the power of an angel. Of Kiel.

"Are you there?" she asked. "Are you really here somewhere?"

Finish him off, Robyn. You're doing just fine. Relief shouted itself, coursed through her, but her elation was short-lived.

"You bet I'm here, you stupid interfering cow!" Crandall hissed, and before she knew what was happening to her had begun to swing a wooden chair at her back.

She screamed and braced for the pounding blow but it never came. She found herself standing behind Crandall. The power of his swing as the chair swept through the spot where she had been, crashing and breaking against the metal storage racks, reverberated in Crandall's body instead.

Knowing Crandall was stunned, she couldn't help the laughter bubbling out of her.

He turned, still holding the jagged back of the chair, more enraged than ever, roaring vile epithets at her. But now she understood he could not hurt her, that Kiel would move her or block Crandall.

"Tell me the truth, Detective Crandall. I want to know it all."

"In hell," he bellowed at her, advancing on her, not getting it yet that nothing he could do could touch her.

"No, now," she said. "Right here, right now. Did you kill Spyder Nielsen?"

He swung at her again and again with the jagged, splintered back of the chair. Each time, she was transported in the blink of an eye to a safe space behind Crandall.

He began to pant, to breathe heavily with the exertion, to fall victim to the confusion. His eyes glazed over in his fury. "He deserved to die," Crandall snarled. "He deserved to die a thousand deaths, and that sanctimonious bitch had the nerve to throw money at my Betsy!"

His pain tore at Robyn, but she had to know the truth. *"Did you kill him, Detective?"*

Enraged even more at what Spyder Nielsen had done to his daughter, he swung at Robyn and missed three more times, like a blind wild man lashing out at a target he couldn't see. In his rage, he hurled the table, and when that didn't work, he pulled down the long row of metal shelving.

There should have been no escape for her, but when the resounding metal clash died away, Crandall standing defeated at one end, Robyn stood unharmed at the other.

"Who the hell are you?" he screamed. "How the hell can you still be standing there?"

Tears seeped into her eyes for this man whose spirit was so warped, and now so crushed by events he must have believed beyond his control. "Please. Just tell me what happened."

He sank to his haunches, covering his face, crying like a brokenhearted child. Kiel materialized somewhere out of sight and walked in. He went to Robyn and put his arm around her shoulders.

She didn't need protection anymore, she needed his support in the face of Crandall's grief.

She looked up at him, sympathy glittering in her eyes, and then she turned her attention back to Crandall.

He wiped his bleary face with the arm of his shirt. "I didn't kill the bastard," he said at last. "Candelaria didn't either."

"Did you know that when my husband was selected as special prosecutor?"

Crandall shook his head. "Not for several weeks afterward."

"How did you find out?"

His face contorted. "That tire. That frigging damn tire. Spent weeks checking it out, combing through sales records of tire dealers all over the state. I thought it was a flat waste of my time, but there was no way your husband was letting it go."

"What happened" Kiel asked.

"I sent photos of the tread imprint to state labs. Came back matching the tread of some woman who drove herself off the highway up in Routt County off the Oak Creek Road."

Robyn swallowed and traded looks with Kiel. "Detective, who was she?"

"Name was Jaclyn Thompson. Another one of Spyder Nielsen's rejects. She lived over outside of Steamboat Springs. No family, not a lot of friends, either, just family money out the ears. Twenty-damn-three years old."

"Then everything Trudi said was true?" Robyn asked. "There *was* a shadowy figure leaving the house that night."

"Bald-faced lie," Crandall snarled. "Do you honestly think she arrived home from that little soiree at 12:17 and saw a shadowy figure but didn't see the car Thompson was driving? I don't think so."

Robyn frowned. "Why would she make up that story, then?"

"Because she's a lying whore—but aside from that, the Thompson woman had to have gotten away clean. Candelaria never saw a car coming back down the mountain when she was on her way home."

"She wouldn't have known there was a tire track to be seen," Kiel guessed.

"Exactly. Candelaria never saw any shadowy figure and she had no alibi after the party. She was making up her story as she went along, lying through her teeth the whole time. And the truth is, she deserved to fry as much as her lover Spyder Nielsen deserved to die."

Kiel shook his head. "Was the tread a perfect match? You're certain it was this Thompson woman?"

"Yeah, I was certain." He laughed unpleasantly. "The tire had a flaw. Chances of it not being the same are about ten billion to one."

Silence reigned in the cold, unheated building. Robyn shivered. "What happened to Jaclyn Thompson?"

"She spent a few days in Routt County Memorial in a coma." Crandall picked himself up off the floor and dusted off the seat of his pants. "Died the day Candelaria was arraigned."

Kiel separated from Robyn, preparing to deck Crandall if he decided to come at them again. "When did you know this?"

Crandall sent them both a look of unmitigated hatred. "Maybe halfway through the trial."

Robyn shivered again. "You never told anyone?"

"Not a soul. Seemed like a good time to keep my trap shut. Far as I was concerned, real justice was bein' handed down by the Lord. Nielsen was a goner, his whore was almost there, and the perp that really bashed ol' Spyder in the head was long since punished, dead and buried. Your husband was doing a fine, upstanding, job, ma'am, and I was happy as a clam to let him do it.''

Her teeth gnashed together. Keller had been lied to and used. "I'm very sorry for what happened to your daughter, Detective Crandall, but none of it justifies putting an innocent woman on trial for her life."

"Save your judgments, lady," he snapped. "Trudi Candelaria didn't get anything she didn't have coming."

The vestiges of Robyn's sympathy for Crandall evaporated. "What about my husband?"

"What about him?"

"Did he finally uncover your lies? Did you have to murder him, too?"

"Well, no. But it was damned accommodating of him to die like he did." Crandall laughed derisively again. "I was bustin' his chops and he knew it—he just didn't know how."

Kiel had never heard the term 'busting his chops' before, but he divined from Robyn's experience that was what the Feds called it when informants or perps were lying to them.

A righteous anger burst into flames inside him, anger that went back to the core of Keller Trueblood's integrity. Without so much as a blink, using only the force of his will, Kiel slammed the detective against the wall.

Robyn clapped her fingers over her mouth to stifle her cry, but Kiel's outrage only magnified. He seemed to grow larger than life and his beautiful bronze-colored hair lengthened. His jeans and sweater were gone, his body was cloaked in a gleaming white robe, tied in the middle with a purple cord.

His wings appeared then, glorious, powerful, more mind-numbingly beautiful than on the night he had taken her to the stars and back. He hovered three feet above the ground; the mighty and fearsome glow around him emanated power. From his eyes he struck a jagged and noisome bolt of lightning at the clumsy, stumbling feet of Detective Crandall.

"Behold, the judgment of the Almighty," he commanded, his voice lifting to the rafters of the old carriage house.

Spellbound by the terrible majesty of Ezekiel, Avenging Angel of the Lord, Robyn watched Crandall slumping to the ground, sobbing for mercy, for his life to be spared, begging to be allowed to turn himself in.

The awesome specter of the angel Ezekiel faded, and in the place where he had rendered the judgment from on high, Kiel stood staring at the pitiful visage of a cop who no longer held himself above the law of his fellow mortals.

THE FOLLOWING MORNING, a beautiful fall Monday morning in one of the most visually stunning and spiritually bereft places on the earth, Kiel and Robyn went to the press conference set up by the district attorney's office.

The word had been put out far and wide that there was a new and stunning development in the old murder case of Spyder Nielsen. Kiel didn't want to make a spectacle of it, but Trudi Candelaria had lately been the woman the public most loved to hate, and the story was big news. Also, the integrity of Keller Trueblood was at stake.

Kiel moved around, feeling more wooden than Pinocchio had been. He was stiff, lifeless and without a single excuse, a solitary reason, why Robyn should trust him or believe in a benevolent God.

He knew she was close to snapping.

He knew her heart was broken and bleeding.

He knew, now, what he had long suspected. That it had been the cruelest of deceptions to try to hide from her the fact that he had been Keller Trueblood. It was true that he had only intended to spare her losing her soulmate twice in one lifetime, but the purest of intentions had not saved her from that fate.

What he should have done was to tell Angelo to take a flying leap at another universe. There was no way that Robyn Delaney was going to fail to recognize her soulmate in whatever guise.

No way.

But he'd gone along with it, and he knew why—because he was just an unevolved-enough angel that there was no way in heaven or hell he was going to pass up another chance to be with the woman who was *his* soulmate. The decision had been his, not Robyn's, and the responsibility for putting her through this—again— weighed squarely on him.

Robyn was taking it all like the class act she was. She could have flatly refused to let him speak at this press conference. She could have refused to stand by his side while he explained that Trudi Candelaria, the target of the special prosecutor in the case of *Colorado v. Candelaria,* had in fact been an innocent woman. These were things, as Keller Trueblood's widow, that she had a right to express on his behalf.

Kiel needed to do this because it was his immortal soul and his integrity, human or angel, that needed restoring. The truth needed to be told, and he was the one to tell it, to clear the names of Trudi Candelaria and Stuart Willetts.

People still whispered. Aspen was still known as the place where John Denver lived and Don Johnson gave wildly expensive parties and Indian princes built gargantuan houses that were a blight on the earth…and where Trudi Candelaria bashed in the head of the great Spyder Nielsen. That lie demanded to be set to rights.

Kiel turned to Robyn at the last second before he stepped up to the podium. She looked so hauntingly beautiful to him it made his sore heart ache. Her shining black hair was pulled back tightly in a French braid.

She wore a deep blue suit and a high-necked, buttoned-down, don't-touch-me white blouse. Everything about her said to him and to anyone looking at her, *don't-touch-me. Don't hurt me. Don't dare hurt me again.*

He didn't know what to say to her. He knew she didn't know what to say to him. It was killing her, having Keller, not having Keller.

"Just make your statement, Kiel."

He could only nod and look for forgiveness in her.

She rolled her eyes and swallowed hard and pursed her lips to keep from crying, and reached to fuss with the knot in his tie. "Don't forget to make yourself photographable."

The knot in his tie was less than perfect. He hadn't cared. But he would have forgotten about the cameras until it was too late, and then he'd have to go around to countless photographers, imprinting his image where it should have been but wasn't on their negatives. Even now this mortal woman was looking after his best interests.

He trapped her hands with his against his chest. "Robyn, you know if this is the injustice I was meant to resolve, I will…I won't be…I'm trying to say I can't stay when this is all over."

She hadn't cried. Not once, but her beautiful doe brown eyes filled now and a tiny noise caught in her throat. She tried to take back her hands but he couldn't let her go.

"I w-won't grieve for you again, Keller. I won't do it. I won't."

He knew it was a lie.

"Robyn."

"Oh . . . Keller." Her eyes brimmed. "Don't go. Please." Her voice was useless, a whisper. An agony. A prayer. "Don't go again, don't leave me again. I won't be able to stand it."

He bowed his head and shut his eyes and clung to her hands. How could he say to this brave and good and honest woman whom he loved beyond life, who loved him, that he must turn away from her and do what he must do to restore justice—because although the pain in him was more fierce than the instant of his death in that accursed mine more than a year ago, he wasn't human and couldn't stay?

"Robyn."

She knew then. Knew he would leave her again. He wasn't human, but dear God, his hands were, and his lips and his eyes and his body, surely they were.

Just as surely, not.

She straightened her shoulders and sniffed and accepted this ultimate blow to her heart and took her hands away. This time he let her go. She touched her fingertips to her lips and then to his, and to her credit, through her own human strength, not that of the power vested in an Avenging Angel, Robyn backed away.

Kiel Alighieri knew to his core, then, what Dante knew—all about the inferno, about paradise lost and the bonfire of vanities.

He had to find the strength Robyn had, and so he turned to speak to the assembled crowd, to say into the microphone and on camera, on Keller Trueblood's behalf, the truth.

That the office of the special prosecutor in the matter of *Colorado v. Candelaria* had determined that the defendant, Trudi Candelaria, had stood wrongly accused of the murder of Spyder Nielsen, that this fact had been raised and unflinchingly supported by Trueblood's cocounsel Stuart Willetts, and that the woman whom they now knew had in fact committed the murder had driven off the road in Eagle County that fateful night and been killed herself.

Kiel went on to state that an investigation had shown Detective Ken Crandall had obstructed justice in this matter, and that his prosecution would be upcoming in the district attorney's office. He thanked Judge Vincent J. Ybarra, the Aspen police department, the county sheriff's department, and lastly, he thanked Trudi Candelaria and Stuart Willetts, who would not be filing civil suits for any and sundry damages to their reputations.

At every moment, in every syllable he spoke, Kiel followed the progress of Robyn Delaney through the assembly of media to her car. She waited, listening, until he was finished. When she left, when she drove away, he was finished. He turned and shook hands with Ybarra and Willetts and Trudi Candelaria, and after he walked away and turned a corner down a long empty echoing hallway in the county courthouse, no one saw Kiel Alighieri again.

it had been before she, and Kiel, left. This morning, two hours forexample to do... somewhere to go... no one to answer to before she pulled out her makeup kit com-pact and sat down to do the only thing that ever took her outside herself.

She began to reapply her carefully composed make-up.

Chapter Fourteen

Robyn drove back to The Chandler House Bed and Breakfast in a blur of tears. Her hosts, a seventy-year-old man and his seventy-two-year-old wife, having listened on the radio to the announcement Kiel made, each gave her a hug. Neither understood her tears.

She let herself into her suite with the key, tossed it on the hearth, then picked it up and put the key in the dish on the table by the door because that's what neatnik Keller would have wanted her to do.

More empty and alone now than in her worst nightmare, her tears dried up. She paced back and forth, and everywhere her glance happened to fall was a memory of Kiel waiting to clean her emotional clock again.

She should have packed her things and left, but she couldn't make herself change a single thing from the way it had been before she and Kiel left it this morning. Three hours into nothing to do, nowhere to go, no one to talk to, no angel to berate, she pulled out her notebook computer and sat down to do the only thing that ever took her outside herself.

She began to write. Furiously.

It began as a Dear God letter, akin to a Dear John one, and grew from there. A cutting indictment against the system whereby injustice flourished and justice was rendered by his Avenging Angels in what appeared to her to be the most random and haphazard of manners.

But, seventeen single-spaced pages into spilling her venom, emptying her soul, of bellyaching and preaching and blistering invective, three hours after she had begun, she stopped.

Her head throbbed and her eyes burned, but worst of all, she knew this Dear God letter was wrong. Keller had not been murdered. The collapse of the Hallelujah was a terrible freak accident, nothing more.

Kiel had been sent to save her life and redeem the injustice perpetrated by Detective Crandall on an innocent woman wrongfully accused—and on Stuart Willetts. Kiel had done both, and she hadn't gotten such a raw deal.

She had loved and been loved and made love with an Avenging Angel. With Kiel. Her heart was still broken, but her mind was clear.

With a few keystrokes, she obliterated the scathing Dear God letter from her computer. In a few days, a few weeks at most, she might take up her vocation and begin again. But there were details here to clean up, like the office in Lucy's building. She shut down the power on the computer and put it away, then changed quickly into slacks and a sweater and walked in the bright midday sun down to Main Street.

She stopped in the Treat Boutique, bought herself a latte, and then walked across the street. On impulse, she turned aside from the door into Lucy's building and continued on instead another three blocks down Main to the newspaper office.

Though the office door had a Closed sign in the window, she tried the door and it opened. She poked her head in. A bell hanging over the door rang out. The owner and editor, Margaret Hollings, came around from behind an old mahogany partition.

"Robyn, hello! I was so hoping you would stop in this morning. Where is your friend Kiel? *What* a stirring speech he gave this morning!"

"It was, wasn't it," Robyn murmured. "From the heart. I'm not really sure where Kiel went to." She did, but how did one explain that an Avenging Angel moved on? "He's not one to hang around."

"Well, we need his kind around here. To keep our moral compass, you know," Margaret pronounced, serious as could be. "Let me get those photocopies for you, while I'm thinking about it."

She ducked back around the partition and invited Robyn to join her. Enjoying the sights and scents, the ambience of the old newspaper office, Robyn went happily.

"Here's the file of articles I copied for you. Why don't you sit down and go through them—then if there's anything else you want, we can dig out the microfilm now." Margaret offered her a chair at an antique rolltop desk.

"Are you sure I won't be in the way?"

"Most definitely not. I've work to do in the back, and everybody knows we're closed on Mondays. You just sing out if you need anything."

"Thanks, Margaret. I'd love to get started." She hadn't intended to stay. The boxes in Lucy's offices needed packing up, but they could wait a little while. The distraction for a few hours couldn't hurt.

She sat down and began to go through the articles dating from December 1892 through April 1893. The passions and rhetoric ran high those days. Amused by the overblown tone of the reporting, which was as blatantly partisan as any she had ever seen, Robyn started a time line on the back of one of the less-informative copies.

She read through all the articles quickly, then settled in to read each again with an eye toward filling in her time line and keeping tabs on how the quotes attributed to Lucien Montbank on the side of the sideliners, and Jerome Clarke for the apexers, changed in those months.

In sociology, the technique was called *caving*. The acronym CAVE stood for content analysis of verbatim explanations. Robyn used CAVE as a sort of time machine where what people said could be proven to predict what they would do. Despite losing the lawsuit in Denver to the superior claims of the apex claimants, which should have been a devastating blow, Lucien Montbank, in his comments to the press, seemed to become more and more optimistic, even elated, over the possibility of a compromise and a return of prosperity to the town of Aspen.

Just why he'd been so optimistic puzzled her. Conversely, Jerome Clarke's statements went downhill over several weeks, from victorious to downright hateful. As far as he was concerned, no compromise would be made. Though such words never appeared in print, Robyn could almost hear Clarke's attitude toward compromising. *Over my dead body...*

KIEL SOARED AROUND the heavens for a long time after he departed the earthly dimension of the county courthouse—but he found no peace of mind. He knew that he had not only saved Robyn Delaney Trueblood's life but corrected an injustice done to Trudi Candelaria and Stuart Willetts. Neither act was insignificant or beneath the attentions of an Avenging Angel, especially not Robyn's life, but he couldn't shake the feeling that his work in Aspen was not done.

He dropped into the DBAA offices on Logan Street, out of respect for Gracie's wishes, materializing out of sight of any mortals hanging around. Grace, however, was on some errand to do with an update of Policies and Procedures.

Bureaucracy, Kiel thought, he could live without. He dashed off an irreverent note to her with a pen only he could see flying across a page of Gracie's notepaper, then bounded up the stairs to Angelo's office.

Kiel was in luck. Angelo was just polishing off the heavenly paper trail transfer to the mortal family that the littlest Avenging Angel Ariel had requested. Jay and Shanna were going to make great parents.

"Ezekiel." He cocked a bushy white brow. "Enjoy your little trek around the heavens?"

Kiel shot him a look. "I know there's plenty to be done around here—"

"Yes, and you're desperately needed. We're critically shorthanded around here what with Samuel getting himself banished to another mortal existence and Dash doing what I told him to do for the first time in recorded history."

"Imagine Dash following orders." Kiel grinned. Dash was notoriously allergic to orders, but then the best detective in all the DBAA, maybe all the branches of the Avenging Angels, could pretty much do what he wanted as long as justice was the end result. Kiel wanted to get around to telling Angelo he wasn't done with Robyn yet, but he had to know what influence Angelo had finally had over the ace detective. "What order did you give him?"

Angelo scowled. "I told him to follow his heart. And what do you know, he did. He and Liz got married."

"That's nice," Kiel muttered automatically, then thought about what he'd just heard come out of Angelo's mouth. "He *what?*"

"He got married."

"He got married."

"Isn't that what I just said?"

"I didn't think, I mean . . . is that possible?"

"Don't even think about it, Ezekiel," Angelo intoned. "Like I said, we're short-staffed enough around here."

Kiel put aside that stunning possibility for the moment, if for no other reason than to get Angelo to let him go back and make sure Robyn would be safe. "I just need another earth day, maybe two, with Robyn."

Angelo didn't bat an eye. The dockets might be full, Kiel realized, but Angelo would not take lightly a lingering threat of injustice. "What's the problem?"

Kiel shook his head. His feelings for Robyn weren't going away. How could they? But that was a matter for another time. "I'm not sure I've done everthing. Spyder Nielsen's death didn't go unavenged. The woman who murdered him wound up driving off the road and getting herself killed."

Angelo heaved a weary sigh. "So many victims to keep track of."

Kiel nodded. "The false accusations against Trudi Candelaria have been resolved."

"And you saved Robyn's life," Angelo pointed out.

"Yes. But there is still the issue of the Hallelujah cave-in."

"What's this?" Dashiell asked, materializing at Angelo's office door with a Camel stuck in his mouth.

"Dash." Kiel grinned, rising to shake hands in the mortal manner with the ace detective. "Good to see you."

"You, too, kid. How's it hanging?"

Kiel laughed but Angelo rolled his eyes and glared at the cigarette smoke wafting around.

Surprised to know that Dash had been following the case, Kiel explained the dilemma.

Out of some overflowing matrimonial good will, Kiel supposed, Dash let his cigarette die and dematerialized the butt. "You're convinced someone did blow up that mine with you and your doll face inside?"

"It's just a hunch. I've got no proof."

"You want a piece of advice? Stick with those hunches, kid. So what's the question? If no one had a motive to murder Keller Trueblood, then who did it?"

"Yeah, that would be the question."

"Classic deduction, kid." Dash grimaced. "if the murder wasn't about Keller, it was about his wife, wouldn't you say?"

Over my dead body.

And then, of course, Jerome Clarke had died, Robyn thought, closing up the file. She was no further along in her thinking about this story than she'd been a year earlier. Even then she'd thought Clarke's death far too convenient. The interesting part was that no one cared what had become of old Jerome once the compromise was put into effect.

But sitting there in the historical old rattletrap of a newspaper building, her imagination caught fire. Spyder Nielsen's death had affected the town in much the same way as Jerome Clarke's. Little more than a week ago Scott had posed the question, what if Abe Lincoln had sneezed in the instant he was killed? Here the question became, What if someone murdered Jerome Clarke? Juxtaposed against the high-profile celebrity murder of Spyder Nielsen, the hypothetical question might make a great book.

She had to bounce this idea off Lucy. Taking the file, she spent a few moments tracking Margaret down to thank her for rekindling her interest in this story and for making the microfilm copies, then took her leave and hurried back to Lucy's building.

She was greeted as she exited the caged elevator on the second floor by a receptionist and Lucy's young sidekick. He stopped her long enough to hand her Adelmeyer's reports, which documented both surface and core residues of ordinary dynamite at the Hallelujah.

"Thanks, Todd. Nothing we hadn't really expected, is it?"

"Sorry about that. Wish we could've been more helpful."

"It is helpful to know this much—but I'm not sure it matters anymore. Is Lucy around?"

He grinned. "Out to a late lunch. Anything I can do?"

"No, thanks, really. I'm just going to tackle the mess in here. Just let her know I'm here, okay?"

"Will do."

The district attorney's office had promised Robyn the return of all Keller's notes once the prosecution of Detective Crandall was over. She tore out one page near the end of his collected notes. The sketch was abstract, but in its lines she saw herself and Keller, hand in hand.

Resolving to keep her heart off her sleeve and back where it belonged, she spent the next hour packing up the rest of the boxes. Lucy Montbank let herself in just as Robyn was taping shut the last box.

Lucy crossed the room and gave Robyn a quick hug. "You could have left this, Robyn. There was no need to do it all by yourself."

She gave a weary smile. "I didn't mind, Lucy. You've been more than wonderful to let us use the space. Packing up was the least I could do."

"What is this little charm you're wearing these days?" Lucy asked.

"This?" She lifted the chain from which Kiel's ivory carving hung. "Angel wings. Why, don't you like it?"

"It's just so commonplace. I'm personally bored silly with all the infatuation with angels these days."

Robyn might have agreed except that Kiel had carved them for her.

"In any case—" Lucy lowered herself into one of the chairs not cluttered with a box "—what will you do now? Go home to Denver?"

"I've been thinking about staying around a few days. I'm really very excited about an idea I had that I wanted to bounce off you."

"Robyn, you're positively glowing! After everything that's happened, I thought I'd find you in a funk. Tell me your idea—but . . . before you do, let me say this. I want you to know how sorry I am that I made such a stink toward Kiel at my party. After the two of you left, I felt like such an idiot. Such a false friend for begrudging you his help and friendship."

Robyn swallowed on a lump of loneliness lodged in her throat. She hadn't known or even thought about exactly what Kiel had done to seal the rift in reality he had made when he whisked them away from the scene Robyn herself had begun to create.

But her friend's apology gave Robyn a sudden new insight. More than any celebrity, Lucy represented this town, its history, its penchant for image, and she wanted nothing, *nothing,* to reflect badly upon her.

"Lucy, please don't worry about it. Kiel was quick to point out to me what wonderful friends I have, how lucky I am in that."

Lucy's impeccable blond brows rose. "Don't tell me he included me among them, Robyn."

He hadn't, not at all. He'd been referring to Mike and Jessie and Scott, but whether Kiel liked Lucy or not, she was a friend and had been long before Kiel came onto the scene. "It doesn't matter, Lucy. Don't give it another thought."

She smiled gratefully. "So, where did our Mr. Alighieri take himself off to so fast?"

Robyn shook her head. "I don't know. Off exploring the Hallelujah for all I know."

Dismay flickered in Lucy's expression. "Surely not!"

"I was just being flippant, Lucy," Robyn rushed to reassure her, wondering why such a ridiculous idea had spilled out of her mouth, anyway. "I really have no idea where Kiel is right now."

"That was quite a speech he made this morning. Reminded me of Keller and that bedrock integrity."

Her throat tightened, but only for a moment. "Kiel did a terrific job. Keller would be—" not pleased, she guessed "—satisfied, I guess. Clear conscience."

"A thing to be desired," Lucy quipped.

"I know Kiel was very disturbed about the treatment Trudi and Stuart got at your party."

Lucy nodded and sighed. "I invited them—and I suppose they came—because we'd hoped this town was ready to shed its holier-than-thou attitude. Anybody would think Spyder Nielsen was some kind of martyred saint, when the truth is, he was a fourteen-karat son of a bitch with more money than scruples or brains."

"Maybe now that Trudi's been exonerated, things will be different." Robyn hoped so, more for Stuart Willetts's sake than Trudi's.

Seeming preoccupied, Lucy flicked one talonlike thumbnail against the other. "Tell me about your idea."

Shifting mental gears, Robyn stacked a few boxes. "I went by Margaret's office earlier today—you knew she went to the trouble a year ago of having those old newspaper accounts of the avalanche that supposedly killed Jerome Clarke printed out for me."

"Supposedly?"

"Yes." She moved a crate of files to the floor and sat down in the chair near Lucy's. Sitting cross-legged, she described her book idea. "The thing is, I think I can draw a really dynamite analogy between Spyder Nielsen's death and Jerome Clarke's. I got to thinking about it this way. People here didn't really care that Spyder had been murdered—wouldn't you say that's accurate?"

Lucy nodded thoughtfully. "He'd become somewhat of an embarrassment with all his drunk and disorderlies, the women, the drugs—"

"Exactly. Where once he was king of Aspen Mountain, his popularity was far more hype than real. He'd actually become a potential liability to the Aspen image.

Jerome Clarke was a perfect example of the same thing, only in a different time and circumstance. If it hadn't been for his apex strike on the very same mountain, this town was Nowhereville—until the ski industry came along, at least. But his welcome wore out, too, especially after winning that court battle. Do you see where I'm going with this?"

Lucy frowned. "I'm afraid I do, Robyn. It sounds like exploitation of image and celebrity to me, not to mention revising history to suit your own purposes."

Bewildered by Lucy's resistance to the whole idea, Robyn decided she must have been less than clever in explaining what she wanted to do with the book. "It's just an analogy, Lucy, a way to point out that the more things change, the more they stay the same. You can't deny this town thrives on its image. That the town as a whole has an idea of itself that commands attention."

"Spyder Nielsen's murder had nothing to do with what image this town holds of itself."

"That's true, Lucy, but the point is, no one *cared*. It gave people an excuse to ostracize Trudi Candelaria, but other than that, his death meant nothing. I think the same is true with Jerome Clarke. He made a tremendous impact here, but when he died—whether he was murdered or not—no one cared."

Expressionless now, Lucy said, "You believe he was murdered."

"*I* do, but that doesn't mean I'm going to haphazardly rewrite history. Don't you see any potential in this story, really?"

"None." Lucy's frown deepened. "Why do you care, Robyn? What is it about this that you can't let go of? Did losing Keller make you believe people care about these things?"

Robyn blanched. "That feels like a cheap shot, Luc."

"I don't intend to be mean-spirited, Robyn, but *something* has stuck you into this frankly morbid bent of mind."

She felt stung. Attacked. "Maybe you're not interested in this kind of thing, but I like to think my books have hit the bestseller lists because the what-ifs really fascinate people. The mystery, the sense of how things go wrong in people."

"You're right, Robyn. I'm not only not interested, I dislike looking for—as you say—the ways things go wrong."

"I'm sorry if it offends you. I thought with all your interest and historical collections—"

"Oh, I quite like all of that, and I'm glad to help you any way that I can. You're a friend, Robyn. But I would suggest that you go home to Denver and see if you can't find something a bit less macabre to fill your time."

Smiling to defuse the tension between them and dispel the disquieting sensation that perhaps Lucy was right on target, she couldn't let go. She didn't know why. "Lucy, this is what I want. Will you help me?"

"How?"

"I would like to go back to the Hallelujah, just once."

Lucy looked aghast. "For God's sake...*why?* You can't be serious!"

"I am, Lucy. I've never been so serious in my life."

"But why? What good can possibly come of it? Let me take you somewhere else, one of the tourist mines, or—"

"No. It's got to be the Hallelujah, Lucy." She took a deep breath. There were important reasons for her to revisit the old silver mine. She wanted to say goodbye to Keller once and for all. She wanted to get over her fears about the dark. The Hallelujah was where all that terror had begun.

Even more important, she wanted to be able to trust her own feelings again. In the wake of Kiel Alighieri, determining the fate of Jerome Clarke, a silver mining mogul who had died or been murdered more than a hundred years ago, had somehow become vital to learning to trust herself again.

She couldn't even write if she couldn't rely upon her instincts.

"If you don't want to go, Lucy, maybe I could ask that old miner friend of yours. Tee Palmer, wasn't it?"

"Robyn, are you absolutely sure this is what you want?"

Her friend's tone made prickles climb her spine. "I'm sure, Lucy."

"Then—" the older woman shrugged "—I will take you."

THE CLAUSTROPHOBIC FEEL of the Hallelujah chilled Robyn to the marrow. Shaking inside, but determined not to show it, she despised it all. The dark. The riveting silence. The way their voices dropped like stones into a bottomless void. Lucy had assured her that the miner's helmets they wore were state of the art, but Robyn thought their light beams pathetically weak against the hellish perpetual night.

Robyn urged that they press on when Lucy would have stopped. She tried to keep track of the shafts and the offshoots, the stopes that dead-ended, the railcar tracks that extended out over virtual cliffs. If what she'd wanted was a sense of the mine, of its enormity and complexity, she had that long ago. By her watch, they'd been plunging deeper and deeper into the mine for an hour.

Creeping along, skittish, just waiting for support beams to groan anywhere near her, breathing the dank, dead air in a fashion that could pass for near-panic on a movie soundtrack, Robyn called out to Lucy to stop.

Her friend turned, and for a moment Robyn was blinded by the light from Lucy's helmet. Breathing heavily, she clutched at the ivory angel wings at her breast.

"The point of this drill is escaping me at the moment." Lucy said nothing, only sank down to her haunches. Robyn went on. "What do I have to prove, and to whom? I don't want to die anymore. Overcoming my fear of the dark here is just ridiculous."

She'd survived, Keller hadn't. What foolishness was it to bid her soulmate goodbye in the place where he had died when his soul had risen again as the Avenging Angel Ezekiel?

Which left her virtually no reason to be down in the yawning depths of the Hallelujah. None but Lucy's tight-lipped resistance to the notion that Jerome Clarke had been murdered. And even that seemed meaningless at the moment.

"Lucy? Say something."

"What did you expect to find down here, Robyn?" Her voice was curiously wooden.

She swallowed hard. "I wish I knew, Lucy. I'm sorry."

"Not sorry enough, are you?"

"I don't understand...."

"You push too hard, Robyn. You won't take a friend's advice. You want to pick things apart for all the ways they can go wrong? Pick this apart. You went looking for trouble like you always do. *This* time," she jeered, "you hit the jackpot."

Chapter Fifteen

"Lucy, wh-what are you talking about? I—"

"I—I—I. *I'm* sick to death of your do-gooder attitude. *I* won't let you ruin me or my name, Robyn. *I'm* putting an end to it, here and now."

Robyn sank to the uneven surface of the stope floor, solid rock to her left, a deadly precipice a few feet to her right. The implication in her friend's words became crystal clear. Panic rose in her on a wave of nausea. "Lucy, are you saying Lucien Montbank murdered Jerome Clarke?"

From across the expanse of blackness came the soft and deadly voice of Kiel Alighieri. "That's what she's saying, Robyn." He switched on a lantern. His stern, handsome face appeared disembodied by the light.

"Kiel?" Robyn cried, her heart alight, her body shaking. "You came back?"

"Oh, brilliant," Lucy mocked. "For all the good it will do either one of you."

"She's always known, Robyn. Jerome Clarke's murder has always been the dirty little family secret, hasn't it?"

"This town is full of dirty little secrets," Lucy spat out. "And without proof—"

"Ahh, but there is proof, you know," he interrupted softly, "in a cage submerged at the depths of this mine. Isn't that right, Lucy?"

He'd struck Lucinda Montbank temporarily speechless.

Clutching her backpack, Robyn looked to her Avenging Angel. "Kiel? What proof?"

"A skeleton, minus one hand, with a slug in the skull."

"Submerged?" She knew the lowest levels of mines often filled when the water table rose. And that cages were the means of lowering and raising whole mining crews to the deepest levels. "How did you ever find—"

His stern visage cracked as he grinned in the lantern light across the chasm that separated them. "Tricks again. Sorry, little earthling. Some things just can't be done any other way."

Lucy snorted. "What gibberish is this?"

Kiel's smile faded. His eyes fixed on Lucy. He withdrew from a breast pocket a slug and tossed it across the cavernous space. The slow gentle arc landed the old bullet in Lucy's hand. "The same rifling," he said, "exactly the same markings as the bullet you dared to put on display in your office. This slug and the one that killed Blackjack Turner came from the same gun."

"My grandfather's Colt .45."

Robyn's flesh crawled. "You knew this," she accused. "You knew."

"I knew," she granted disdainfully, shedding her backpack at her feet. "Of course I knew. And I put that slug and that gun in the display case and I laughed."

"Why? Why did he resort to murder?"

"Why?" she mocked, laughing her contempt. "Figure it out, Robyn. You're the high-and-mighty author."

She remembered, then, the research she'd done, the pieces that didn't fit. "Lucien Montbank outsmarted himself, didn't he. How many times, Lucy? How many surface claims did he sell to Clarke for pennies on the dollar and think he'd swindled an easy mark?"

"You do have a gift for the obvious, Robyn." Lucy's features twisted in derision. "Too bad it's going to be wasted."

"I don't think so, Lucy," Kiel intoned.

She swore at him and pulled a handgun from her backpack, swung around and shot off her weapon, aiming perfectly at Kiel's lantern. A horrible crack of gunfire resounded. The slug shattered the lantern and cast Kiel's side of the tunnel into blackness. "Die, you meddling clod!"

A scream caught in Robyn's throat as the light of the lantern sprang to life again. "The truth, Lucinda Montbank," he commanded, pointing at her.

Lucy's face slackened in disbelief. With both hands she leveled the pistol at the lantern again and fired. Kiel deadened the noise and plucked the slug from thin air and held it up. Awestruck by his might and power, Robyn swallowed.

"The truth, Lucinda Montbank," he intoned again.

"Who are you?" she shrilled.

He stood then, clothed in his magnificent male human form, legs spread wide, arms outstretched, the light of the lantern setting a glow around his body and bronze hair. "Ezekiel," he pronounced, "Avenging Angel of the Almighty."

Shrieking her disbelief, Lucy stood and aimed and fired into the chest of Kiel, but the bullet slowed, slowed, and fell away into the yawning pit at his feet.

Lucy's hand dropped, and she stumbled backward.

"I'll ask you one more time," he said, pointing a finger at her. "Say it! Unless Jerome Clarke died, your great-grandfather was a ruined man. Your empire comes tumbling down when the truth is known!"

She hurled the gun down, and it clattered out of her reach. "I have *nothing* to lose! I could never be held accountable for things that happened a hundred years ago."

Robyn stared in the beam of the light of her helmet lamp at the woman she had believed to be a friend. Lucinda Montbank had profited immensely from the fruits of a poisoned tree. Robyn saw that whether her fortune was at stake or not, Lucy could never bear the onus, the derision, the snickers and disparagement and sheer stigma of being a false claimant in a town like Aspen.

"But you are now called to account for the attempted murder of Robyn Delaney, and the murder of Keller Trueblood," Kiel charged. "You sent Tee Palmer on a fool's errand so he could not witness your treachery. You set those charges, and you must pay."

Her pulse racing, her throat locked in fear of what Lucy would do next, Robyn knew this must be a bluff—there was no proof, no evidence of whatever charges Lucy had set off that couldn't be attributed to mining operations a century ago.

But Lucy couldn't know for sure. Kiel had found proof where she'd believed none would ever be found of her great-grandfather's crime. She stood, shaking her head sadly. "How many times, how many ways, did I try to stop you, Robyn? You would not stop! You wouldn't let it go, you refused, even to die when you should have."

Overcome as she always was by the tortured reasons of tortured souls for their crimes, Robyn shivered hard. "All you ever had to do was tell me the truth, Lucy."

"And go down in ignominious disgrace?"

"Lucy, you were not responsible for what your ancestors did!"

But Lucinda Montbank was beyond reasoning. "Do you think I've lived my whole life for that end, you idiot woman? Do you think I'll stand for it?"

Her face contorted and she screamed in her fury and grabbed a grenade from her backpack. Horrified, frozen, Robyn watched as she pulled the pin and stood there shrieking until the last possible second. She hurled the live explosive with all her might at Robyn's feet and then ran for cover.

Kiel's furious roar filled the stope. The grenade went flying but exploded in a horrendous blast that shook the earth and rattled the skeletal remains of the mine to its core. Beams splintered and crashed and the earth rumbled.

"No-o-o-o-o!" Kiel bellowed, but Robyn was thrown into the wall at her back, her helmet was ripped from her head and the lamp shattered. Tossed around like a doll in a violent, nightmarish black conflagration, she screamed for Kiel.

Desperately he searched for her life form by the ivory angel wings around her neck. In the instant a rock slide would have crushed her to death, he cast a force field around her and flew to her side.

He materialized in his human form at her side. Rocks hurtled and crashed down all around them, but in the eye of the fury, she was safe. By the eerie, hot red-orange glow surrounding him, Robyn saw the anger in his body and the fear that he had not reacted quickly enough to prevent the crashing, collapsing disaster. She saw the overpoweringly vulnerable position he was in of loving her as a mortal man and what a colossal, terrible drain it was on his powers to hold back the tons of rock from crushing her then and there.

"I'm all right, Kiel," she cried. "Go after Lucy. She's not in her right mind. Don't let her be killed."

"I love you, Robyn Delaney." He grabbed her shoulders and kissed her hard and fast. Then, in a split second, he was transformed to the manifestation of the Avenging Angel Ezekiel.

When he left her with a powerful beat of his wings, she was in the darkness again, her worst nightmare unfolding, buried alive again, her life hanging by a thread in the space of a force field she didn't know if Kiel could sustain, or for how long.

Her life passed before her eyes, her girlhood, standing at that chalkboard scribbling, *Fighting is never the answer,* her endless hours interviewing twisted murdering souls, her brief moments in the spotlight when her books hit the bestseller lists, her all-too-brief, too-precious hours with her beloved Keller.

She had brought this calamitous and death-dealing moment upon herself because she'd been looking for trouble and refused to see the danger, but she knew in her heart that if she made it out again this time, if Kiel could save her this once, she would look for the good instead and use the power of her words for the cause of real and abiding justice on earth.

She heard Lucy's screaming rage and Kiel's booming, heavenly commands. Another blast rocked the earth and then another. In some zone she had never known, she saw in her mind's eye the terrible battle being waged. She saw Kiel try again and again to save Lucy from herself, but it was as if the forces of evil had consumed her and invested in her powers equal to Kiel's.

In a mighty sweep of his wings Kiel deflected an avalanche of rock, and the power of her own furious attack turned back on Lucinda Montbank, rained down on her and crushed from her human body all life.

And all the evil power at her command turned tail and fled in the face of the might of Ezekiel's heavenly wrath.

THE ARGUMENT GOT HEATED in Angelo's office at the DBAA.

"The rescue teams will reach her in another few hours," Angelo stated.

"I won't leave her there another five minutes," Kiel snapped. "I won't do it."

Angelo glowered. "She's human, Ezekiel. You are not. You have saved her life. That, and that alone, was your obligation. She has found peace with herself, and she will now fulfill her destiny. For you to go back to her now is to make a grave error."

"May I say something, here?" Clarence interrupted persistently.

"No!" Angelo bellowed.

"No," Kiel snapped, meeting the awesome power in Angelo's eyes with an awesome strength of his own. "What destiny? The child you spoke of?"

"Yes," Angelo equivocated. "Among other things."

Kiel stared hard, the Adam's apple of his human manifestation pitching. "About the child," he demanded.

Angelo's mighty head rolled on his shoulders. He knew exactly where this was leading, to an even more critically depleted staff of Avenging Angels. One more heretofore unutilized exception to the rules, when a miracle occurred and a mortal woman's mating with an angel produced a life inside her body. "The child is yours."

Such a profound joy pervaded Kiel's heart and mind and soul and physical presence that his earthly tear ducts emptied. He jammed his fingers into his mortal's jeans, and his head fell forward in deepest gratitude.

"Surely," Clarence piped in during the first available silence, clacking the beads of his abacus in a frenzy, "surely even you can see that the odds of such a love as is shared by Ezekiel and the mortal Robyn Delaney are one in eighty-nine trillion... and six," he added, trembling, clearing his throat in the face of Angelo's mighty scowl. "In the next fourteen millennia," he finished defiantly.

The numbers astounded even Angelo, rendering him speechless for a time. Kiel met his fierce and penetrating blue eyes. "I don't want to hear anything about it when her mortal life expires in seventy years," he warned. "You're mine, then, and for all time."

Kiel's thousand-candle smile nearly blinded the crusty old angel. "We'll both be yours to command then."

"Don't toy with me, Ezekiel," Angelo thundered.

"Never happen, sir," Kiel cracked.

Eavesdropping behind the door, Gracie clapped her hands.

The kiss to end all kisses, better than any princess bride had ever known, was recorded that day in history, and what do you know?

The spirit of Kiel and Robyn's baby clapped her tiny hands, too.

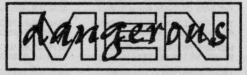

HARLEQUIN®

Don't miss these Harlequin favorites by some of our most distinguished authors!

And now, you can receive a discount by ordering two or more titles!

HT #25645	THREE GROOMS AND A WIFE by JoAnn Ross	$3.25 U.S./$3.75 CAN. ☐
HT #25648	JESSIE'S LAWMAN by Kristine Rolofson	$3.25 U.S./$3.75 CAN. ☐
HP #11725	THE WRONG KIND OF WIFE by Roberta Leigh	$3.25 U.S./$3.75 CAN. ☐
HP #11755	TIGER EYES by Robyn Donald	$3.25 U.S./$3.75 CAN. ☐
HR #03362	THE BABY BUSINESS by Rebecca Winters	$2.99 U.S./$3.50 CAN. ☐
HR #03375	THE BABY CAPER by Emma Goldrick	$2.99 U.S./$3.50 CAN. ☐
HS #70638	THE SECRET YEARS by Margot Dalton	$3.75 U.S./$4.25 CAN. ☐
HS #70655	PEACEKEEPER by Marisa Carroll	$3.75 U.S./$4.25 CAN. ☐
HI #22280	MIDNIGHT RIDER by Laura Pender	$2.99 U.S./$3.50 CAN. ☐
HI #22235	BEAUTY VS THE BEAST by M.J. Rogers	$3.50 U.S./$3.99 CAN. ☐
HAR #16531	TEDDY BEAR HEIR by Elda Minger	$3.50 U.S./$3.99 CAN. ☐
HAR #16596	COUNTERFEIT HUSBAND by Linda Randall Wisdom	$3.50 U.S./$3.99 CAN. ☐
HH #28795	PIECES OF SKY by Marianne Willman	$3.99 U.S./$4.50 CAN. ☐
HH #28855	SWEET SURRENDER by Julie Tetel	$4.50 U.S./$4.99 CAN. ☐

(limited quantities available on certain titles)

	AMOUNT	$
DEDUCT:	10% DISCOUNT FOR 2+ BOOKS	$
ADD:	POSTAGE & HANDLING	$
	($1.00 for one book, 50¢ for each additional)	
	APPLICABLE TAXES**	$_____
	TOTAL PAYABLE	$_____
	(check or money order—please do not send cash)	

To order, complete this form and send it, along with a check or money order for the total above, payable to Harlequin Books, to: **In the U.S.:** 3010 Walden Avenue, P.O. Box 9047, Buffalo, NY 14269-9047; **in Canada:** P.O. Box 613, Fort Erie, Ontario, L2A 5X3.

Name: _____

Address: _____ City: _____

State/Prov.: _____ Zip/Postal Code: _____

**New York residents remit applicable sales taxes.
Canadian residents remit applicable GST and provincial taxes.

HBACK-AJ3

BRIDE'S BAY RESORT

UNLOCK THE DOOR TO GREAT ROMANCE AT BRIDE'S BAY RESORT

Join Harlequin's new across-the-lines series, set in an exclusive hotel on an island off the coast of South Carolina.

Seven of your favorite authors will bring you exciting stories about fascinating heroes and heroines discovering love at Bride's Bay Resort.

Look for these fabulous stories coming to a store near you beginning in January 1996.

Harlequin American Romance #613 in January
Matchmaking Baby by Cathy Gillen Thacker

Harlequin Presents #1794 in February
Indiscretions by Robyn Donald

Harlequin Intrigue #362 in March
Love and Lies by Dawn Stewardson

Harlequin Romance #3404 in April
Make Believe Engagement by Day Leclaire

Harlequin Temptation #588 in May
Stranger in the Night by Roseanne Williams

Harlequin Superromance #695 in June
Married to a Stranger by Connie Bennett

Harlequin Historicals #324 in July
Dulcie's Gift by Ruth Langan

Visit Bride's Bay Resort each month wherever
Harlequin books are sold.

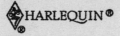

HARLEQUIN ®

BBAYG

**The wedding celebration was so nice...
too bad the bride wasn't there!**

Runaway Brides

Find out what happens when three brides have a
change of heart.

Three complete stories by some of your favorite
authors—all in one special collection!

YESTERDAY ONCE MORE
by Debbie Macomber

FULL CIRCLE
by Paula Detmer Riggs

THAT'S WHAT FRIENDS ARE FOR
by Annette Broadrick

Available this June wherever books are sold.

Look us up on-line at:http://www.romance.net

V *Silhouette*®
™

SREQ696

Bestselling authors

ELAINE COFFMAN
RUTH LANGAN

and

MARY McBRIDE

Together in one fabulous collection!

OUTLAW Brides

Available in June wherever Harlequin
books are sold.

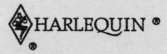

HARLEQUIN ®